Folk'd

LAURENCE DONAGHY

D1355394

BLACKSTAFF PRESS

First published in 2012 by Last Passage

This edition published in 2013 by Blackstaff Press
4D Weavers Court
Linfield Road
Belfast BT12 5GH

With the assistance of
The Arts Council of Northern Ireland

© Laurence Donaghy , 2013

Laurence Donaghy has asserted his right under the
Copyright, Designs and Patents Act 1988 to be
identified as the author of this work.

Typeset by CJWT Solutions, St Helens, England

Printed and bound by CPI Group UK (Ltd), Croydon CR0 4YY

A CIP catalogue for this book is available from the British Library

ISBN 978 0 85640 918 9

www.blackstaffpress.com
www.laurencedonaghy.co.uk

For Kath: who made me feel such love that the thought of losing it inspired this book

The Future

'Tell me a story,' said the child.

The mother sighed. 'It's late. It's almost midnight.'

Alert eyes met hers. 'I know,' the child informed her, as bright light streamed into the bedroom from the street outside. 'Not time to flip yet, but. Please, Mummy.'

'You've school in the morning,' the mother said sternly.

'Will you and Daddy flip with me?' the child asked, putting just the right soupçon of whine into the words. 'I don't like being there by myself. It's dark.'

'It's always dark there,' her mother said mildly. 'There are no Suns.'

'And there are the wolves,' the child said, with eyes as big as dinner plates. 'I can hear the wolves. I can hear them moving outside in the dark, Mummy.'

'Well then,' the mother shrugged. 'What is there to be afraid of?'

The child's jaw set. 'I want a story,' she pouted, making it seem as though storytime would be all that would prevent an immediate call to the nearest child welfare office.

'Okay,' her mother said. 'Story circles.'

'Yay!' the child cheered, as her mother drew circles in the air, leaving behind solid lines of different colours, until little brightly-coloured spheroids bobbed up and down all over the bedroom. They pulsed with an inner light and were soft to the touch.

Her mother playfully swatted a bubble, a great purple one, and it crashed into a smaller green neighbour, for a moment creating a blackish-brown mixture.

A small thunderclap resounded in the bedroom.

The child shrieked and vanished under her duvet. Hurriedly, the mother reached out with her hands and pulled at both ends of the compound bubble, separating the two colours once more.

'It's okay now,' the mother said, patting the quivering, child-shaped lump on the bed.

A head emerged from the bed, looking this way and that. 'Mummy, what happened?'

Her mother was holding a bubble securely in each palm, keeping them apart. Other bubbles bounced off surfaces with ponderous slowness. The whole bedroom was like a rave for tortoises.

'I'm sorry, wee love. That story isn't suitable for you.'

'What story?' the child's nervousness was forgotten now. She was sitting up in bed, peering at the two bubbles. Her mother tried not to show the strain involved in keeping them apart.

'It's the story of how this place came to be,' her mother said quickly, all in a rush, and then called a gorgeous, diamond-clear bubble down from the ceiling. 'This one would be much bet–'

'The Origin!' the child shrieked. 'You made the Origin didn't you?'

'You're not ready,' her mother said firmly. 'You'll hear that story someday, wee love. I promise. But it's not like the other stories you're used to. It's dark and dangerous and very scary and … oh, fuck me, I'm not helping myself here am I?'

The child giggled in delight at hearing her mother let loose with a bad word. She was kneeling on the bed now, completely out of the covers. If this had been a Tex Avery cartoon, her heart would have been leaping three feet out of her chest with every beat.

'Please …?'

'No. Not up for discussion. Now pick a different story circle or you can flip right this minute, young lady, and go sleep in the dark with the wolves. Look at this one,' her mother said, pointing at the diamond bubble, 'this one is all about a princess …'

The purple bubble escaped her grasp. She tried to snap it closed, but too late; it resonated like a rung bell and shot past her, looping over her outstretched hand even as the green bubble saw its own opportunity and wriggled free. The story circles were not tame.

This time, the child was ready for the thunderclap, and had her fingers plugged into her ears when it rumbled and rolled in the confines of the bedroom. Before her mother could stop her, the child had unplugged her ears and reached out her cupped palms, and the brownish bubble – not nearly so pretty as many of those still floating around – dropped into her hand like a felled tree. The child's expression froze as the bubble made contact with her skin.

The pretty bubbles still floating around the room popped, all at once.

No going back. The mother sighed. She had Sky Plussed

The X Factor. No chance of watching that tonight. She put her hands over the child's, and as she spoke, the bubble pulsed in perfect rhythm with her words.

'It was a dark and stormy night ...'

The Birth

The darkness was almost complete.

Light filtered through from above, but it was too diffuse to do anything but suggest the outline of the four or five hulking, squat shapes sitting in the blackness.

The odour of death pervaded the scene. The smell of rotting meat.

A rumbling sound began to build, from distant murmur to thundering rattle. With a *whp-crak*, a bolt was drawn back. In the blackness, nothing seemed to stir.

Several groaning creaks signified the stop-start opening of a reluctant door.

'Sure, when's it *not* my fuckin' turn?'

Muttering this and other dark utterances, Danny Morrigan reversed into his back alley, dragging the bastard wheelie bin behind him.

He emerged into The Alley of Eternal Damnation and Sporadic Dogshit thoroughly fucked off with life, shivering in his T-shirt and shorts, regretting the decision to do this in his comfy night gear and wishing he'd done it in daylight instead of coming home and thudding gratefully into the depths of the sofa.

'Might have been an idea to have done this a few hours ago. When it was light? When you still had your jeans on?' a voice called to him. A voice that was young, female and so chock-full of smugness that if someone had pricked it with a pin it would have exploded in a shower of iPhones.

'*Might* be an idea to go and fuck?' he growled back. But not too loudly.

This fucker of a bin – curse it, curse it and its demonic seed for a hundred generations – was, as ever, a complete ballix to navigate. Some unidentifiable but unmistakably gloopy shadow-material at his feet gave the wheels the merest flicker of a nudge and, despite being big and solid and heavy, the bin wobbled and bobbled, and the whole thing came within a whisker of capsizing.

If it did, it would vomit black bags into the darkness and they, being about as sturdy as the Old Woman Who Lived in the Shoe's grasp of birth control, would gratefully release their unspeakable loads and he'd spend hours, honest to God *hours*, out here in the black, ankle deep in his own crap lest he earn the disapproval of the entire street.

Not gonna fuckin' happen. Danny strained every sinew and let loose with a string of very bad words before he finally managed to get the bin righted and set down in a suitable parking spot.

Job done, Danny risked a quick glance up and down the alley. Intellectually, of course, he knew it was just a narrow passage between two identikit rows of terraced houses, a very mundane and urban thing. Some other part of him knew it was a very narrow space, extremely poorly lit, at fuck-knows o'clock. No one even had their bedroom lights on at either adjoining house, making the darkness especially oppressive.

But …

But he was a man. And men do not nervously scamper and skip like ballerina crabs through alleys. Men don't think of how easy it would be for something to hide between these ugly oul bins, something small and brown and scuttly and diseased, its smell blending in with the eye-watering stench.

Danny was thinking *very hard indeed* of how much men didn't think of any of this.

He moved as casually, yet purposefully, as his ego allowed to return through the alleyway entrance and into the safety of his own back yard.

With perfect comic timing, something that cast a large black shadow dropped down right in front of him.

'GEERRRWAYACHRISTABASTARD!' he screamed before immediately embarking upon a whistle-stop journey of the five stages of male recovery from a fright.

Relief: It was a cat. Not some hitherto-unknown-to-nature alleyway horror.

Calm: A cat. A cat. Stop the heart pounding, Danny, for fuck's sake. Simmer down, son.

Reflection: Just a cat.

Embarrassment: You just got on like a big woman over a cat …

Anger: 'Stupid fuckin' cat! Bastard, ye!'

How dare it, Danny thought, wrapping the anger around him like the big fluffy comfort blanket of masculinity it was. How dare the big bastard flit across his vision like that? Who did it think it was, making him momentarily, if completely understandably, startled?

The fucker didn't give him so much as a backward glance thrown contemptuously over its shoulder as it slunk off into its nocturnal alley kingdom, flowing from one bin to the next.

Deciding he'd had enough, Danny fairly dived back through his alley door. He bolted it first time – his brain telling his fingers in no uncertain terms that this was no time to fuck about coordination wise – and was through his kitchen door in a few strides.

Not far away (the kitchen's size guaranteed that anyone, anywhere in it, wasn't far away) at the sink, washing a day-long, three-lane pile-up of dishes was Ellie, his girlfriend.

Like many of the fairer sex, to Danny's way of thinking, Ellie rather fancied herself as a guru-like purveyor of sage advice. Unfortunately, also to Danny's way of thinking, her particular brand of advice was mostly of the 'shutting the stable door after the horse has not only bolted, but been caught, lived to a ripe old age, fathered a massive brood, and been taken away to be turned into Pritt Stick' variety.

Ellie was petite, pretty and raven-haired. And she had a smile that … well, he couldn't explain it. Most likely, the smile was just the most visibly adorable thing about her that summed up everything else. But that didn't sound as romantic as 'she had a smile that lit up the room' or some such nonsense.

Pragmatism like that rarely showed up in the *Cosmo* relationship surveys she sometimes made him do. In his mind, no matter what the actual title of the survey was, the bottom line was always something like, 'Are you destined to be a super-happy couple who stay together forever or are you, frankly, a bit shit?'

On the 'What's her best feature?' question on those surveys, he always went for 'lovely smile' or 'great sense of humour', which was a nice safe option, and made sure to *tut-tut* at option D, which was usually something about 'size of tits'.

Danny himself was nothing special: medium height, medium build, neither particularly handsome nor homely in the looks department. His defining feature as a person wasn't physical, but was instead a sort of lolloping, genial manner which made everyone surmise (correctly) that he was harmless and (incorrectly) that he was not all that sharp.

'Did you say something? When you were outside? Thought I heard …' Ellie began, with altogether too much merriment in her eyes for Danny's liking.

'Fuckin' bin. Hate putting it out. Did I mention that?' Danny replied, shivering as he poured himself a drink from the fridge. 'It's pitch black out there.'

'Ach, it is not pitch black,' Ellie retorted mildly, swabbing a plate with her trademark counter-clockwise motion. 'Don't exaggerate. You're always exaggerating, you.'

'I'm not exaggerating!' Danny said indignantly, between swallows of apple and raspberry juice (on the verge of turning, by the taste of it). 'It's that dark out there the fuckin' bats are wearin' night-vision goggles. They should have flare-gun emplacements rigged up every ten yards down that alley. It's not safe. And that fuckin' cat … oooh' – and he took a moment to physically shake with rage and animal cruelty fantasies – 'I hate that big black bastard.'

'What are you afraid of?' Ellie asked, bemused.

'Don't talk daft,' he retorted instantly, getting himself a suitably manly mini-Snickers bar from the leftover-from-Christmas-Celebrations tin on the countertop. He thought about biting into it in as masculine a way as possible but given its reduced size, this would have carried the serious risk of chomping off fingertips. He settled for simply swallowing it whole with as gangsta a look as he could muster.

Ellie continued innocently washing the dishes. 'Could it be the huge rats out there?' she said, lingering over every word. 'Is that it? You should be glad of that cat, because I saw a rat the other week, swear to God, coulda mangled a Labrador.'

He grabbed her by the waist and made as if to bite off her ears. She wriggled in protest, letting the plate slip with a *blooopsh* into the almond and coconut scented dishwater. She scrabbled at him with wet hands and he spun her around until, given their positions, she was more or less (but not really) forced to kiss him.

Her supposed resistance evaporated after the first few seconds and he enjoyed the taste of her, as if her lips were warming him again after the dark uncertainty of his epic quest to Put the Wheelie Bin Out.

Danny broke the kiss and tilted his head, as if listening for something.

'What?'

'Isn't this when the wee fella's supposed to start crying and we look at each other and sigh?'

'I bribed him with the emergency fiver,' Ellie replied, grinning.

Danny padded out of the kitchen to peek into the living room. Lying on a squashy blue baby mat, covered in soft blankets and surrounded by squeaky toys, was – in Danny's unbiased opinion – an extremely cute eight-month-old boy. Little Luke. Their son. Currently flat out asleep. All was silent, all was still.

The only noise in the room, in fact, was coming from the television news which had been given the task of lulling Luke those last few inches to sleep while Ellie did the dishes and Danny was dragged to bin duty. Set to low volume, it had done its job brilliantly. He felt like kissing the screen, until he saw what was occupying it.

'… and so in one week's time, Ireland will usher in a new era of telecommunications when the Lircom network goes live, delivering what's been termed "the information hyper-highway", a super-high-speed Ethernet connection from Rathlin in the North to Cape Clear, leaving the rest of Europe in the slow lane. This is Terry Irvine, for UTV News in Belfast.'

Danny made a face. Even at home he couldn't escape reminders of work. That fuckin' super-duper-Ethernet project accounted for 90 per cent of their support calls, and it hadn't even gone live yet. Next week was going to be a nightmare.

An almond and coconut scented goddess appeared at Danny's shoulder. He had to hand it to her; they might not have two quid to rub together most weeks, but she wasn't prepared to let standards drop when it came to dishwashing aromas. The legacy of her less-modest upbringing.

'Look at him,' Ellie said softly. 'I could sit and stare at him for hours.'

'Yeah,' Danny agreed, leaning on the doorframe and taking in the peaceful scene before him, one that had seemed scarcely possible only an hour before. 'I know. I could too.'

Ellie looked across at him, her eyebrow raised.

Seconds later, they were bounding to the stairs, Ellie leading, offering her outstretched hand to Danny, who reached forward and grabbed it, hopping happily as he moved, singing their traditional foreplay ditty as he went.

'Sex, sex, sex, sex!'

Ellie laughed.

To the untrained eye, it must have looked like he and Ellie were trying to defuse the world's cutest bomb.

Danny entered the (cough) master bedroom (you couldn't have swung a cat in there, and Christ knew after tonight he had a suitable candidate in mind) with a fluffy blue package draped over one shoulder. Between the package first getting picked up and now, it had gone from immobile, peaceful and still to kicking, jerking and emitting noises from all ranges of the auditory spectrum, although it seemed to be expressing a preference for those near the high-pitched end.

Danny carefully lowered the package into the cot that had been pushed up alongside their bed. Luke stared up at him with one of his, I've-only-just-remembered-the-world-is-utterly-amazing expressions, and gave an involuntary spasmodic jerk of his limbs before smiling gummily and farting onto his daddy's hand through three layers of nappy, sleepsuit and wraparound blanket. Danny knew instantly that it would be a yellow-green, little to no smell since the noise-to-smell ratio was tilted too far towards the noise end.

He paused for a second to reflect on how singularly odd it was to know something like that about another human being; something that, when you got down to it, was downright disgusting. It didn't feel like that, though. It just felt like one of those things you know.

'Dere's my liddle man! Where is ya? Where is ya liddle man, eh?'

As Luke burbled excitedly, Ellie entered the room carrying a kettle and a jug containing bottles of milk. She put the kettle on the high shelf with the guard, the furthest place away from the cot in the room, and placed the empty jug with the bottles on the bedside dresser.

She'd had kittens about bringing a kettle upstairs at night and keeping it in the same room as a sleeping baby until Danny had explained, very slowly and very patiently, and with the help of some diagrams, that Luke would have to be a ninja to perform the acrobatics necessary to extricate himself from his wooden prison, traverse the room, climb the dresser, execute a textbook backflip up onto the shelf, switch on the kettle, and *then* burn his widdle hands on it.

'And besides,' he'd added, 'I can't be fucked going downstairs in the middle of the night to the kitchen to get hot water to heat the bottles any more. It's a pain in the hole.'

Oh, for the day when they could afford two kettles.

'Is he tired?' she asked him, as he performed the 'red wire / blue wire'-esque task of changing the night-time nappy.

Danny snorted. 'What do you think?'

Ellie looked down at the UXBaby, currently engaged in examining his left thumb which, as was evident by his expression, held the key to the secrets of the cosmos.

'All right, let's do this. Nurse?'

A distinct air of medical professionalism descended on proceedings.

'Yes, doctor?'

'Dim the lights.'

The dimmer switch was rotated. Another flake of white paint broke loose from the knob and floated gently to the carpet. Danny pretended not to see it.

'Lights dimmed.'

'Teddy bear?'

'Teddy bear.'

Gar-gah was inserted. He had been a hippo at some point in the distant past but eight months of being industriously chewed and showered in lakes of baby drool meant Gar-gah now looked like Jeff Goldblum about fifteen minutes from the end of *The Fly*.

'Rattle?'

'Rattle.'

They waited a few moments. The happy squeals and babbling continued unabated, and actually increased in volume.

'Doctor, he's going hyper.'

Danny wiped his brow dramatically. 'The mobile, dammit!

14

The mobile! Now!'

Ellie wound it up.

'Clear!'

A circle of dangling plastic jungle animals suspended eighteen inches above Luke began to slowly rotate as the strains of 'Brahms' Lullaby' creaked out. Danny and Ellie sat in the dimly lit room, two silhouettes on the end of the bed. Luke's gaze went from the animals to them, to the animals, to them …

The lullaby wound down. Luke's gurgles and burbles wound up and were joined midway through by a distinct *waaaaa*, precursor to the full-on wail that would follow.

'Again, dammit! Hit him again!' Danny said.

As she reached over to re-wind the mobile, Ellie looked at Danny with what could charitably be described as a quizzical expression.

'I'm banning you from watching any more hospital dramas,' she said matter-of-factly.

Moments later, they watched in hardly-daring-to-breathe triumph as little eyes drooped … opened … drooped … and finally closed.

Ellie and Danny breathed a simultaneous sigh of relief. Danny slipped his mobile into the pocket of his bed shorts and then, gingerly, making no sudden movements lest they disturb a creaky floorboard or other such hitherto unknown hazard, they got into bed. Kissing ensued.

'Oh, I almost forgot,' Ellie said, breaking away from Danny. 'We got another notice today from the Risra.'

'The wha-ra?'

'The Regent Street Residents Association. R-S-R-A,' she explained, with infinite patience.

'Oh. Imagine my embarrassment at not getting that.' Danny rolled his eyes. 'So what do the Risra want this time? Death squads? Sniper turret? Probably a robot-operated one with a targeting computer programmed to shoot-to-kill anyone wearing Burberry, or who's under the age of sixty. I told you we were the only young people in this street, didn't I?'

'Ach, don't start.'

Danny sat up in bed, not a trace of a smile on his face. 'It's true. This place is like the *Antiques Roadshow* sponsored by Stalin.'

'Anyway … apparently the old couple at number 42 had their back windows broken. And the *really* old pair at the end house …'

'Davros and the Fat Controller?'

'… their windows are out too. Eight houses in the last fortnight.' Ellie paused, curiosity having settled upon her lovely features like snow. 'Which one's which?' she asked.

'I'm sorry?'

'Davros and the Fat Controller. Which is which?'

Danny looked at her incredulously. 'Which one of them's in the wheelchair?' he said.

'Wee Agnes, of course. She gets some speed up in that thing. I seen her chasin' after the postman last month and I swear she overtook a kid on a bike.'

'Right,' Danny said. He looked at Ellie. The curious expression had not abated. 'And …' he prompted, ever so gently, '… that doesn't give you a clue?'

'Should it?'

'D'you even know who Davros is?'

Ellie, sensing the ammonia-like whiff of piss-taking in the air, immediately retracted her arms and legs into her defensive shell. 'The magician?' she said, cautiously.

Danny's mouth moved silently for a second or two, as if decoding something. A facial tic was all that betrayed the fact he was having to keep a lid on a huge laugh. 'Davros,' he said, slowly and painstakingly, 'megalomaniacal creator of the Daleks. Not Bobby *Davro*, creator of a second-rate impersonation of Victor Meldrew.'

Ellie didn't miss a beat. 'Oh right,' she shrugged. 'So who's the Fat Controller?'

'Agnes' husband, obviously!' Danny exploded. 'Fuck me, by the process of elimination he fuckin' well has to be doesn't he?! Who else would it be! The fuckin' cat?!'

'Well I guessed that!' Ellie snapped back. 'I mean who *is* the Fat Controller!'

This was too much. 'The fuckin' fat cunt off *Thomas the Tank Engine*, name of fuck! "You have caused confusion and delay."'

'Well sorry! I was only fuckin' askin!'

'No that's what *he* says!' Danny said, genuinely beginning to believe he was going to spend the rest of his life having this argument.

Silence descended. Ellie stared at the ceiling as Danny went over the last few minutes of conversation in his mind as if checking that, yes, they were real. He forced himself to calm down slightly, and rather than asking the question he really wanted to ask – 'If you didn't know who either of the two characters were why in the name of Christ did it matter who was who?' – instead searched his memory for how they'd been sidetracked in the first place.

'I've told you and I'll tell them,' he offered, 'it's that fuckin' alleyway. Some group of wee hoods must have a key to one of the gates and they're goin' in there at night to fuck about. And no, before you say it, it's not rats.'

'It is rats,' she replied evenly. There was a distinctive smidge of sulk in her voice.

'Ah fer fuck's sake, Ellie. Where do we live? Chernobyl? How d'you explain the broken windows then? Constructing some sort of rudimentary catapult are they?'

'Well, you can tell that to the next meeting of the Risra!'

'My hole!' Danny spluttered. 'I'm not goin' anywhere near them geriatrics! Especially Chairwoman Mystic-fuckin'-Meg herself. Jesus. You know she gives me the willies. When Satan was a wee boy he probably had his da check under the bed in case she was there.'

Ellie dissolved into laughter. Danny tried not to glory in it and then gave in and gloried to his heart's content. Making Ellie laugh was how he'd won her in the first place, after all. She'd been well out of his league back then.

She still is.

Luke stirred and moaned softly in his sleep, causing Ellie to quickly muffle her mirth. She affected a mask of disapproval and poked Danny in the shoulder, causing him to simulate a wounded expression in reprisal.

'Ach, now c'mon. Just cos you don't like her cat. Wee Bea's a lovely woman. She was asking to do my tea leaves the other day when she saw me in the Spar.'

'She was asking to do yer what? What'd you tell her?' Danny asked. The thought repulsed him, far more than it had any real right to.

Ellie shrugged. 'I says aye, why not. Sure it might be a laugh.'

Danny rolled his eyes. 'Gettin' your tea leaves read? A laugh? Serious? What part of the physics degree did they teach that in? Idiot Particles 101?'

Ellie's good humour vanished. Her eyes flashed. And just like that, Danny knew he'd made a mistake.

'I didn't mean you were an–'

'Well we'll never know, will we?'

He should have left it there. He didn't. 'It's not my fault you didn't finish it,' he said. 'I didn't finish my degree either, in case you didn't fuckin' notice. I had to get that wanker of a job. There's not a lot of applications out there that say *we'll let you in with half a degree.*'

Ellie looked away, her jaw jutting. He thought of it as her anti-smile: just as the smile melted him, this expression never failed to irk him.

'You *had* to get that job?' she said. 'You didn't *have* to do anything.'

'Yeah? Well you didn't *have* to get fuckin' pregnant, did ye?'

As soon as the words were out he wanted to pluck them from the air, crumple them into a ball, burn them, bury the ashes and salt the earth under which they lay. Ellie didn't even react, which told him how bad it was. Fuck. Fuck fuck *fuck*, why did it always come down to this?

The silence was all-encompassing. He found himself willing

Luke to wake up, to fill the air with comfortingly familiar stressful noises, to put them both into the autopilot of parental routine into which he might be able to slip an olive branch. But his son was flat out and snoring gently, and nothing would wake him, and the silence just kept on stretching.

Why should you apologise?

He could see the argument stretching out in front of him. You should have used something. So should you. Well we didn't, so there's point in crying about it. Oh, so you want to cry? So it's a bad thing? No, it's not a fuckin' bad thing, but don't blame me for you not finishing your degree and I'll not blame you for me doing the same. Oh that's real fuckin' decent of you, thanks so much for that, what a brilliant basis for a relationship. On and on and on, the same old dance, the same words.

And then she'd drop the nuke: *Why are you here? For me? For him? Or because you're too scared to be called a bastard for not being here?*

All of that lay before him. And so Danny said absolutely nothing, and instead simply lay down and stared at the wall.

His father's words came to him, unbidden, as they always did at times like this.

And I'm glad I did.

Her hand dropped on to his shoulder some time later. His foot curled backward to rest against her leg. They fell asleep.

Light crept back into the corners of the world, illuminating Belfast street by street, dog turd by dog turd. In a house in Regent Street, in a bedroom smelling faintly of words unspoken and night-vintage baby wee, an alarm clock displayed 6.29 a.m.

The bedroom was still and silent. All three occupants dozed peacefully; Luke with a heroically sized puddle of baby drool beside his pudgy little cheeks. Gar-gah was clutched in a deathgrip headlock. The once-a-hippo's eyes pleaded silently for a quick death that would never come.

6.30 a.m. No alarm sounded. However a very low noise, as if a pneumatic drill had been switched on several streets away, began to rumble. Danny's face twitched. As the low noise continued, his nose wrinkled. His eyes struggled open. He grunted in alarm and roused Ellie, who greeted the world with the grace of a bluejay bursting into song.

'Wha?' she huffed. 'Whadayafucawan?'

Danny's eyes were wild and sleep-drunk. 'Somethin' got me! Somethin's in bed! Eatin' me!'

This seemed to blow away the cobwebs from his beloved. 'It's your phone.'

After much uncoordinated rummaging beneath the covers, Danny succeeded in fishing out his mobile phone which was vibrating like crazy. He looked at it in much the same way as his baby son might have examined a nuclear fission reactor instruction manual written in Mandarin.

Ellie rolled over. 'Dickhead,' he heard her mutter.

He stabbed buttons until this angry buzzy thing stopped being angry. Memories swam back to him, including his own name, the name and purpose of objects, and the concepts associated with them. The Equation of Life assembled itself in his mind. It went something like *phone = alarm = work = money = existence = ???*

And last night. Oh yes, he remembered last night all right.

Danny struggled out of bed, eyes open only as slits. He staggered towards the wardrobe. Compared to the general shittiness of the rest of the room, it was fairly impressive – one of those tall double-tiered jobs with a large double-door compartment below a smaller one. His clothes hung very clearly and very visibly indeed on the handle of the upper compartment.

Danny failed to see this. He opened the lower doors … they pushed the clothes hanging from the upper door handles out … the hangers fell off the handle …

A shirt, tie and pair of trousers fell on his head with a *clatter* … *whump*.

'Find your clothes?' Ellie's voice came from the depths of the bed.

Luckily, Danny's reply was muffled.

A short time later, a washed, dressed and combed Danny poked his head back into the bedroom. Luke was having one of his rare sleep-ins, and he expected to find Ellie still turned resolutely away from him. She wasn't. She was sitting up in bed, and she was looking directly at him. He found this confounding of his expectations to be a little unfair.

He sat on the bed and met her eyes. 'I'm sorry about last night.'

She nodded. Didn't say anything else, just nodded. 'Don't forget about tonight.'

He blinked. 'Tonight?'

'Dinner with my mum and dad?'

'Oh,' said Danny in the Leaden Tones of Doom, 'God, I nearly

22

forgot. Well … today at work can't fly in quickly enough to get me back here for that.'

It was a risky approach. But while the Baby-Making Incident and its associated topics and sub-topics were strictly off-limits when it came to Big Conversations, her parents were safe targets. She smiled and he felt that big bag of tension unloosen itself from around his shoulders.

'Mmm. I'll bet. C'mere.'

Danny moved to her. They kissed. As always, her lips tasted of purple.

'I promise it'll go fine. It'll be fun.'

'Mmm. I'll bet,' he replied.

She snuggled back under the covers. He was envious in a way, but he knew that a ticking time bomb of feeds and changes and bottle-making lay in the cot beside them. He leant inside the cot and brushed as substantial a kiss as he dared across his son's cheek, knowing that if he woke the little boy he'd be forced to leave for work through the upstairs window, courtesy of the deceptively slight girl lying in bed.

Pulling the front door gently shut behind him, Danny heard the snib *clack* into the locked position. He glanced up the street, eyes resting on Bea's house. Maybe Ellie's interest in the old lady wasn't about the tea leaves. Maybe it was about finding some company during the daylight hours with someone who had bladder control.

Davros and the Fat Controller walked past his gate. He inclined his head. They gave him A Look.

If that's what she's after, we're living in the wrong street.

*

Danny walked past desk after desk of PC-fixated people, headpieces attached to each one of them like some insanely successful alien symbiote invader. Fingers chattered busily across keyboards. Voices droned. You never knew what a background hum was, not really, not down to the very depths of your soul, until you worked in a call centre. To Danny, the sound had always been brown in colour, which was apt in several ways.

A huge banner was emblazoned with a reminder, as if anyone needed it, that there were only '[2]DAYS TO …'

Danny stopped. He motioned toward the sign as Stuart, one of the guys from the IT department, shambled past. 'Jesus, Stuart,' he whistled. 'Bit on the nose, innit?'

'Huh?' Stuart offered. His eyes drifted upwards in the direction of Danny's gesturing. 'Two days to live,' he intoned.

There was a pause. Danny could see the problem working its way through the Rube Goldberg machine that made up Stuart's thought processes.

'There's a word gone,' Stuart said, in much the same way as Da Vinci must have thought, I'm gonna let the bastards just guess her expression.

Danny was searching on the floor. He let out a triumphant squawk and straightened up, holding a large card with the word 'GO' written on it in big, bold letters.

'That's gonna bug me all day now, wondering what word's missing,' Stuart said, and wandered off.

Danny watched him go. He considered re-attaching the card to the rest of the sign, but when he looked up, he saw that underneath the main message, in a heavily-researched and 'statistics-show-it's-perceived-as-fun' font, they'd added, 'GAME FACES ON, PEOPLE!!!' Fuck them, he decided, flinging the card that said 'GO' like a Frisbee and watching it sail jaggedly through the air.

He plonked himself down at a free desk, going through his hot-desking ritual of hanging his coat over the back of his chair, taking out his wallet and fishing out a small photograph to place on his PC. Ellie and Luke, faces pressed together, stared back at him. He hit a few buttons on the PC and the system thrummed to life, adding its own mournful voice to the cacophony.

'All right, Danny?' said Alice, terminating her call with a shudder of relief. They got twenty-eight seconds of wrap-up time between calls. Not thirty. Twenty-eight. Presumably thirty seemed far too rounded-off and arbitrary a number, whereas twenty-eight seconds suggested a figure that had been thoroughly researched by consultants, at great expense.

'Alice. How's life on the front lines of telephony customer service lookin'?'

'Like I'd need a stepladder to get to hell.'

Danny glanced at the empty seat between them. 'Is Cal not in?'

She coloured instantly. 'No,' she replied. There was a pause, which she obviously felt compelled to fill. 'He's … uh, he's probably sleeping off some drinking session.'

'Aye. So, did you two …?'

Time was up. Alice's headpiece began to bleep. She shrugged apologetically, but looked relieved to be interrupted.

'Good morning,' she said in that horrible sing-song telephonist voice. 'You're through to Lircom. My name is Alice, can I take your customer account number please?'

Danny fitted his headpiece with a silent sigh. Hand resting on his mouse, he teased the cursor over the 'active' button for a few seconds. Finally he took a breath and clicked. Within a heartbeat, his headpiece was beeping.

'Good morning,' Danny sang, in an altogether more reluctant voice than Alice had just used. 'You're through to Lircom. My name is Danny, can I take your ...'

Time passed in gulps, like he was coming up for air every so often.

'... your customer account number is the one with the numbers in, yes... when I say double click I mean you have to click twice, you see ... there was a power cut? And when did it end? I see. Well, I'd advise that you wait until it *does* end before ringing us ... no, click *twice* ...'

Danny went offline with gusto, feeling aggrieved yet again that no matter how firmly you press a mouse button it still just makes a wimpy 'click' noise. There should be a pressure sensor on the fuckers for really vehement clicks that generated more of a *fuck you* type of sound effect – just like there should be a BOOM sound effect that goes down the phone line when you slam down a phone instead of the same standard *click-bmmmmm*.

He was about to leave his desk when a middle-aged man with an unfortunate hairstyle and a comfortable paunch meandered over. Thomas, Danny's boss. He had the office buzzword cliché textbook out and he was running through it step-by-step.

'Danny, mind if we touch base?'

'Well, actually I was just gonna go on lun–'

'It *is* important.'

'Sure,' Danny said.

They walked over to an unoccupied nest of desks. Danny sat down and glanced at the clock. Thomas sat opposite him, flashed him a quarter-second smile, and steepled his fingers in what, presumably, his *Line Management for Dicks* book told him was an 'authoritative yet friendly' pose. Danny always got that one mixed up with the 'cockhead' pose.

'You know I like to give you guys a heads-up.'

'Yes …'

'Let's discuss your utilisation levels. Do you feel they're satisfactory?'

Danny wondered how obvious it was that he was about to pluck an answer out of the air. Should he mime using a pair of chopsticks to try and pluck a bluebottle from mid-flight, Mr Miyagi style? 'Yes?'

'We have a major go-live date approaching fast. Mr Black has made it clear that he wants the very best from the organisation. He wants us to drill down to the bedrock of results, to ramp up our performances. Our target ceilings have shifted, Danny. It's important to keep ahead. I can't function if I'm not sure my agents are being kept up to speed with what's being expected of them on the ground.'

A long pause. Danny's expression was so blank he was surprised Thomas didn't simply get a marker and draw his expression on. That would have been helpful, come to think of it.

'I'll leave that with you,' Thomas continued. 'Your appraisal is coming soon, and you need to identify your change inhibitors. Can we expect to see a little more focus on your change enablers?'

'Count on it!' Danny said, all but mock-saluting.

Thomas nodded, satisfied, and walked away. He loved to dangle the threat of Mr Black in front of the staff; like the chief executive was going to take a personal interest in Danny's call answering rates and utilisation levels anytime soon. Yeah, right. He probably couldn't have picked Danny out of a one-man line-up. He sighed, rose from the identikit desk in the midst of the ghost town of workstations awaiting more drones, and bumped into a young lad of about his age walking in, red-eyed and with deliberately dishevelled hair.

'All right, Cal?'

'All right? I'm sitting on the cusp of damnation staring down into the crimson pit of Hades with nine demons sitting on my back playing cup and ball with my eternal soul. God save me, Danny, from this purgatory of mediocrity.'

Cal had watched *Withnail and I* some years before whilst high on what could only be described as a smorgasbord of drugs, and hadn't just liked the Richard E. Grant Withnail character, but had sort of absorbed him through a screen-to-person osmosis.

'So, did you and Alice …?'

'Danny, please! I can't possibly listen to this!' Cal replied, putting his fingers an inch from his ears and brushing past him in the general direction of the staffroom. He could see Alice's head swivelling to follow him even as her eyes remained fixed on the computer monitor, which was a pretty impressive trick, he had to admit.

'Good luck with the demons thing!' Danny called after him.

Cal turned, all traces of trained actor gone. 'Ach, cheers,' he said in a genuinely pleased way, as if Danny had just wished him luck on a driving test.

Danny rolled his eyes and blew out. This, he thought, was why call centres didn't work. On one side, you had overeducated employees doing complex work for monkey-hit-feeder-bar wages and having to invent interesting personality quirks to pass the time between regretfully shagging one another.

Meanwhile, on the other side, you had incredibly nervous bosses, with much less education, suddenly promoted way beyond the capabilities of their interpersonal skills on the basis that their stunned gratitude would guarantee some infinitesimal degree of employee loyalty. This in an industry where toilet rolls had longer terms of service than staff. And had to put up with less shit.

Danny left the office floor for the adjoining corridor, walking past a poster which happily proclaimed the company slogan: LIRCOM – YOUR GATEWAY TO A BETTER WORLD.

That evening, the home phone rang. Danny picked it up, grateful as ever for a last-minute out from persuading Luke that baby rice was not his sworn enemy. 'Hello?'

'What the Christ about ye?'

Danny grinned. A typical Steve greeting, that. He could just picture him now, the tosser, in that dopey jacket and those ninety-five pound trainers. He'd been heartbroken to have to take the price tag off the fucking things. 'Not bad, mucker. What's up?'

'Not much. Few of us gonna go out later tonight.' Steve paused. 'It's an … uh, it's a special occasion.'

'Oh aye? What's that?'

There was a slight pause.

'Um …'

'Forgot the rest of the joke again haven't ye,' Danny said, his grin only broadening.

'Sorta.'

To give Steve credit, there wasn't a hint of embarrassment in his voice at admitting it. Danny thought for a moment, but only a moment. 'Day with a Y in it?' he suggested.

'Nah.'

'Opening of an envelope?'

'No.'

'Jesus, we've been through your entire back catalogue. Don't ask me.'

'Ach fuck it,' Steve said cheerfully, undaunted. 'I'll remember it later. Anyway, ya comin'?'

Danny licked his lips. 'Um …'

Right on cue, Ellie entered the hallway, baby Luke in her arms. Well, mostly in her arms. Clearly 'Operation Rice' had been abandoned – Luke's teething pangs had been slowly inching up the severity scale over the last few days and currently he was hanging about 70 per cent out of her arms, red-faced and squealing indignantly at the unfairness of existence.

Ellie registered Danny on the phone and instantly deduced the caller and purpose of the call. She managed to raise an eyebrow without actually raising one, hefting baby Luke up like some sort of anti-beer talisman. A long curl of drool ran from his mouth to the thin carpet below.

'Ah Christ,' Steve swore, 'she's there, eh? Code-talkin' time?'

'Most certainly.'

'What do you call them things without backbones?'

Danny wondered for a moment how much of Shakespeare's collected works those monkeys at the typewriters would be able to produce before Steve would come anywhere close to identifying the word invertebrates. 'All right, I get the point,' he said.

Ellie smiled sweetly. 'Who is it, love?'

'It's Steve, ya demented fishwife! You fuckin' tell her I said that, lad!'

Danny smiled back, just as sweetly. 'It's Steven. He says hello.'

'That's nice,' Ellie replied, juggling Luke effortlessly from one shoulder to another in a manoeuvre Danny had never mastered.

'Tell her you're going out with yer mates to get plastered! Big fuckin' wimpy bastard, ye!'

'Well, you know Steven,' Danny said, his hand clamped firmly over the speaker.

'Is he asking you to go out?'

Danny blinked as if flabbergasted by her clairvoyance. 'Why, yes … yes, I believe he is.'

From somewhere around his chin came a muffled, 'Fuckin' better believe it!'

'Shame it's tonight. We're going to dinner,' she said, smiling sweetly until she clocked his blank expression and her mask of uber-niceness slipped for a moment, revealing hidden pits of

Hades he had no wish to explore. 'You know, the dinner you've been so eagerly anticipating all this time. At my parents. Tonight. And anyway,' she carried on briskly, as even little Luke seemed to sense this was a wise time to limit the decibel level, 'even when that's over you promised you'd smooth out that bump in the garden for me – Michelle was tellin' me about a wee green fountain in B&Q that would be lovely there.'

'Oh yeah, so I did,' Danny admitted. Balls. Why did he agree to these things? In what parallel universe was humping a fucking fountain from B&Q and then trying to install the inevitably awkward bastard a reward for working in the garden in the first place?

Ellie winked at him and swept out of sight, bringing Luke with her, ready to plonk him in his high chair and wave watery brownish muck under his nose for an hour until he realised that a) it was food and b) that he was meant to eat it. Danny put the phone back to his ear.

'Prick! You're a prick! Why don't ya just stick on a saddle and sit with a wee nosebag on, eh? Jesus Christ. Pathetic, man. Pathetic.'

Danny was composing a reply along the lines of *fuck you* when Ellie poked her head back into view again, Luke having been safely deposited in his Throne of Despair.

'Danny?'

'What?'

'Can you feed wee Luke a second? I want a word with Steven.'

All the colour drained from Steve's voice.

'She wants a what?' he said.

*

Even his in-laws' front door was posh, Danny thought glumly, examining the fancy glass and brass knockers and wind chimes and all that oul shit all over it. Ellie rang the doorbell and after a few seconds he could see a shape scurrying to answer it. He half expected it to a maid or something but no, it was Christina, Ellie's mother. As always when he saw her the taste of tin flooded his mouth.

'Darling!'

'Hello, Mummy,' Ellie replied. They kissed on both cheeks, each standing too far apart so they had to lean in in an exaggerated way. Danny tried not to roll his eyes at this, or notice the change in her accent. She didn't like having the *posh voice* thing pointed out. Didn't like it with italics on.

'And here's my widdle mansy-wansy woo-woo!' Christina exclaimed, enthusiasm positively dripping out of her as she poked her head into the pram and fussed over Luke. Danny, his face a mask of neutrality as he watched this, wondered if she had practised in the mirror before they arrived. For his part, Luke looked up dubiously at her.

Danny could practically see his tiny, mad little baby brain working. On the plus side, she was paying him attention, and little Luke was nothing if not an unapologetic narcissist. On the minus side, she was clearly mentally ill. Kids aren't mugs. They can spot nutters.

The wailing began. Danny did a fist pump, fist hidden safely in his pocket at the time. Christina hurriedly removed her head.

'Ah, ha ha …' Christina said, nervously wringing her hands as Ellie reached in to coo at and soothe the wee fella. 'Probably finding it all a bit strange to be at a big house!'

Danny gritted his teeth at this. One-nil. He expected nothing short of a whitewash tonight. Christina turned, appearing to acknowledge him for the first time – as if he'd been standing behind a fucking bush or something, when he'd been in plain sight the whole time. Was that two-nil? Oh what the hell. Give them it. This was their sport, and they were fucking world-class at it.

'Christina,' Danny nodded, the metallic tang squatting on his tongue. 'Good to see ya.'

'Danny,' she returned, so very, very politely, so very like her daughter had sounded earlier when he'd been on the phone to Steve. Danny pushed that particular memory away.

'How goes the … call-answering?' she inquired, as though she was a member of the medieval Spanish court asking him was he absolutely sure that was really the fastest way to India?

'Ach, same old, same old. How goes the …' and Danny realised he was going down a conversational dead end. Christina didn't have a job, unless arranging luncheons and appearing in the *Ulster Tatler* could be counted as one, and if it could, she was seriously overworked.

'How's life?' he amended weakly. Ellie flashed him a warning look. He gave her an eyebrow-shrug in return.

'Is Daddy putting the finishing touches on?' Ellie interrupted, seemingly unconcerned about whether Christina was intending to answer Danny or not.

'Oh, you know him. Everything has to be just perfect for his little girl and his darling grandchild.'

Danny resisted the urge to cup his balls and belch loudly just to reassure himself that, yes, he was still here, and, yes, he existed.

'Look at us all, out here on the doorstep!' Christina cackled merrily at this hilarious situation. She had a wonderful laugh. It was like the noise a dog made just before it threw up. 'We'll all freeze! Let's go in and get settled, shall we?'

Unwisely, she chose to intercept her daughter's gentle lift of Luke from the pram, scooping him up from her daughter's arms before she could squeak a warning. Luke goggled in surprise and promptly decided he didn't like this at all. After a few 'awws' and swooshes up and down (not a help) she was forced to give him back to Ellie, who carried him into the house. Danny noted he was on the receiving end of a glance from Christina that seemed to say – *enjoy that, did you?*

Yep. Yep I fuckin' did, he thought right back at her retreating form as she performanced her way down the hallway, Ellie a few steps behind. Danny noticed belatedly that he was all but alone at the doorstep with only the pram for company. He glanced in Ellie's direction, and was surprised to see that she'd stopped.

She smiled and tilted her head in what could only be an embarrassed apology of sorts. He smiled back at her and rolled his eyes, but in a casual, *tuh! parents!* way, far more nonchalant than he was actually feeling. Ellie accepted this and turned again, quickly vanishing from sight into the general living quarters of the house.

'Daddy!' he heard her squeal.

'Bon appétit,' Danny sighed, lugging the pram over the threshold behind him.

*

It should have been a lovely dinner. The food was excellent. The setting – what *Good Homes* magazine would doubtlessly have described as the Quinn's 'delightfully rustic dining room' – was gorgeous.

Instead, it was a bus ride to bollocks.

Danny took in the tableau of dysfunction before him from the comfortable and privileged position of 'outsider' while at the same knowing that his being that outsider was a major cause of what he was witnessing.

Ellie was eating – that is, alternating between smiling manically and jabbing her neck downward to nip at food, casting uncomfortable glances this way and that.

'Daddy' was Mr Michael Quinn, a suave executive in his mid-forties with iron-on respectability. He was head of a small telecommunications company, FormorTech, a minor rival of Lircom's. Currently Daddy was sawing into a steak so thick it looked like tyrannosaur thigh with a large serrated knife in impeccably observed silence. You had to hand it to the man. Even his moments of social awkwardness were professionally done.

Christina, pecking daintily at some vegetables, had her eyes cast down. Christina was a strange one around food at the best of times: from what Danny had been able to discern from the few times they'd met, she must have been able to draw fat content from oxygen itself, for he had never seen anything larger or more fattening than a broccoli stalk pass her lips, and yet she wasn't exactly stick thin.

He suspected that deep in chez Quinn's attic terrified families of chocolate products were awaiting the day when they too would be frogmarched onto the trains to Christinavitz.

For his own part, Danny found himself glumly pushing his food around the plate. He had waited until Ellie had picked up her knife and fork before choosing one of his sets. When he was younger he'd been to a wedding where they'd had more than one pair of each implement, and he and the other kids had marvelled at the forethought of the hotel to lay on spares for when you dropped the other one on the carpet and it got manky.

Besides, he didn't like eating anywhere but his own house, truth be told. It wasn't that the cooking wasn't as good as it was at home, or even at his mother's. Danny loved his mother dearly, but the nearest she was ever going to get to being Jamie Oliver was if she developed a lisp, stole Turkey Twizzlers off schoolkids and started annoying millions of people at once.

No, it was the synaesthesia that was the problem. He'd been seventeen years old and almost at Queen's before he'd even known the condition had a name. He'd been thirteen before he even realised he had a condition, come to that. To Danny, it was just how things were. Colours had a smell, smells had a taste, and nearly everything and everyone generated their own little sensory footprints. Ellie tasted of purple. Sunday mornings smelled like chips. Numbers were coloured and some were ugly while some were beautiful.

His whole life, it had generated puzzled frowns and pats on the head from kindly people he'd tried to explain it to. He'd learnt to keep it to himself; it wasn't that hard, after all, it wasn't as though it was debilitating … most of the time, anyway, and that was the crux of the problem with eating out. More than any other

37

sensation, synaesthesia reacted to taste. In another person's house, tasting their food, it could be wildly unpredictable. He didn't fancy trying to keep a straight face when an innocent mouthful of vegetables set off a series of flashes in his mind, anything from a childhood memory to an overpowering smell.

But it wasn't like the dinner was a total loss for everyone.

'ASSSAawwwwwasszzzzaaahhhhbbbaaa!'

Little Luke, in a wooden high chair that looked like an *Antiques Roadshow* castoff (and that Ellie had twice inspected for splinters), was having the time of his life. He was within reach of most of the food, for one. He had twice as many targets as normal. He was currently mashing his plastic plate of baby-gruel with his palm and squealing with delight. Huge globules of food were hanging off his nose and chin. He was completely filthy, a street urchin amid the finery, and Danny had never loved him more than he did right then.

As if picking up on this, Luke chose that moment to smile gummily at his dad. Danny grinned right back and winked at his son. Dear old Daddy, seeing this exchange, seemed less enthused. He cleared his throat ostentatiously.

'Did I tell you that FormorTech's output is up by 12 per cent this fiscal year, Ellie?'

Ellie almost fainted with relief at having something verbal to respond to. 'Oh, that's great, Daddy!'

'Oh well … you know. I've been insisting to the board that we push up the sales envelope these past twelve months. In fact I've been drilling it into them so consistently that some of my directors, ah ha ha, have taken to calling me "Duracell Man".'

Pushing up an envelope? Danny wondered how that worked. He had a mental image of Michael Quinn being eaten by a huge envelope, its mighty flap opening up hungrily and swallowing him whole, leaving only a slight gummy tang in the air and a world rejoicing.

Ellie was doing her best to laugh at the Duracell Man thing.

'Because, you see, the Duracell slogan was "just keeps going and going and going".'

Ellie's smile wilted slightly under the strain. 'Yeah, Dad, I get it.'

'Lircom have been sniffing around us again, of course. I know Black would love to get his hands on our patents. But there's no way I'm going to sell to him.'

'Danny works for Lircom,' said Ellie, the eternal conversational optimist.

'Yes,' Michael said neutrally, 'well, I'm not sure how privy you'd be to senior management decisions, Danny. You're still in the' – slight pause – 'customer service team?'

'Yep.'

'Team leader at least, I assume?'

'No,' Danny replied evenly. 'No, just a regular call-answerer guy.'

'And how do you find that?'

'Wonderful. Every day seems like a blessing.'

'The way FormorTech is performing, I wouldn't be surprised if one day you found yourself working for me.'

With immaculate comic timing, Luke let rip with an enormous belch.

Who says you can't train a baby? Danny thought, redirecting his gaze from Michael to the food on his plate as he tried, not particularly hard, to suppress a smile.

'Goodness!' Christina said. 'Someone's enjoying dinner, aren't they?'

Danny lifted his head, trusting himself to resume eye contact. Michael was staring directly at him with a look of such naked contempt that it actually staggered him for a moment; there was nothing in those eyes but disgust. Danny felt a chill go down to his bones. He'd always known that Ellie's parents didn't exactly approve of the relationship, that they suspected he'd deliberately sabotaged their only darling daughter's incredibly bright future and dragged her down to his level.

But it wasn't mere dislike he saw in Michael Quinn's eyes. It was hate, pure and simple. The bastard hadn't even the common decency to look away when he'd been caught in the act – he kept the eye contact right on going. Only when Ellie glanced over in their direction did the temperature of the look rise to something approaching civilised and his lip uncurled.

Danny was reeling. He'd never been hated by anyone or anything in his life. He had no idea how to react, except that a hot little ball of anger and humiliation was kindling in his stomach.

'Where were we? Oh yes, your career, Danny!' Michael Quinn burst forth, all professionalism and cheeriness. 'You're still on the lookout for a better job?'

'I've a few irons in the fire,' Danny heard himself reply. It was his standard reply for anyone who asked him about his shitty job in that shitty call centre. His brain wasn't in the game yet. He tried to prod himself back. He wasn't about to give this fucker the satisfaction.

'Well, that's excellent news. After all, student jobs are for students – you can't seriously expect to support a family on a call centre salary?'

Danny felt a *thrummm* as his mind stepped back into the game. He narrowed his eyes. If Michael Quinn wanted to play, so be it.

'I agree with ye totally. Trouble was, you see, when Ellie here found out she was pregnant, my first thought was that we needed to get some money behind us, get somewhere to live, give the baby a roof over its head. Lircom was hiring, they were handy on the bus, and they offered flexible hours while the wee fella's so young. It's not world-beatin' in terms of wages, but we're all fed and watered, and everyone has to start somewhere. I'm sure a great businessman like yourself appreciates that, Mr Quinn.'

He glanced at Ellie, not knowing what to expect. A corner of her mouth lifted. It wasn't exactly a resounding standing ovation, but it'd do.

'Oh I do,' the reply came. 'But you'll appreciate that I want the best for my daughter and my grandson. I wish you'd reconsider my offer to accept a little financial help.'

And be indebted to you the rest of my days? Not fuckin' likely.

'It's appreciated, but we do okay,' he lied. Any household that needed an emergency fiver wasn't exactly breaststroking idly through a sea of opulence.

Quinn wasn't done yet, it seemed. 'Perhaps your father could put in a good word for you at … I'm sorry, where does he work again?'

That little ball inside Danny began to burn. In his peripheral vision he could see Ellie stiffen and he knew she'd be preparing to intervene, trying to think of some way to defuse the oncoming storm. All he had to do was stall, give her time to think of something.

'He doesn't.'

'Doesn't ...?'

'Work.'

'Oh yes, of course, my mistake. Ellie mentioned this to me some time ago. Health issues, I understand?'

The table was silent now. Ellie knew it was too late to intervene, that any such attempt would only be so blatant as to make the awkwardness even more pronounced. It was just the two of them now, with Ellie and Christina looking on, observers in this back-and-forth.

'He's an alcoholic,' Danny said. He said it quietly, but he didn't mumble the word. The low volume in his voice wasn't born of shame but from the effort of keeping his emotions in check.

'Oh.' Michael absorbed this supposed revelation with such false, wide-eyed sympathy that for a moment Danny expected him to clasp his hands over his heart and swoon. 'That must have been difficult for you. Growing up.'

'Daddy ...'

'Ellie,' Danny said, holding up a placating hand. 'It's fine.'

'No,' she said firmly, ignoring the gesture. 'No, it's not fine. Daddy, is this really something we want to talk about at the dinner table? Unless you'd like me to talk about Granda Quinn? Or Uncle Dermot? How's he doing?'

It was as if she'd stuck a pin in her father. His pomposity seemed to *wheeeeee* out of him like air from an escaping balloon. He gave his daughter a look of shocked betrayal. Ellie simply returned the look, before very deliberately turning her eyes away from her father and addressing her mother with forced casualness.

'So, Mummy, what do you think of the little man? Isn't he growing fast?'

Christina all but threw herself for the conversational life-raft. 'Oh he certainly is!' she exclaimed. 'And he just loves his food! Don't you my widdle man? Yes you do! Yes you do!'

Michael seemed to sense the moment had passed. 'I'll bet his granddad can get a big kiss from him,' he said with such stiff spontaneity that it was a wonder he hadn't filled out a permission slip. 'Let's see what–'

He leant in close to Luke. Luke, quite reasonably in Danny's view, interpreted this not as a desire for a kiss but as a way of saying, *mmm that gloop all over your hands looks tasty, mind if I take a bite?*

Ever happy to oblige, the little fella promptly smeared his food-covered chubby fingers all over his grandfather's face. Michael Quinn recoiled as if shot, his face covered in carrot and potatoes.

'Oh! Daddy!'

Ellie scurried from her seat, a baby-wipe already in her hand. Where she fished them out from Danny could never say; he was beginning to suspect she dispensed them from a slot in her stomach. He watched as a middle-aged businessman allowed his face to be cleaned, meek as a toddler.

Sometimes it was the little things in life you learned to appreciate.

The Call

There's something therapeutic about hard graft, people who haven't done a hard day's graft in their entire lives often say.

Danny wiped some dirt from the bridge of his nose and leant on the spade. The late evening breeze cooled the sweat beading on his forehead.

'Know what?' Steve pronounced grandly. 'It's at times like this that ye ...'

Danny glanced bemusedly at his partner-in-sod, who was leaning on his own implement with less of a devil-may-care pose and more of a holy-fuck-I'm-ballixed slump. Steve had been a bit of a sportsman in school, but school had been almost six years ago now. He was cultivating a comfortable belly and, by the looks of him, he was quite the botanist.

'That you ... what?'

Steve shrugged. 'Ach, I've lost my train of thought.'

'It's at times like this, with the moon on your back and only the honest toil of good manual labour to keep you warm that you look around, and you think to yourself, *fuck me, I wish she'd let us go to the pub?*'

44

Steve grinned. 'Aye, somethin' like that, lad.'

Danny let his gaze drift upward, away from the garden hump they were manfully attacking, away from Regent Street in the balmy late evening moonlight, to the starry sky above. It was a gorgeous night. Belfast wasn't usually much for starfields with all the light pollution, but tonight was an exception: they could have turned off the streetlamps and you could have almost read a book, such was the stellar lightshow going on above their heads. The air sparkled.

'Here, back to work, you,' Steve rebuked him indignantly. 'Get the missus to rope me into your chain gang and then slack off, will ye? Cheeky fucker.'

Danny swung into reluctant action, but his momentum had been lost somewhat. He caught his friend's eye and sighed. 'You should have seen them two dickheads earlier.'

'Who's this?'

'Her ones.'

Steve *tsk'd* disapprovingly. As tradition demanded, since they were no longer talking about football or tits and instead about real emotions, they avoided eye contact, and so Steve was ostensibly staring down at the soil below as he hacked into the uneven surface. 'Ach, that pair o' fuckwits. They need their heads surgically extracted from their holes, them two. Sure you've always known that, lad. No surprises there.'

'Her da brought up my da's drinkin',' Danny said quietly.

Steve looked up, his surprise overriding the usual taboos. 'Fuck. What'd ya do?'

'Not much I could do, was there? Not like I could call him a liar.'

'No, but you could have told him that your family was none of his fuckin' business. Pencil-necked shite.'

'It is sorta his business but, isn't it? I'm goin' out with his daughter. I'm supposed to be the provider and the husband and the father and all that. And there's him, Mr Chief Exec, Mr Fuckin' Success Story, and me ...'

He trailed off, then shook himself out of it and went back to safer pastures. 'Besides, it woulda been kind of ironic – me stickin' up for my da.'

'Blood's thicker than water to a blind donkey,' Steve intoned.

Despite the general shittiness of the topic, Danny laughed. He couldn't help it. Steve had the most ridiculous way of mixing his metaphors that never failed to crack Danny up; and if in doubt, he would stick 'to a blind donkey' on the end. They had remarkable wisdom, the visually impaired *Equus africanus asinus*.

'You've a perfect right to call your da all the names you want,' Steve went on, 'but some power-suited ganch who knows fuck all about you or your family doesn't.'

They went back to the digging for a while. Danny didn't much feel like saying more on the subject, and Steve sensed it with the practised ease of a man who'd known his friend for well over a decade.

'Right. Back's broke on this fucker. I'm havin' a break,' Steve said. It was true; they had been at it for almost an hour now, and the little hump of earth that had been a source of consternation to Ellie since they moved in to Regent Street just over a year back had been all but eradicated. Danny was quite proud of his efforts, but slightly worried too; was he setting a precedent here? Was she going to expect him to do things like put up shelves now?

Or – his blood chilled even at the thought – *redecorate*?

A sweet smoky smell made his nose twitch. A familiar smell. He glanced sidelong at Steve, who was bent over, shielding something from the elements. When he straightened up again, Danny's suspicions were confirmed.

'You're jokin' me, aren't ya?'

Steve blinked, having just taken his first long inhalation. 'Jesus Christ, lad, it's only a wee joint sure.' He patted his pockets. 'Ya wantin' one?'

Danny looked shocked and affronted. 'What's this? Peer pressure?'

Steve gave his best devilish grin. 'Yep. All the cool kids are doing drugs, you know,' he said, and snickered evilly. 'If you don't take one, you're a big fuckin' girl's blouse and the girls won't like you. Actually,' he paused judiciously and took another draw, 'I'd better not say that part to Ellie. She'd never let me within ten miles of your house with a joint in case some big busty blonde stole ye away.'

'Aye,' Danny agreed, 'she's the jealous type all right.'

'Fuck knows why. You're an ugly cunt.'

'Cheers.'

'Not a worry,' Steve said. He fished out another joint and offered it to Danny. Danny looked down at the little white tube, unevenly rolled (Steve never had been the best at it), and shook his head.

'That horse has bolted, lad. It's not for me.'

'Horse has bolted!' Steve cried in despair. 'Listen to ye! You're twenty-three years old for the love of fuck! Just because you've a ball and chain now and a wee fella doesn't mean you can't have a laugh now and again!'

Danny sighed. 'Steve, it was only fun because we were nineteen and we lived in a flat the size of your Danielle's thong.'

Steve spluttered indignantly. 'You leave my sister's knickers outta this!'

Danny shrugged. 'I try, but my mind keeps goin' back to them. Anyway,' he added quickly, seeing Mount Steve was about to erupt in a shower of brotherly rage, 'my point is, things have changed.'

Steve lifted the spade pointedly. 'Yep. This is nightlife for you now.'

'Ach away,' Danny replied, 'if I'd wanted to go out tonight, Steve, I would've.'

Seeing his chance, Steve nodded animatedly. 'Same with me sure, same with me,' he said. 'I mean when she came on the phone and says about comin' and helpin' you out tonight I didn't say yeah cos I'm afraid of her.'

'Nahhhhhh.' Danny pooh-poohed this ridiculous notion.

'If I'd wanted to go out I would've, like,' Steve concluded.

'Yeah,' Danny agreed. 'It's not like she says jump and we–'

'Hey!' a familiar female voice called.

In one smooth in-unison motion both scrambled into action, chins off spades, cutting surfaces stuck back into the ground with renewed vigour. In a moment of panic Steve flapped the joint from his mouth, kicking it behind him with a brilliantly executed mid-air back-heel volley even as it fell from his lips.

'Boys?'

They turned and beheld Ellie, holding a tray of goodies featuring Wotsits and beer – a six-pack of cans sitting proudly, giving off rays of frosted-ice goodness.

Like ravenous wolves, spades cast aside, Danny and Steve descended on their prey.

A short time later, Danny was allowing another long draught of cold beer to wash down his throat. Ellie's hands were wrapped around his waist from behind. She smelled of apricots and baby milk. Steve was standing off to one side, staring up at the stars.

Danny wondered if his friend was all right. It had been, what, a few months now, just, since the big break-up of Steve and Maggie. Before Maggie, Steve had always done all right, women-wise. He'd a mouth like a sanitation plant and a mind like the Readers' Letters pages in dirty magazines, but girls had a way of sensing that he was a decent fella beneath it, that it was all bluff and bluster.

Since Maggie, Steve had had a few bits of luck here and there, but Danny had sensed that his friend's heart wasn't quite in it. Even the camera-phone pictures he'd sent of the sleeping girls' tits had seemed somehow hollow.

Not for the first time, Danny contemplated bringing up what had happened between Steve and Maggie, broaching the subject of the cause of the break-up. They were fellas, not girls, which meant traumatic life experiences weren't immediately the cause for a ring-around of close mates, a crying session, loud music, vodka, soppy DVDs and the general consensus that all men were cunts anyway.

Danny was quite thankful for that in many ways, but the whole male wall of silence thing did make it hard to know what was going on inside his mate's mind. Assuming, of course, there was much going on in there beyond sexual fantasies and pondering matters of universal truth, like 'if all the Premiership managers had a fight, who'd win, and why?'

He'd have asked Maggie herself, of course, but that wasn't really an option either now, was it?

As Danny considered this, something seemed to pull Steve's mind from the murky depths. 'What about the wee man?' he said. Danny looked at his friend – from time to time, Steve would surprise him by displaying genuine concern for the baby.

'D'you wanna listen for yourself?'

Ellie handed him the transmitting end of the baby monitor. Steve raised it to his ear and absorbed the soft, cute, snuffly baby breathing noises emanating from within. Danny grinned. Tonight was one of Luke's rare 'play ball' nights, it seemed.

'Finally went over fifteen minutes ago. Gave him enough Calpol to knock out Jabba the Hutt.'

'That's my clever girl,' Danny said. 'Mother of the yearrrow!' as her fingers dug painfully into his sides and she made as if to snap off one of his earlobes with her teeth.

'Get a room, yous two cunts,' Steve said mildly.

'Get a room? We're standin' in front of our house,' Danny pointed out.

'Aye well,' Steve said, and left it at that. Danny lifted his hands to Ellie's and gently de-coupled her from him, turning as he did so to give her an eyebrow wiggle and nod in Steve's direction. Ellie got it, thankfully, and did not protest.

'It's not usually this starry, is it?' Steve said, once again looking upward to the thousands of tiny pinpricks bleeding silver light into the orbital tapestry suspended above.

'I was thinkin' the same thing earlier,' Danny admitted.

'There's not even any midges about,' Ellie observed.

She was right. Ordinarily they'd be swarming all over the garden at this time of night at this time of year. But tonight, not a one. Even the main road into town, only a street or so away, was quiet. The occasional car purred past, but the city was all but silent around them. It was beautiful, if slightly eerie. The sort of night, Danny thought to himself, where you could imagine seeing figures lurch out of the mists in the distance and realise the quiet was due to an oncoming zombie apocalypse.

'My granny used to tell me stories about the stars,' Ellie said softly. 'She used to say that every single one of them was a soul on its way to Paradise.'

'Really?' Danny said, unable to stop himself. 'I heard an oul folk tale that they're all vast cauldrons of nuclear fusion brought together by gravitational pull, where hydrogen is turned into helium and the resulting waste energy is given off as heat. Silly superstitions, eh?'

'And you an English student?' Ellie said. 'You're about as poetic as a kick in the balls.'

'Ach I just hate all that shite. Souls on their way to heaven,' Danny snorted. 'My hole.'

Ellie rolled her eyes. 'Mister Misery guts. Just for that you don't get to hear any of my nanny's stories.'

Danny put a hand to his heart. 'And after me and my colleague here doing such a sterling job tonight. I am offended.'

Ellie cast an appraising glance around the garden and nodded approvingly. 'So yous did,' she admitted, and her eyes glinted mischievously in the moonlight. 'Just think how much satisfaction you'll get from standing back and admiring the lovely wee fountain when you pick it up from B&Q on Saturday.'

A mouthful of cold beer arced out of Steve's mouth.

'Do what now?' he spluttered.

'Hold firm, lad,' Danny ordered him. 'Don't cave in. She needs to sweeten the deal. Them's the rules, sweetheart.'

Ellie coughed delicately. 'Well. Ah, obviously I can't promise you both the same incentives …'

Steve gave an, *I could live with that* shrug. 'I dunno.'

'Shut it, you.'

'Here wait a minute.'

'Want me to start talkin' about your sister's thong again?' Danny went on, ignoring the look on Ellie's face and knowing he was going to have to explain that one later.

'How about a promise of more cold mead for my favourite warriors, upon completion of their mythical task?' Ellie offered.

'Me like way serving wench thinks!' Steve replied, giving the thumbs-up.

'Watch it with the "serving wench",' Ellie replied instantly, flashing him a sweet little smile, 'or your balls will be Mighty Thor.'

Plop.

Plopplop.

Huge drops of rain started to land on Danny's head and nose. He looked up and got one right in his left eye, the world blurring for a moment, the garden around them turning into a warped version of itself. He let loose with a reflexive string of curses and threw his arms above his head before they gathered the various implements and goodies from around them, shouting chaotic instructions to each other as they made a beeline for the shelter of the house.

Once inside, Danny stared out in disbelief. It was pissing down. Rain danced off the path. Already the flat surface of the garden they'd worked so hard to create was beginning to swampify.

'Where'd that come from?' Steve said, craning his head to catch a glimpse of the skies as he looked out of the front windows. Ellie had gone upstairs to check on the wee fella. 'I coulda sworn there wasn't a cloud up there.'

Danny nodded in agreement. 'At least we got everything done before it came on,' he said, rotating his shoulders, feeling an ache begin to throb there. He grabbed the phone. 'Taxi?'

Steve nodded. 'Cheers. Might take tomorrow off like.'

Must be nice to be able to afford to, Danny thought, even as his mouth worked to order the taxi.

The wailing penetrated his peaceful slumber, a hook baited with obligation that, try as he might to swim away from it, he eventually had to clamp down on and hang on as it jerked him to the surface.

The bedroom was lit only by the soft glow of the nightlight –

all long shadows and hulking squat shapes. He could sense Ellie beside him similarly rousing herself, even through the wailing, all-pervading siren. Danny saw her head lift off the pillow, maybe an inch, and a moan issued forth from her lips. She turned her head and gave him a pitiful *would you mind?* look, and for just a moment, he hated her.

This was her thing. She didn't … WAAHHHHH … work she didn't have to … WAHHHH WAHHHH … trail herself off to that fucking … WAHHHH … call centre, so she was supposed to … WAHHHHH-HAHHHHH … pick this slack up, but here she was now giving him the pleading eyes because he seemed to be marginally more awake than she was.

He closed his eyes and sighed. She must have taken this as a sign of victory, because a half-second later, when his eyes opened, he was looking at a fast-asleep Ellie once again, as Luke continued to renew his wailing vows to the universe at large.

Of all the shocks of parenthood, the myriad of little 'oh shit' moments that lined themselves up one after the other when a baby surfaced in your life – changing a nappy, making a bottle, burping, dressing them … all of that – nothing had quite prepared him for the crying.

He'd been an only child so he'd never had a brother or sister, but he'd been around babies – who hadn't? – and had heard them cry loads of times. Only those babies would be shushed by their parents and then taken away to calm down …

It was the *taking away* bit that had lulled him into that false sense of security.

Those first few nights after they had brought Luke home

from the hospital, the little fella (so tiny and so cute) had let rip with the wailing. They'd fed him. Sometimes this worked. They'd burped him. Sometimes this worked. They'd changed his nappy. Sometimes this worked.

Sometimes, none of them worked.

And when they hadn't, when all avenues had been exhausted and still the crying continued – not every day but enough days, not every night but enough nights – the realisation had crept up on Danny that there was no *taking away* now. All there was was listening to this noise, this incredible undulating howl that went up and down, got louder and quieter, hit pitches that reverberated inside the head and the teeth.

It was torture. A special kind of torment that got worse if you acknowledged it or let your frustration with it show – not just because losing your temper and snapping at the tiny little form you were responsible for inevitably made it wail all the more, but also because the horrible realisation that you'd just shouted at a baby settled on you, so now not only did you have the crying to deal with, you had the knowledge that you were a horrible human being too. Knowledge that only served to increase your despair.

Thankfully, this wasn't one of those times.

The wee man had quietened when, after a brief delay to knock on the kettle and start the bottle-warming process, his daddy had lifted him from the cot. Now, as Luke softly glugged the freshly made bottle down, his little eyes went from wide open and staring, to half-open and relaxed, to closed. Danny, his back propped up against the soft headboard, considered navigating past his partner's sleeping form to perform the 'replace-the-golden-idol' scene from the beginning of *Raiders of the Lost Ark*; but one rash move laying Luke down flat in his cot and a giant rolling boulder'd seem like a fucking birthday present.

Instead he sat there holding his son in the crook of his arm, Luke's ridiculously small head resting against his chest. The little fella was breathing raggedly in and out with a barely-audible *hnff*, the result of a full stomach.

He was so tired. The dinner with her parents. Flattening the mound in the garden. Having a few beers with Steve. They hadn't gone to bed until well after midnight.

Luke needed burped … all that milk. He shouldn't be held while he slept … body heat … wasn't good for …

… so tired …

… Danny's head lolled to the side as sleep claimed him. Moments later, only the slow, rhythmic sound of sleep-breathing could be heard in the quiet dark of the bedroom.

The residents of Regent Street awoke to the clanking and rattling of bin collection day, and, moments later, were treated to the whooping and hollering of Danny Morrigan, as he charged down the back alleyway, his face red with indignation.

'Oy!'

The binman turned. This took him longer than it should have done, for he was a very large specimen of humankind, a fact that wasn't lost on the young man currently skidding to a halt in front of him, his righteous anger wilting somewhat in the face of the odds.

'Aye?' rumbled the binman. Two of his co-binmen behind him, who until this moment had been flinging bins onto the back of the lorry, paused to regard Danny keenly. He didn't like being regarded keenly by big hulking binpeople. It wasn't him, he decided.

Danny indicated the bin behind him. Ellie had insisted on putting a big fucking sticky plastic picture of a daisy on the side of the thing, presumably on the basis that the local hoods would be less likely to steal a gay bin. His cheeks burned with shame.

'You ah …' he mumbled, 'you … you didn't empty this.'

A huge finger descended and indicated a plastic sticker on the bin lid.

'Cos it's contaminated.'

Danny looked. There was a sin bin list on the note of unrecyclable materials and someone had ringed 'plastic bags' with what looked like blood.

'There's no plastic bags in it!' he protested. 'Look!'

He opened the bin lid to prove his point. Plastic bags sailed free in their droves, whirling out into the chilly morning air like happy little polyurethane helicopters. All that was missing was a 'yippee, freedom!'-style cartoon sound effect.

A particularly delighted Asda bag, whipped by a spirited breeze, *whapped* through the air and attached itself to Mount Binman's north face. A hand with fingers like aerosol cans reached up and removed the offending object.

Danny closed the bin lid.

'Ah,' was all he said.

The walk of contrition back to his back yard was long indeed, made all the longer as he had to pass several of his neighbours out to collect their freshly-emptied bins. Danny prayed to the gods that they would all curl up and die horribly somewhere, and then a presence at his left arm and a distinctive smell of Shake 'n' Vac made his heart sink.

'Ye can't recycle the wee plastic bags, son.'

'Yes, thanks, Mrs Dunwoody.' *Fuck off, Mrs Dunwoody.*

'They give ye a wee list of things you can recycle. I think I have a spare one, if you need–'

'No thanks, Mrs Dunwoody.' *FUCK OFF, MRS DUNWOODY!*

'You should– ' but the rest of her latest pearl of wisdom was swallowed up by the door separating his yard from the alley scraping shut in her wizened old face. Did she seriously think he was that daft? His eyes flashed. *Speaking* of daft …

'Ellie!'

She poked her head over the landing, her hair wrapped in a towel. 'Did you catch them in time?'

He took a breath. 'Yes I did – for all the fuckin' good it did me! You put plastic bags in again?!'

Her head drew back defensively. 'No! I put them in the black bin!'

'When?'

'A few nights back!'

'In the dark …?'

Realisation dawned on her. 'Did I pick the wrong bin?' she said, grimacing. 'Oops … sorry, love.'

'Why d'you think I put the fucker out a day early?' Danny

demanded. 'You know what that alley's like the night before collection. Now I'll have to phone them to arrange an extra collection, meaning I'll probably have to go out tonight and do it all over again!'

She rolled her eyes. 'Jesus Christ!' she exclaimed. 'It's bringin' a bin out to an alley! I'll do it if it bothers ye that much!'

His jaw set. She'd pulled that bluff before and he'd backed down. Not this time. 'Righto,' he called up. 'Seeing as how I did your night feed last night, yeah?'

The head and towel flounced from sight above. He trudged upstairs, taking off the makeshift bin-chasing outfit he'd thrown on in a panic when they'd espied the lack of emptying going on from the window. It was 8.21, one of his least favourite times – all horrible browns and greens. By rights he should have left for work ten minutes ago, so now he was going to be late and, in all likeliness, would have to endure another one of Boss Thomas' mystifying lectures. Wonderful. Superb.

She was in the bathroom, the door shut, making approximately 40 per cent more noise than was necessary just to let him know she was, in fact, fucked off with him. Luke was lying in his cot, awake, sucking mightily on his fist, baby spit covering everything around his head like a deleted scene from *Ghostbusters*. He gurgled in Danny's direction as his daddy swept this way and that above his head, but Danny was too busy trying to find a work outfit to pay much heed.

Ellie emerged from the bathroom, discarding her towel and walking in front of him naked, not even looking in his direction. She smelled of apricots. He could practically see the beckoning fingers of aroma curling under his nostrils, pulling his head up, making him look.

No. *No*. He'd told her a million fuckin' times not to throw stuff out in the dark because the two bins sat beside each other (they'd little choice given the size of the yard) and a blue recycling bin looked like a black rubbish bin in the darkness. She never listened. She just nodded and looked cute and he thought it was going in, but in truth she was too busy thinking of what she was going to say when his lips stopped moving, merely biding her time until that happened.

And he was sick of it.

Sick of her not listening. Sick of her fuckin' parents making him feel like a piece of dogshit that their daughter had unwittingly stepped in whilst out shopping in her Jimmy Choos, to be scraped off at all costs.

Sick of having to find a white shirt with as few visible creases as possible (because she – somehow or fucking other – hadn't time to iron and he baulked at the very notion) to go to a job he despised.

Sick of being talked down to by people who, rather than enquiring whether he was serious about managing his fucking utilisation levels, in a fairer world, in a *just* world, would instead be asking him if he wanted fries with that.

Sick of falling asleep half-propped on a headboard at ridiculous o'clock in the morning because he'd unleash an air-raid siren if, God forbid, he went three feet to the right and tried to put Luke where he belonged.

Sick of the smell of night-old piss greeting him every morning.

He stood up, and felt something brush his arm. Ellie had reached out a hand and touched him. He met her eyes and saw that her face had softened. Her lips were parting, and he could tell she was going to attempt to quell the disagreement before he left for work.

'I don't know if I can do this,' he said, before she could speak.

And with that, he walked out of the room, out of the house, closing the front door behind him then slamming the gate shut.

' … No, sir, you have to click *twice*… what's your contract number? … is that N for November? Okay.'

As his mouth moved, he watched Alice and Cal. She would take calls and be all business, but her eyes would drift to him over and over. He was doing something similar, and occasionally, the oh-so-casual sweeping glances they were casting at each other would lock, and for a moment they would stare at each other and both would falter for a heartbeat on their scripted speech to the customers on the telephone.

He wanted to reach across the table and shake them.

Instead he logged out and made his way to the vending machine. A3. Mars bar. As he watched it corkscrew lazily from its holder, he could feel the weight of his mobile in his back pocket. All morning he'd had it sitting on the desk in front of him, in a mild flouting of the rules, waiting for it to light up and vibrate across the polished, sterile tabletop. But it had remained steadfastly immobile.

He'd been composing replies to the inevitable text from her all morning in his mind, ranging from rude to conciliatory to long and rambling. But now it seemed the 'inevitable' text wasn't quite living up to billing. *And why would she text you? It was you who came out with it, wasn't it, and then walked out like a big yellow bastard …*

In the time it took Danny to stoop down and retrieve the Mars, a reflection had appeared in the glass of the vending machine.

'Hey, Thomas,' Danny said, without looking around.

'Danny. A word?'

'I just want to get back on the calls,' he said weakly. He nodded in the direction of the wallboard, reflecting how ridiculous this all was as he did so. 'The queues are up to sixteen minutes and–'

'I know what the queues are, Danny,' Thomas said quietly.

They walked away from the main bank of desks and towards the inactive part of the floor. There wasn't even a room you could go into for a private chat in this place – only the chief exec had one, and that was on the floor above.

Danny hovered near the area where they usually stopped, but Thomas was walking past, stopping only when he reached the vacant desks and chairs adjacent to the windows overlooking the city centre. Danny felt his stomach knot. He sat down anyway.

'Sorry about coming in late there,' he said, as offhandedly as he could manage. A feeling of numb inevitability was spreading through him. He wiggled his fingers on the desk in front of him, to ensure he could still feel the realness around him. He cast a glance around the floor. He wanted to stand up. He just wanted to take a call.

'Danny, your probation period was extended because of your lateness and your sick record. We're going live with the biggest contract in Lircom's history in two days time. Management doesn't want anyone who might prove to be a liability. Your probationary period expires on Friday week. We're not going to renew it. I'm sorry.'

Thomas the laughable wanker. How they'd sat around the desks and chuckled at his antics. Thomas the worst manager ever. And he was looking at Danny with sympathy in his eyes. No, not sympathy.

Pity.

If he'd thought he was going through the motions before, what he was doing now would have made his previous form look scintillating. Nothing like hearing you were going to be sacked for putting some verve into your voice.

As his mouth moved, Danny found himself looking out of the windows at the Belfast vista. He'd always found it grimly amusing that a call centre he mostly viewed as a prison should have such glorious wraparound floor-to-ceiling views. About a hundred yards away, was a rail bridge that crossed the River Lagan. Sometime during the last few minutes, a train had ground to a halt on it, exactly in the middle of the bridge. It was suspended, caught like a fly in amber over the waters below.

Although he wasn't a regular train traveller by any means, Danny knew that trains had to stop occasionally to allow others using the same track ahead of them to switch. It wasn't the first time he'd looked out to see one parked over the river, in fact. And yet the sight never failed to raise an ever-so-slight chill of excitement within him. There was something inherently wrong about seeing a train immobile over the water. From this distance, he could just about make out heads at windows, the occasional ripple of movement within.

While telling someone how to reinitialise their network connection, Danny found his mind idly picking at the scab of the world outside his window, pulling it aside to reveal an apocalyptic wound. Under red skies, the train had stopped mid-track because that was when the power had died, that was when someone had hit the button. The passengers were rotting corpses on chewing-gum spattered seats. Never to arrive, it was a time capsule of humanity, strewn with newspapers and snack-size Pringles tubes. How long would it remain there, he wondered, parked and still. How much time would pass before a combination of wind and wave eroded those bridge supports and the silent train would come tumbling down into an indifferent river below ...?

'... and that,' he said to his caller, 'should solve your problem. Is there anything else I can help you with?'

As the caller mumbled something or other in reply, the train began to pull away. His apocalyptic vision took a little longer to do the same.

When lunchtime rolled around, three hundred and eighty-seven years later, Danny logged out, ignored Cal and Alice and their questioning looks, and walked from his desk to the common room (Lircom was far too achingly hip to call its canteen a canteen). He sat on one of the ergonomically moulded chairs supposedly designed for comfort, but really designed to induce crippling back pain in any staff members tempted to lollygag there for longer than their allotted break, and he stared into oblivion.

He had five days of holiday left and had planned to take them in July. He, Ellie and Luke would get one of those bus & rail family tickets and just go somewhere, even if it was some shitty wee one-street resort town; even if it was mizzling with warm rain most of the time. It would have been their first proper family holiday, and he'd been looking forward to it. But by the time July rolled around, he'd be unemployed. Long gone.

Thomas had told him he could either take the leave, which would make tomorrow his final day in work and give him next week off, or he could work right up to his final day and get the holiday money as extra. He hadn't been here long enough to qualify for any sort of severance pay.

He wanted to take the leave. He wanted to walk out of here, right now. And yet there was a huge cloud of panic all around him that kept him nailed to the chair on which he quasi-sat. He felt as if every door he opened, every corner he turned, would bring him face to face with that panic cloud and it would rush into him, envelop him, overwhelm whatever rationality he had remaining and make him give in to the urge just to sit and wallow in misery.

His brain kept presenting him with facts he didn't want to think about – the state of the job market, the fact that he didn't have a degree. He kept visualising the awfulness of what lay ahead. The final day. The card. Starting to look in newspapers for jobs. Going to a fucking recruitment agency and filling out those fucking forms and doing one of their fucking typing fucking exams to see how many fucking words he could fucking type in a fucking minute.

But it was more than that. And he knew it.

He was right about you, wasn't he?

He was right to look at you that way.

He had dialled the number before he quite knew what was happening.

'Hello?'

'Hey.'

'Oh.' Ellie hesitated, clearly wondering what voice or tone to adopt. He sighed. He felt so tired.

'I'm sorry,' he said.

'So am I.'

You should be sorry. If you hadn't put plastic bags in the bin, I wouldn't have had to chase the binman and waste all that time, and I wouldn't have been late for work. If you listened to me, if you ever listened, I wouldn't be feeling like I was deemed not good enough for the worst job in the world.

'What are you sorry for?' Danny said aloud.

She didn't reply for a moment, which only made him feel worse. 'Just …' she sighed. 'Just, I'm sorry.'

Danny realised with horror that he was crying. He tilted the phone away from his face a little and swiped quickly, ashamedly, at his eyes with his sleeves. *How am I going to tell her?*

'You won't believe what happened this morning,' Ellie was saying.

He tried to clear his throat as quietly as possible. Keeping his voice steady was key. And in a flash of relief, or pragmatism, or just plain cowardice, he realised that he couldn't possibly deliver the news over the phone. He would wait until tonight. Or maybe – yes, maybe he could look into a few new jobs between now and the weekend, line up an interview even. And then when he told her, he could seem proactive, already on top of it.

'What?' he asked, almost absent-mindedly, all of this whirling around in his head.

'Guess who said *Daddy*.'

He blinked. Had she just …?

'Luke?' he said. 'Luke said …?'

'Aye,' she confirmed.

'You're sure? It wasn't just baby babble? He didn't have a mouthful of food at the time?'

She laughed. 'I sat him on his arse on the sofa and he just looked up at me, looked out the living room window, and said it, plain as you like. *Da-ddy?* He was asking where you were.'

He might be seeing a lot more of me. He submerged that thought quickly. 'Put him on,' he said urgently. 'Put him on, see if he does it again.'

In a few seconds heavy breathing replaced the sound of her voice on the phone. Danny knew this was his cue. He talked baby-talk down the phone and Luke's breathing stopped for a second (he knew from long practice that this was because he'd be looking around him, puzzled, for the source of the voice) before, after much prompting from stage left, he eventually let loose with an ear-splitting shriek of delight and frantic babbling, all of it cute but none of it intelligible.

'Sorry' – Ellie's voice returned – 'you know our Luke. He's no one's performing seal. Anyway, how's the day at work?'

Just like that, reality came flooding back in to his momentary oasis. 'Ach … all right,' Danny said carefully. No. It *wasn't* cowardice – you didn't impart news like this over the phone. Besides, he wanted a wee while to get his own head wrapped around it and dispel the panic cloud. No sense in both of them flailing around.

But she wouldn't. You know what she'd do. Where she'd go …

'Listen, um,' Ellie said. It wasn't a good *um*, the way she said it. Danny frowned. 'I think we should maybe have a chat tonight, when the wee fella's asleep.'

'What about?'

'Just … um, things.'

Double *um*. Fuck, this was getting worse by the minute. What was she … no. No, surely he couldn't be the only one who didn't want to deliver bad news over the phone? She wasn't going to tell him …

'Things about … us?' he asked. He had to. She didn't reply, but that was as good as an answer, wasn't it?

There was a soft *bump* in the background from her end, and the sound of Luke's little crying engine *bub-blub-waahing* its way up to full throttle. 'I'd better go,' Ellie said.

'Wait, I want–'

'I have to go,' she repeated. 'I'll talk to y–'

And he was suddenly forced to hold the phone away from his ear, almost dropping it to the ground altogether, as an eardrum-piercing squeal rent the air. He saw a few of the other common room patrons flinch, such was the noise level.

His first panicked thought was that Luke had hurt himself

badly and that the squeal had come from him, but after a moment's consideration he dismissed that – it had clearly been some kind of electronic feedback. That sound could not have come from a throat.

He carefully brought the phone back to his ear, comically slowly, as if it were a live grenade. The call had ended. Ellie must have hung up or been cut off as the interference came through; well, she'd said she would have to go anyway, hadn't she, with the wee fella crying?

Ellie was still at the stage of picking Luke up every time his big bottom lip so much as threatened to curl, something which, according to anyone they'd met with parenting experience, all but guaranteed their son would grow up to be worse than Hitler and Darth Vader rolled into one.

For a moment he considered ringing back. It was, he supposed, a little ironic that he was so affronted at the notion of her keeping something from him until she saw him tonight in person; but he couldn't have done anything about his news, could he?

Yes you could, you could have been better at your fucking job.

Wonderful day so far. Nothing like a potential break-up conversation with your girlfriend for taking your mind off getting the sack.

Cal was at the sandwich machine when Danny walked over. He stepped aside. 'What ya after?'

'Oh I dunno,' Danny said breezily, picking through the shrapnel he'd dug out of his pocket. 'Cyanide pill? Sawn-off shotgun?'

'I think they're still waitin' on them being restocked,' Cal said. 'Although it's nice they've taken the first aid kits out of the machines and made them available for free again.'

'You know Mr Black,' Danny said, 'he's all heart.'

He picked out a sandwich that looked as if the butter spread across it had been churned pre-WWII. As he popped the coins into the slot, he glanced across at Cal.

'They sacked me today,' he said, in a conversational tone.

Cal stamped his foot and pointed a finger straight up in the air. 'The swine! They shall rue the day …!'

'Cal … I'm serious. They're not renewing my contract.'

Withnail melted away rather sheepishly. 'Nah? For real? ' Cal said, shocked.

He stuck an arm inside the machine, feeling vaguely like your man from *All Creatures Great and Small* and expecting to pull out a bloodied newborn calf. 'Yep.'

'But they can't sack you …' Cal said, in what was clearly a light-bulb-above-the-head moment. 'You could take them to court! Claim discrimination!'

'Discrimination?'

'You can say they sacked ye cos of your disability!'

Danny sighed. He rubbed his eyes with his fingers. 'Cal,' he said patiently, 'as I've told ya before mate, synaesthesia is not a disability.'

Now it was Cal's turn to look doubtful. 'Hearin' colours and smellin' days of the week? Not a disability?' he said, in what he probably assumed was a kindly tone. 'I dunno. It always sounded like a bit of a fuckin' Christy Brown job to me, man. Sorta *My Left Brain* 'stead of *My Left Foot*.'

It was time for the speech. 'It's a neurological condition. When my brain is stimulated by a sense, it can – *sometimes* – cross-associate it with another sense. It's harmless, trust me. Sometimes it's even useful.'

Cal didn't try particularly hard to disguise his scepticism. 'Like when?'

Danny rhymed off a series of numbers.

'Whoopdee-doo,' Cal said, twirling a finger in the air. 'You can say loads of numbers in a row.'

'Look at your credit card, Cal.'

He took out the card and looked at Danny. Danny obediently rhymed off the numbers once more. By the end, Cal's jaw was hanging down so far he felt like reaching across and tying it back on with string.

'Relax, lad,' Danny assured him. 'I'm not planning on identity fraud. I just glanced at it when you left it on your desk. The synaesthesia makes it real easy to remember numbers and sequences and things, that's all.'

Cal breathed again. 'Well,' he said, 'even if you did steal my identity, if you wanted anything dearer than a fuckin' Mars bar and a packet of cheese and onion, you'd be ballixed.'

The number thing was good for a laugh and it impressed people, but it was old news for Danny. Numbers were coloured in his mind; 2 was dark blue, 9 was red, 5 was yellow, and so on. Somehow it just made recalling them simple.

'We'll have to have a leaving do for you, man. When's your last day?'

'Friday week. Or tomorrow. I haven't decided yet. But Cal, listen … I really don't want a leaving do. Honestly, I struggle to express to you how much I don't want a leaving do. Words fail me.'

Seeing Cal's questioning expression, he sighed and elaborated. 'Look,' he said, as kindly as he could. 'You and Alice, you're all right. But, not to put too fine a point on it, I despise pretty much everyone else in here. So the thought of being surrounded by them and having to listen to them talk a lot of oul shit about how much they're going to miss me fills me with what I can only describe as horrified bile.'

Cal considered this. 'Fair enough,' he said. 'But …' and, bless him, Danny could see the fella was actually struggling to say this in an acceptable way, 'well … it's not gonna the same without ya.'

'Wise up,' Danny said, not unkindly. 'Okay, so I won't be there to run interference between you two star-crossed lovers any more, but I'm sure you'll cope.'

Cal flushed so hotly at that Danny almost burst out laughing. 'It's not that …' he said. 'It's …' he shrugged. 'I don't know. I mean, I sorta like working here. All right, the pay is shit, the bosses are wankers, I know all that.'

Danny nodded, knowing it was true, knowing that Cal only worked part time, and for part-timers Lircom was heaven – a microwave dinner of a job, as disposable and forgettable as it was unappetising. Cal had it all. He lived in a student house with eight other fellas. As a group they had won some sort of competition in the first year of university – he'd told Danny what the competition was numerous times but Danny always forgot almost instantly; it was some beer thing or other – and had landed an absolutely amazing house, newly built, rent free for the first year and for a reduced rate until all of them left uni. So naturally they were hell-bent on extending their degrees by fair means or foul.

Danny had been to the house only once, just before the Lircom Christmas do last year. When he'd walked in through the doors he appreciated how those first conquistadors must have felt when they took the virgin steps onto the Americas. It was a hedonistic paradise of soft drugs, Xbox Live tournaments and girls disappearing into rooms. Most nights of the week randoms would fill its hallways.

He'd looked around, remembering his own student days, when he'd lived in an almost identical setup. The memories had come flooding – or in some cases, oozing – back. He'd left early, making some excuse about the wee fella not being well, unable to stand there for a moment longer watching these fuckers drift about in this palace and resist the urge to grab one of them, all of them, by the shoulders and scream, *Do you know what you've got here? Do you appreciate it? Do you?*

Cal was still trying to formulate his sentence. 'You'll be all right,' he said lamely. 'I know you will, man. Don't let the bastards get ya down and all that.'

Danny took a bite of the sandwich.

Danny very carefully set the sandwich back down again.

With some considerable effort of will, Danny swallowed.

'Cheers,' he told Cal, rising from his seat, his voice slightly strained. 'I'm gonna get something to wash the taste of that away. Nice warm glass of piss, maybe.'

He passed Alice on the way out, but confined himself to a nod and headed on. No doubt Cal would fill her in on his departure.

Weird, actually. From what he knew of Alice, she'd never been to Sodom (aka Cal's house). She wasn't the sort. So why Cal was so interested in her and she in him … well, another one of those complexities of love, he supposed. Some people just didn't realise the grass always looked greener on the other side.

The irony bypassed him entirely.

Naturally, there wasn't a seat to be had on the bus. Danny resigned himself to standing, and reached up for one of those handhold things that hung down and left you looking like a *Thunderbirds* puppet on drugs if the bus picked up any speed going round corners. Although from the look of things, the chances of them picking up speed were minimal – the road was clogged, or 'chockerblock' as the taxi men would have it. Those loveable ruffians.

To pass the time – and to distract himself from stray thoughts of strangling a small girl who seemed determined to pass the journey time by singing one of those fuckin' Disney songs at a pitch that by all rights should have shattered every window on the vehicle – he decided to bite the bullet and phone home. He didn't usually ring on the journey, but he couldn't wait any longer to see what the 'chat' about 'things' really was. He could cover it up by asking Ellie if she needed anything from the shop – bread, milk, new life?

EEEEEEEEeeeeeeeeeeeeeeeeeEEEEEEEEEEEEEEEE!

'Jesus fuck!'

Another horrendous electronic squeal had ripped forth from the phone. Though Danny was concerned only with his own hearing, had he been able to glance up, he would have seen every single passenger with their hands over their ears. In an impressive feat of self-control the driver managed to confine his automatic reaction to a wince, keeping his hands on the wheel, although he did indulge himself by sending Danny a truly withering look in the rear-view mirror when the opportunity presented itself.

Danny saw none of this. He was repeatedly jabbing the 'end call' button on his mobile to kill the noise; he could have sworn it took him about five attempts to hang up. He was left with a loud ringing in both his ears, and a feeling that hot needles had been forced into his brain. The silence when the noise eventually did stop was absolute; even the bus engine seemed to have taken a break, and now that the other passengers could stop cradling their heads in their hands, they were able to throw some really juicy hate-filled looks in his direction.

'Sorry,' he mumbled. 'I don't know what's wrong with this thing … I'm sorry.'

This seemed to mollify no one. On the plus side, though, the annoying little girl was now curled up in her mother's arms, sobbing mightily about the bad bad noise and how much it had hurt her poor wee ears. This cheered him somewhat, but it was with some relief that he stepped off a few stops later, leaving the lingering hostility of the bus passengers (and driver, he noted) behind.

Ah well. Fuck the bus driver. If Beelzebub and his halls of hell really existed, and if the jobs we held in life had an infernal ranking system to determine the length of time we spent with red-hot pokers lodged firmly up our crinkly eyes, then bus driver would be second only to concentration camp guard.

More importantly, was his phone fucked? That really would be the cherry on the slagpile. Danny glanced upwards at the heavens he'd been staring at in wonderment only the night before. *What's next on the inexorable merry-go-round of fun, God? Resurrect my beloved childhood pet and have it eat my granny in a murder-suicide pact?*

No, fuck it. He wasn't gonna give in to self-pity. The key was to seem in control of the situation. So he'd go home, all business, do the necessary with the wee fella, get him off to sleep and then break the news to Ellie and lay out his carefully structured plan, which was:

1.   Take next week off, take the gamble, and use the time to hit every single recruitment agency in town.

2.   Distribute his CV to so many potential employers that he'd inevitably score a success, no matter what it was – Jesus, he'd stuck near a year at Lircom after all. If his next job was down a fuckin' salt mine he could consider himself on an upward trajectory.

3.   Move smoothly from Lircom to his next job with nary a break in wages, bills continuing to be paid – he might even get a payrise out of it. He might even land a job he didn't despise. Unlikely, yes, but possible.

His step quickened. And if after all that she … she …

Well.

Well, he'd …

He paused at the gate. Something in the recesses of his mind was pulling its trousers down and mooning at him, but he ignored it and kept his gaze on the front door ahead. Normally he would either have seen Ellie moving around in the front room, or she'd have the door opened with the wee fella in her arms waiting for Daddy to arrive home (half the time for the cuteness of it, half the time because she couldn't wait another minute to get rid of him for a while). Not today it seemed.

Striding into the house with as much manly purpose as possible, he succeeded only in almost knackering his shoulder. The door was locked. She kept it locked at his insistence, given the rare but occasional daylight break-ins in the area, but she always unlocked before he was due home. He felt a wave of annoyance but forced it down – this wasn't the time and today wasn't the day to let little dopey things bog them down; he'd learned that from this morning.

Fishing in his pockets turned up four different chocolate bar wrappers, a bus pass that had expired three years ago, and an AAA battery – all before his fingers found the keyring. He turned the key in the lock and walked inside, wrinkling his nose. Luke had been busy, recently by the smell of it. Maybe that explained the absence of a greeting.

'Ellie?' he called, unshouldering his jacket and hanging it over the banister. No, wait. She'd kill him for that, it was a pet peeve. He went a few steps further, opened the cupboard under the stairs, hung the jacket up in there and felt proud of himself.

'Ellie?' He ducked his head into the living room. The television was on, albeit on mute. Brightly coloured things were capering about and frantically miming brightly coloured songs. Maybe it wasn't pokers that bus drivers were meant to endure in the ninth circle of hell after all.

The kitchen was empty, but the kettle had just come to the boil. A tin of formula milk was out. The microwave suddenly *bee-beeped* for attention, announcing that the steriliser inside had finished its cycle. And as he cocked his head to the side and listened, he detected the low gurgle of water running. Of course. Bath time. With the bathroom door closed and the water running, noises from the rest of the house were pretty muffled.

He started towards the stairs, then checked himself, looking at the equipment before him. An opportunity for further proactivity points presented itself.

'Bottle filling time for Daddy ...' he said, and set about his work. Danny had it down to a fine art.

Remove steriliser from microwave using safety grips. Spin. Grab tea towel from oven door. Wrap around hand. Unscrew steriliser top. Yank hand away from escaping steam. Place lid on draining board. Allow bottles to cool while popping top off formula milk tin and boiling kettle. Line up bottles in a neat little row with their safety seals and teats lined up above them, also in a neat little row (this was optional, and slightly psychotic, but damn it was eye-pleasing).

Pour in the boiled water from the kettle – Luke was on 7oz of milk now per bottle so he poured in the water to the right level (amazing, he could remember the days of 3oz, when Luke was just a little peachy fuzz ball with the fattest little back). One scoop of milk per ounce. Place safety seals on. Screw on bottle tops. Shake mixtures, doing dance of choice (again, optional and psychotic, but fun). Pop on bottle tops and place in a row in the fridge door. Bask in glory as Ellie opens fridge and remarks on how wonderful a partner you are.

All of this completed, he walked to the bottom of the stairs and frowned. He could still hear the faint rumble of running water from upstairs. Was this one of Ellie's luxury baths containing between four and six unique bath-foaming products? He was continually amazed she actually sank in those things, the water was so gravid with oils. Maybe Luke was asleep and she'd decided to treat herself.

He bounded up the stairs and checked the bedroom. Just as he opened the door, the final two notes of the mobile above the cot had pling-plonged out in a weak little drawn-out squawk, but there were no wet snuffles emanating from the cot, no baby inside. She must have used the mobile to keep the wee fella distracted while she was in next door, filling the bath.

He knocked on the bathroom door, rather absurdly, and then shook his head at his own folly and opened it.

'Ellie, I've …'

He trailed off. The room was empty. And the bath was about a quarter-inch from overflowing. No steam was rising from the taps. The water had long since gone cold. In one long stride he was at the taps, turning them off as fast as he could, stemming the flow of water just in time.

'Ellie!' he called. 'Are you in the spare room or what? This fuckin' bath was near overflowing! Do you want the whole upstairs flooded?'

He plunged his arm into the eighteen inches or so of tepid water and retrieved the plug (the chain had perished three months back and 'fix the bastarding bathplug' had been on his to-do list ever since). And still there was no answer from Ellie. What the fuck was she doing in the spare room anyway? There wasn't anything in there but boxes and unpacked stuff and …

… and nothing else.

Danny stood at the doorway to the spare room, for the first time feeling a twisting in his stomach. She wasn't in there, and it wasn't like there was anywhere to hide. Luke wasn't in there either.

His mind worked through the options. If they weren't in the house, then they were out of the house. Ellie took her mobile with her everywhere, mostly in the hope that one of her mates would text her, which lately … not so much.

He double-pressed the green call button on his mobile. As it flashed up the 'connecting' graphic he had his first niggling thought – *something's wrong. Something's wrong with Luke, something that came up so suddenly she had to leave the house straight away and forgot about the bath running. Something so serious she hasn't even had time to phone me yet. Jesus Christ, Jesus Christ … what could be that serious? What could have happened so quickly?*

Images of ambulances and Ellie flashed through his mind, and his stomach gave another lurch. He forced down the panic with a conscious effort, waiting for the click to indicate his phone was connected.

EEEEEEEEeeeeeeeeeeeeeeeeeeEEEEEEEEEEEEEEEE!

'FUCK SAKE!'

He held back the urge to throw his mobile against the nearest wall only with some difficulty. Once the noise ended, and his fresh headache from the teeth-jattering sound was blooming nicely inside his cerebrum, he stood and took a few deep breaths, trying to think what the next step was. His mobile was fucked, that much was pretty certain.

Home phone.

He took the stairs two at a time and was just U-turning at the bottom to make a beeline for the home phone when he heard a knock at the front door. Relief flooded over him. He'd locked the door automatically upon entering the house. Stupid. And this was Ellie, returning from whatever errand she'd been called out on.

The door was unlocked. It wasn't Ellie.

'Uh,' Danny said to the old woman standing on his doorstep, watching him with rheumy eyes. 'Bea ... sorry, love, if it's about the tea leaves thing, you've called at a really bad time. Can ya call back?'

Beatrice O'Malley blinked. He could almost hear those dry old lids sliding over her eyes. At any other time he'd have had the presence of mind to be creeped out by her, but right now he had more pressing matters at hand.

'I'll call back,' she croaked. 'I'll call back tomorrow night, Danny.'

'Right, right,' Danny said, as Bea closed the door behind her. He could feel bad about being just short of rude later on, when Ellie and Luke were home. Or, he mused as he called Ellie's mobile from the home phone, he could fail to feel bad entirely – that was an option he was leaving open.

EEEEEEEEeeeeeeeeeeeeeeeeeeEEEEEEEEEEEEEEEE!

'Name of sweet fuckin' Jesus Christ, what the fuck is goin' on?'

Danny shouted to the universe at large. He stood there in the hall, a useless phone in each useless hand.

Okay. All right. Panicking wasn't fucking helping anyone, and besides, it wasn't like they could have gone far – the bath hadn't overflowed before he'd reached it and, Jesus, that mobile only played for about four minutes or something even when it was fully wound. It was a wonder he hadn't seen them leave … *in the ambulance* … the street as he'd come home from work … *he's hurt, she's hurt* …

He took a breath, settled himself – and almost shit a brick when his mobile started chirruping merrily in his hand. Adrenalin flooded through his body and, in that glorious moment, the world went back to making sense even as he stabbed 'accept call' and pressed it to his ear.

'Ellie! Fuckin' hell, love, I was starting to–'

''Fraid not,' Steve's easy voice replied. Danny's shoulders slumped. He rubbed his temple with his fingers.

'I don't have time to talk right now, lad,' he said.

'You haven't even heard wh–'

'I don't have *time*, Steve,' Danny repeated. He dropped his hand from his temple and started spinning the wheels of Luke's pram, folded up in the alcove beside where he stood. He itched to be in motion.

'Ach all right. Fuck ye then. I'll call ye when you're in better form sure.'

An idea occurred to him then. 'Wait!'

'What?' Steve asked, still sounding a bit irked.

'Haven't heard anything from Ellie have ya?' Danny asked,

knowing even as he said the words that it was the longest of long shots. The best you could say about Ellie and Steve was that they tolerated each other's company and had not, as yet, resorted to pistols at dawn. 'Recently like?' *Like in the last four minutes?*

'No … not since last night. Why? Somethin' the matter?'

'I'm just back from work and she's not here. Neither's wee Luke.' Danny said, realising this was the first time he'd spoken it aloud. Somehow it felt better to do that. It made it sound smaller than it felt.

'Fuck's sake,' Steve said, obviously thinking the same thing about the size of the problem. 'She's probably taken the wee man for a walk to the shops!'

Danny's eyes drifted downward to his free hand, seemingly noticing what he was doing for the first time. 'The pram's here,' he said slowly.

'So she's carryin' him then. Fuckin' hell, lad. Do you want me to send up a flare? Should I get on the blower to Tracy Island? Big panicky muppet, ye.'

Danny wanted to reach down the phone and throttle his smug fucking face. He didn't understand. 'No,' he said firmly. 'No, you don't know Ellie. She spends ten minutes packing a baby bag for a trip to the fuckin' corner shop. Something's wrong.'

Some of the jokiness dropped from his friend's voice as he finally seemed to get the message that Danny was genuinely concerned. 'Ring her and see, then.'

'I can't. There's somethin' wrong with my mobile and the house phone. I can't connect to her number.'

Steve paused. 'I'm on my mobile to you now,' he pointed out.

'You try her. Please?'

He heard a small sigh from the other end of the line, but considering the circumstances, that was small beer for asking Steve voluntarily to speak to Ellie. 'Right. I'll ring you back sure, or I'll get her to ring.'

'Cheers, lad.'

'No problem. And Danny?' Steve added, putting on his best sage advice tone. 'Calm down for Christ's sake. They'll be back and crampin' your style before you know it.'

With that parting shot, he was gone, and Danny was alone once again. It had been nice to be talking to someone, even if it hadn't been Ellie or Luke. Without the TV blaring or Luke's constant stream of baby babble he'd rarely heard the house this quiet.

Through the stained glass panels at the top of the front door he could see a dark shape at the bottom of the garden path. Hope surged in him for a moment, but after taking a few steps so he could look through one of the adjacent transparent panels, that hope was quashed – it was Bea, only just now reaching the bottom of the garden path.

She turned to close his gate, and seemed to sense his eyes upon her, because she looked up and stared directly at him for a moment. His mind flashed back to the stare he'd endured from Michael Quinn the previous night, except this one wasn't full of hatred. It looked almost like she was sad. But then, if he had to look in the mirror and see that face staring back at him, he'd look fairly fuckin' miserable too.

And then she broke the glance, and her head turned towards,

of all fuckin' things, his garden. He followed her gaze and felt that tug as if something was …

His phone buzzed. He had it answered almost before it had started to shake. 'Hello?'

'Danny.' It was Steve.

'What'd she say? Did you talk to her? Is the wee man all right?'

'Sorry, lad,' Steve began, causing Danny's heart to palpitate, 'I phoned her number, but there was some sort of crazy interference. Probably just this useless phone of mine.'

'Interference? Like someone squealing? Loud as fuck?'

'Yeah.'

'Something must be wrong with her mobile, then. It's been doing that all day.'

'I dunno,' Steve replied, 'I've never heard that before. And the call's being picked up, like – she's answering. It's not going to voicemail. But as you say, it's just that squeal.'

Danny tried to think of something to say, but found that he couldn't stop thinking about the conversation he and Ellie had had earlier that day, at lunchtime. When she'd told him she wanted to have a word with him. He'd known what that word would be. Maybe she'd known he'd known that. Maybe she'd decided to skip the conversation altogether.

He tried to stop his father's words from bubbling to the surface of his mind. As ever, he failed.

And I'm glad I did.

Steve was talking on, to fill the silence. 'Must just be interference where she is. Look … I hate to say this, but when I was visiting my ma in hospital they told us to switch off …'

Hospitals. Hospitals fucked with mobiles. Of course they did. It was a relief, in a perverse kind of way, to consider that possibility; at least for a moment until the unpleasant ramifications of what that would mean had kicked in. As he stood in the tiny hallway, his eyes swept over every available surface, looking for evidence. Blood. Anything.

'Do you want me to …'

'No,' Danny replied, softly but insistently, surprising himself as much as anyone else. 'I'm gonna check a few things out – ask the neighbours, ring her ones, my ma, her mates. Then' – he paused, and made himself say the words – 'I'll phone the hospitals.'

'Right. Are you … you all right, like?'

'Me? Aye,' Danny said. He forced a note of lightness into his voice, as much for Steve's sake as his own. 'As you say, she's probably nipped off somewhere and her mobile's on the blink. I'll kill her when I get her.'

He walked to the front door, opened it, pulled it shut behind him, intending to begin rapping on the doors of the neighbours. The air was colder than it had been on the walk from the bus to here. He considered going back in for a coat, but decided against it. He'd only be knocking on a few doors after all.

'Aye, lad, keep it relaxed,' Steve said. 'There'll be some daft explanation for it all.'

Seconds ticked past.

'Lad …? You there?'

'Yeah,' Danny said absently. He had spotted what Bea had been looking at, what had been vying for his attention since he first walked up the path.

They'd busted their balls flattening that hump of earth, that wee mound. He still had the calluses on his right hand from the spade. And yet there it was, sitting pristine and undisturbed and looking as if no one had ever been near it with a toothpick let alone a garden implement.

Compared to, say, finding his girlfriend and his baby son, solving this puzzle paled into insignificance. And yet, as he bade Steve farewell and made his way to the first of his neighbours, Danny felt his eyes drawn back to his garden.

There must be a daft explanation.

Had to be.

The First Threshold

The hardwood floor was cold beneath his feet. They'd talked about putting carpets down because that would be better for the wee fella when he became properly mobile – softer on his wee knees and elbows for all the spills and tumbles that would come with the toddler stage. But, as with the sofa against which he now sat, the sofa where old springs went to die; as with the freezer that needed defrosting every fortnight because the thermostat was fucked, intrusive financial reality prohibited the achievement of such laudable goals.

At some point over the last few hours he'd removed his socks. He couldn't actually remember doing it, but since he was now in his bare feet the evidence was fairly incontrovertible. Probably to pass fifteen seconds worth of time without glancing at the clock or at the phone, without cradling his mobile and staring at it, willing it to light up with an incoming call and the caller ID picture of Ellie sticking her tongue out and crossing her eyes – a photo that she had asked him forty-seven times to delete and about which he'd lied forty-seven times.

He sat on the hard floor, the phone book weighing on his left leg, but he didn't mind that, just as he didn't mind the cold floor freezing his toes or slowly leeching all feeling from his arse. Danny didn't care. Right now he just wanted to feel something that wasn't the overpowering sensation of wrongness that Ellie and Luke's absence was creating within him.

His finger moved down the page to the next hospital on the list, and he dialled the number. He spoke to the receptionist for a few moments, even as he heard his front door open and people enter the house. He scrambled to his feet, hope surging in him even though he had identified the voices as those of his mother and father. He knew it was futile, but nonetheless when they entered the room, he couldn't help but look behind them, as if Ellie and Luke would be there and the whole thing would turn out to be a gag.

'... no, no, I understand that,' he said, completing the phone call robotically. 'Yes, I'm sure I should. Thank you.'

'Well? Any word, love?' Linda Morrigan asked the question, though she must have already known the answer.

Danny shook his head. 'No one's seen or heard from them–'

He got no further, interrupted by the impact of his mother enveloping him in an embrace. He remembered those sorts of hugs from growing up, and how quickly he'd outgrown the days when they could make anything seem better. But he'd never dream of telling his mother that, because he knew she was hugging him for her own benefit as well.

Sure enough, when after a few seconds she pulled away, she hid her face and dabbed at her eyes before looking back at him, as if this would disguise the fact that she was upset. He loved her for trying anyway. To the side, his father Tony watched all of this and said nothing.

'Don't you worry, love. Don't you worry. They'll be fine.'

He nodded in what he hoped was a sincere way. What else could he do?

'Have you told her ones?'

Danny regarded his da. Tony was a soft-spoken sort – quiet and reflective, always staring out the window, always lost in thought. His ma maintained that this just meant he was a deep thinker. Danny was not unkind enough to point out that, while not a stupid man, his da was far from an intellectual. Anyone who counted solving a *Countdown* conundrum as a lifetime goal was not going to trouble the Nobel prize committees anytime soon.

'Phoned them an hour ago. Just after I rang you,' he said aloud. 'They're coming over. Wanted to try a few places first.'

He was going red just remembering that conversation. He'd been dreading making the call, naturally, but he had to check and see if Ellie had gone to her mum and dad's for whatever reason, and when he discovered that she hadn't, well, he more or less had to tell them what was up.

Ellie's mother had passed the phone to Michael Quinn in short order and a series of clipped questions had followed – the sort of questions that had probably helped Duracell Man climb the corporate ladder. What had killed Danny about it was that the bastard hadn't even sounded that surprised; as if his daughter and grandson's disappearance had been an inevitable happening, the long-awaited crashing of a fuck-up juggernaut with Danny Morrigan at the wheel.

'They're coming here?' his ma said and Danny watched, exasperated, as she checked her reflection in the hallway mirror. Seeming satisfied, she turned her attention to her husband and tugged at various invisible threads on his jacket. Tony fixed her with a warning look and directed her back to Danny as subtly as he could, causing her to stop. Danny couldn't summon up the energy to be angry. His ma had always been terrified in any situation where she suspected she'd be propping up the social ladder.

'I'll … I'll go and stick the kettle on,' she stammered.

Her husband smiled at her briefly. 'Aye, Linda love, you do that.'

'Yeah, great,' Danny echoed. Wonderful. A cup of tea. All problems solved.

His mother walked into the kitchen, already with a slightly springier step since she now had a purpose. Maybe that was the key to tea – not the cuppa itself, but the comforting ritual of making it. Danny was too tired to ponder much on it, which only made him feel worse, more useless. Shouldn't he be running on adrenalin now? A barely contained explosion of affirmative action and plans and ideas? For the last three hours all he'd wanted to do was sit down somewhere and stare into empty space, or even better lie down somewhere and sleep, and wake up to find that this was all one extended nightmare that would slip through his fingers in the first few seconds of wakefulness.

Tony moved hesitantly towards him. Danny caught his expression and instantly knew what was on his father's mind.

'Don't,' he warned.

'You don't know what I'm–'

'Oh I do, Da. I do. Don't even fuckin' go there, all right? Although that's your speciality come to think of it, yeah? Going.'

He sat down heavily and snatched up the phone book from the floor, staring resentfully at its big yellow *thereness*. He flicked through pages of hospitals and horticulturalists and hypnotists and fuck knows what else, but saw fuck-all entries for 'Phone Here for Location of Missing Family'. With a sudden burst of energy he hurled the phone book against the wall of the living room which it hit with a papery *whump*, and then fell to the floor.

His da was watching him, not speaking, but Danny knew the silence wouldn't last.

'Maybe I deserve that,' Tony said quietly.

'*Maybe* you do?' Danny said incredulously, before shaking his head. 'Don't do the Irish martyr act, Dad. I don't feel like listenin' to it just now, OK?'

'Don't do it? What else have I got?'

He was on his feet before he even realised it, toe to toe with his father, shouting in his face. It was all too much. 'My family are fuckin' *missing*, Dad!' he shouted, right into his stupid fuckin' da's stupid fuckin' face. 'My family are GONE! Can we make this not about you? Just for once?'

And like a gunshot, in the quiet that followed his outburst, came the sound of a cup shattering in the kitchen. Both men glanced in that direction. Danny looked away, walked to the fireplace and put his head down on the cool marble just to feel something cold against his skin. He felt hot and dirty and tired and less than human. He felt guilty.

'I'm sorry,' his da said softly behind him.

'Yeah, I know,' Danny sighed. 'Fuck … it doesn't matter. Not now. I just want them back.'

'Son, there's … I don't know how to start, or even if I should start, or if this is the time …' Something was different in his da's voice all of a sudden. Curious despite the maelstrom of emotions raging inside him, Danny straightened up and turned. 'There's things we need to talk about.'

'Now?'

'Yes now. *Especially* now. I just …' and he blew out a long breath and ran his hands through his hair, sitting down and standing up and sitting down again, as if not sure what to do with his own body. 'I'm fucked if I even know how to start.'

'Unless it's an explanation for where Ellie and Luke might be, Da, I can't say as I'm particularly interested.'

'I don't know, son,' Tony said helplessly. 'I'm probably just making all this worse. I probably shouldn't be saying anything. But I'd never forgive myself if … if it turned out that … and I hadn't told you, you understand?'

'Understand? Understand *what*? You're talking out your arse, Da, that's as much as I can make out. If you've something to say, say it.'

All Tony did in response was stare at him. He could see something was going on behind his father's eyes, some inner turmoil, and once or twice the older man's mouth opened, as if he were about to speak … but then it closed again.

'Well?' Danny snapped.

His father's shoulders slumped. 'Did you ever think Ellie might have joined a cult?' he said.

Danny stared.

'A cult,' he repeated.

'Yeah,' his father said wretchedly. 'Run off to a commune or something ...'

'You think this is fuckin' *funny?*' Danny snarled, and stepped forward. As he did, he felt the floor beneath his feet, soft and warm rather than hard and cold. He glanced down, and saw that he'd stepped on the collection of blankets they kept in the middle of the living room floor. Lying on top was the wraparound blue one that Luke slept in.

Tony stepped aside as his son flew past him and upstairs in a series of long strides, not bothering to explain his sudden burst of motion. No explanation was necessary. He knew what Danny was going up there to do – he had seen it in his son's eyes as he registered what he was standing on.

Linda emerged from the kitchen with a tray. The cups on it rattled as her hands shook. Tony smiled at her and took the tray, setting it down safely on the sideboard. He saw the questioning look on his wife's face.

'Upstairs,' Tony said, by way of an answer. 'He'll be back in a minute.'

'I'll go up ...'

Tony moved forward a half-step to block her exit from the room. 'Let him be up there, love. Please. He'll be down in a wee second.'

She nodded, if a little reluctantly, and then started in surprise when she felt her husband's hand settle on her shoulder.

'What is it?'

He had to ask. Christ he didn't want to, but he had to.

'Was this what it was like for you?'

She looked away. He'd anticipated that she would, but it still hurt him to see it. 'Aye,' she said, and he didn't mistake the softness in her voice for affection. 'More or less. I remember throwing up. But that was just me. Danny … he just kept looking at the door, out the windows. You know, he never even cried? Everyone said he was being so grown up about it, but I wanted him to just …'

She stopped, unable to go on, and stepped away from his touch, leaving his hand to fall by his side.

'I'm sorry,' was all he could think of to say.

'The worst thing … the worst thing was when he got your letter instead of me. If only I hadn't have been asleep …' she said, the anger in her voice directed solely at herself now as the memory came back. 'I didn't see him for the best part of two weeks after that.'

'I had to try and explain–'

'It's not something you can explain.' She cut him off. Linda Morrigan did not raise her voice very often, and this was not one of those times. Nevertheless, you could have cut glass with every word she spoke.

'I'm sorry,' Tony said again, staring out the window, unable to meet her eyes.

'Then why'd you do it?' she burst out. 'Why'd you leave us?'

'I came back, didn't I?'

He was hoping for a smile, even a hint of one, but none was

forthcoming. 'Yeah. You came back,' she simply said, and walked to the window to stand beside him, but not too close. A shiver went through her then, and while Tony's first instinct was to comfort her, his second instinct was to realise that this might not be the best time.

'It's weird,' she went on, talking as much to herself as to him. 'My first thought should be that it's something simple, like she's upped and left him and taken wee Luke with her. I know them two weren't exactly a picture book couple – who is? – but I know she wouldn't leave him. Not with the wee one. Not like this. And sure even if she had, why hasn't she just gone to her ones or her mates or somethin' and told him about it? No one's seen sight nor sound of them since this morning.'

'Sometimes it's not that simple,' Tony replied. His expression was troubled, and when his wife glanced over to him, she thought it was guilt she was seeing upon his face.

It wasn't that simple.

Throwing up was vastly overrated, Danny decided. He remembered when he'd caught a stomach bug or some such as a kid, his ma would have been practically cheerleading the vomit on, telling him that he'd 'feel a lot better after'.

Of course he fuckin' would. After the ordeal of throwing up – the feeling of your digestive system reversing its modus operandi, the flooding of your mouth with spittle, the hot sticky foul-smelling mess spewing forth from your throat, and the small fact that in blowing chunks into the toilet you were putting your head into a place that was only ever meant to be plugged up by your arse – sticking your cock into a glory hole in the Camp Crystal Lake toilets during a Jason Voorhees rampage would seem like a fantastic voyage of fun and frolics.

He groggily got to his feet and flushed. Mouthwash. He was fucked if he was going to smell of puke when her ones arrived. He swilled it around his mouth and spat it into the sink, about to wash it away when he stopped for a fraction of a second and noticed how the pattern of mouthwash gunk looked a bit like tea leaf patterns in a cup.

Maybe he should get Bea over here to read his sink. Or maybe she hung out round bars on weekends, reading teenage girls' futures in their barf-splashes. World's first practising nauseomancer. Assuming people took her seriously, and didn't think it was all a gag.

That should have been his cue to start laughing uncontrollably, a therapeutic release for all the built-up tension within. He stood there for a moment in the hope this might happen. He flushed the toilet again and faced the fact that he was going to have to go back downstairs.

The doorbell sounded. Again, he couldn't suppress the surge of hope. He was out of the room in a second, bounding down the stairs. His father was already at the door but he shouldered him aside – fuck that, if anyone was going to welcome his girlfriend and wee son home first, it was going to be–

Steve.

'All right, lad.'

Much as Danny's hopes were dashed, on some level it was

good to see him. Steve stepped into the house and Danny stepped forward, and they came together in an embrace that wasn't self-conscious in the slightest. He didn't see his father's eyes settling on the gesture of easy closeness, and wouldn't have cared less if he had.

'Phoned everyone I could think of,' Steve said, as they broke apart and headed for the living room. 'All the rest of the lads – although as ya know most of them are away …'

'Away?'

'Ach ya all right, Mrs Morrigan?' Steve grinned as Linda beamed back at him. 'Haven't seen ye in ages. Aye, all of them except Flan and Vic are away in Fuerteventura for the week – one of them off-season deals.'

'Ach that's nice,' Linda said. 'Did you not want to head away too?'

Steve shook his head with a goofy grin, the same grin he'd worn talking to Danny's ma since he was about four. 'Nah. Not my scene these days, Mrs M. Behavin' myself. Bein' a good boy.'

'You?' her eyebrows skyrocketed theatrically. 'A good boy?'

Danny cleared his throat. Both had the decency to look slightly embarrassed. Steve went back to being all business. 'Aye so the rest of them are on the case, ringin' anyone they know. Flan and Vic wanted to come down here with me but I sorta thought you'd probably be getting a pretty full house and …'

He didn't have to continue, but if he had finished the sentence it would have probably have gone something along the lines of … *and I didn't want to bring them two dickheads along and add a double murder charge to your current list of woes.* Flanagan and Vic were good fellas for a night out, but in a crisis situation they could be relied on for two things – getting shitfaced, and playing first-person shooters with frightening excellence, often at the same time. Neither skill would prove particularly useful right now.

'Ellie's ma and da are on their way,' Danny said.

'Oh. Great,' Steve said, clearly as thrilled at the prospect of this as everyone else.

'Want a wee cup of tea, love?'

'Ach that'd be great Mrs M. Cheers.'

Danny rolled his eyes. 'Have mine,' he said, indicating the tray. His mouth still tasted of Listerine, and his ma couldn't make tea for shit. Even if she could, he hated tea.

Steve took a sip from his cup. 'Lovely tea, Mrs M,' he said brightly. Danny could have stabbed him.

'How's wee Maggie doin'?'

At any other time, Danny would have winced at the awkwardness that innocent question was sure to generate. Right now he had more pressing things on his mind, but he still cast a reflective glance at Steve, who met his eyes with a *here we go again* look that they'd shared many times before.

'Sure we broke up, Mrs M,' Steve said, forcing some joviality into his voice.

'Ach!' she coloured. 'So yis did. Sorry love, I keep forgetting don't I?'

'Yeah …' Danny and Steve chorused together.

'I thought yis were a lovely wee couple as well.'

Steve's forced smile wilted. 'Yeah,' he replied. 'So did I. Um. So, are the police …?'

'I phoned them earlier,' Danny said. Another phone call he'd been thrilled to make. 'They said normally it'd be too early for them to declare them missing, but because there's a … because there's …' he hesitated, fighting to keep his composure. His stomach lurched again. Every time he let reality back in fully he couldn't handle it. Jesus. He was a fuckin' mess.

'Because there's a baby …' he finally completed the sentence, 'they've taken the details, and they're comin' over to have a look around sometime tonight, assuming …'

Assuming they don't turn up safe and well before then.

He couldn't even say it. It was as if every time he dared to say it, it became less powerful.

'Fuck,' he said, remembering something, 'the police said not to touch anything …'

His ma almost choked on her Tetley, looking around in horror as if the windows were about to be kicked in by a SWAT team ready to take her down for a heinous crime. 'Danny, I didn't know … I'm so sorry,' she said.

Danny held up a hand to calm her down. 'Not your fault, Ma, it's mine. Just … from now on, no one touch anything.'

'Did they say anything else?'

It was the first time his da had spoken since Steve had shown up. Danny looked over at him, fighting a rush of anger as the *maybe she's joined a cult* conversation came back to him. Whether because of that or because more and more time was ticking by with no sign of Ellie or Luke, his da seemed tenser now than before.

'Just the same oul shite I've been gettin' from the hospitals – very early days, try to remain calm, try phoning everyone you can think of, they'll probably turn up in the next few hours.'

'It's good advice,' his da said.

'Yeah, they're probably right, love,' his ma chimed in.

'Aye,' Steve agreed. 'Spot on.'

Danny couldn't hold it in any longer. 'Jesus Christ, they've fuckin' *vanished*!' he cried, as if talking to morons. 'No coats. No purse. No pram. No nappies. No nothin'. I checked the neighbours. No one saw them leave. Everyone sees everythin' in this fuckin' street. If she didn't take the pram, she was either carrying Luke or she phoned for a taxi. I phoned round the local taxi depots. Only one booking for here today – for you.' Steve's eyes widened in alarm as Danny gestured towards him. 'The taxi we phoned for you last night – it was after twelve,' Danny elaborated.

Steve deflated with relief. 'Aye, that's right,' he said.

'Proper wee fuckin' mystery, isn't it? Isn't it just?' Danny said bitterly. He didn't exactly feel better for the outburst, because it had solved nothing, but he did feel some relief from the pressure of having to pretend everything was almost normal. 'Come on, you have to admit – it's ab … sol …. ute… ly fascinating! It's like the *Marie* fucking *Celeste*!'

'Danny …' his ma said. She tried to put a hand on his arm to calm him down. Fuck that. He moved away. He was only just getting started.

'What, Ma?' he asked, bright-eyed, feeling energised properly for the first time. 'What? I haven't finished. Ellie's mobile has been giving me the same weird static signal since lunchtime. I thought it was my mobile but it's not. Wait til ya hear this …'

As Danny hit keys on his phone, Steve took a step back and

covered his ears. He turned to Linda and Tony. 'Copy me,' he advised.

Tony frowned. 'Why, what's–'

His question was answered a moment later as the electronic shriek filled the air. Danny let it blare for a few seconds. He'd been ringing Ellie's mobile every fifteen minutes or so over the last few hours so its pitch no longer caused him to flinch. It had become the central symbol of this whole fuckin' puzzle, the start of it all. And so he made no move to cut it off, almost revelling in the noise. Only when he saw the pain on his mother's face did he cut the call.

Surprisingly, Danny noticed, the noise seemed to have hit his father hard too. Tony had sunk into a nearby chair and was doing his best to chew his fingernails down to stubs and, by the look of it, was taking a fair whack of his fingers along too. If his da had come here to try to get Danny to relax, he needed to work on his bedside manner a bit more. Seeming to notice Danny's stare, Tony glanced up. Father and son locked eyes for a moment. Again, Danny had the strangest feeling wash over him, but when his father eventually looked away he shrugged it off – Christ knows his synaesthesia had been screaming at him these past few hours.

Luke would be asleep by now, on a normal night. He'd have lifted him up the stairs like a wee sack of coal over one shoulder and laid him gently in his cot. And then he'd have come downstairs and had that chat with Ellie about the two of them, and Christ he'd been scared to think of it, but he wanted to have it now so badly, even if she really was going to give him The Talk. He would fight it. He would refuse. He wasn't finished yet.

'I called her network,' he told them. 'They ran checks. There are no network problems. They haven't got a fucking clue what's causing the static.'

'Jesus Christ,' his father said softly. Danny ignored him. He'd heard enough of his father's theories. Something was pulling up outside. He moved to the window.

'Her ones are here,' he said simply, and moved to the door to let them in, leaving his parents and his best friend standing in silence.

It was going about as well as could be expected, Danny thought as he stood by the front window. Night was falling fast.

'… think that would be sensible.'

'It's pretty fuckin' hard to be sensible at a time like this …'

'Well, we're just as worried as everyone else! This is my daughter! Our only grandchild! We've spent the last – haven't we Michael? haven't we? – the last four hours ringing every single person we can think of, and not a single one has heard from her.'

'God help us!' Danny's mother burst out. It was her go-to exclamation in times of crisis.

'This isn't her. Not her at all. She was always a headstrong girl, God knows. She had her rebellious streak, as I think we're all *well* aware, but she was never one to up and leave,' Michael Quinn said.

Danny could feel the eyes boring into his back even as fuckface spoke. He still didn't turn. Apart from an initial few words when Michael and Christina had entered, he had lost the energy for the conversation entirely.

'Well, she's gone,' Tony said, stating the obvious.

'Clearly she's gone,' Michael snapped back. 'I don't think we're gathered here to look for her in the fucking cupboards or beneath the patio.'

'Beneath the patio? Now what the fuck is that supposed to mean?' asked his father.

And then the foul-mouthed cavalry bugles rang through the air.

'Come on, folks, for fuck's sake. Jesus Christ. Fuck me. I know tensions are runnin' high but c'mon, y'know … pull together and all that fuckin' oul balls. Too many cooks spoil the broth to a blind donkey. Danny … Danny?'

Danny glanced back over his shoulder at Steve, who was pleading with him to intervene. He should. He knew he should. But he simply didn't have the energy. And like that, the armistice was gone and hostilities resumed. Danny could see Steve throw up his hands in disgust without him actually having to do it.

'We rang the police,' Christina announced.

Michael harrumphed. 'They weren't very helpful.'

'So has Danny,' Linda piped up. 'They're coming over shortly.'

There must have been some sort of exchange of facial expressions, Danny realised, because within a fraction of a second the temperature in the room had dropped by about a hundred degrees and both of his parents were shouting and asking what the fuck that look was meant to mean and were met with outraged reiterations of how serious this situation was and how they were not going to be instructed how to behave when their only daughter and grandchild vanished–

Danny turned. 'Stop it.'

He must have hit the right tone for, even though his voice was quiet compared to the accusations and counter-accusations being hurled across the battlements before him, all four combatants fell silent immediately. Everyone turned to him.

'The police say,' he said slowly, 'that they're doing all they can. They'll be along later to take a statement from me and a full description from all of you, as well as to inspect the house for … well … for whatever turns up,' he finished, unable to bring himself to say the word clues.

He paused to take a long breath. It felt like the first one he'd taken in about a decade. And when he spoke again, it was as quietly as before.

'Now I'll say this once, and not again. My girlfriend and my son are missing, and I don't know where they've gone. All I want to do is get out there and look for them, turn the fucking world upside-fucking-down for them, but I can't because I have to wait for the police to arrive. So I stand here. Feeling useless. So useless I want to tear myself apart. If I am made, in my misery, to listen to you bickering amongst yourselves with your pointless, pedantic, posturing piss-fucking bullshit for one single second more than I have already had to endure, then I will take no pleasure at all from throwing you the fuck out of my house right then and there, but I will fucking do it. Am I making myself absolutely clear to you?'

At any other time, he might have found the sheer scale of Michael Quinn's fury at being spoken to in such a way hilarious. But not now. He thought he saw respect in his own da's eyes, but unfortunately gaining his long-absent father's approval was not high on his list of priorities either. Steve looked as if he were about to spontaneously combust into some sort of firework display of pride, though.

'Please, no nodding. Speak up.'

His da spoke up first. 'Yes, son, I'm sorry,'.

'Son, I'm ... '

His ma was upset, and his heart softened to see it. He stepped forward and squeezed her arm with his hand. 'I know, Ma,' he said, and managed to give her a semi-smile.

The remainder of the room was silent. He turned his attention to Michael and Christina. As ever, she let her husband speak for them both.

'Very eloquently put. Perhaps that half a degree of yours wasn't a total loss.'

Steve, perhaps believing himself to be whispering, very clearly said the word wanker in response to this. The reactions of everyone else in the room quickly established that he'd spoken a bit more loudly than he'd thought. He went crimson, but not as red as Michael Quinn.

As the police pulled up outside, wonder of wonders, it was Christina who prevented their first act being to charge Danny with assault. 'What my husband *meant* to say was yes,' she said, arching her eyebrows at Michael as if daring him to disagree.

'Yes. Yes, I did,' he agreed, but only after he'd seen the officers moving up the path. The doorbell rang a second later.

He thinks I had something to do with this. There was no getting round it, and even as Danny opened the door and waved the police inside, he knew that if it were possible, his day had just become more complicated.

*

He had just gone to sleep when she did it. For a moment, the sensations of coldness and wetness became part of his dreamscape and then his mind, as if underwater, kicked up towards the surface. As he broke through, he was presented with the sight of her standing above the bed, holding a wet towel a few feet above his head, allowing it to drip water onto his face. Another huge droplet landed on his nose and splashed, sending little frigid fingers of shock through him.

Seeing he was awake now, Ellie jerked the towel away like a matador and stuck her tongue out at him. He came to terms with the scene in only a few seconds and his first urge was to howl in outrage and lunge from the bed, seeking his revenge. She squealed in delighted terror and scampered for the stairs, with him in hot pursuit. She was begging him not to catch her and get her, warning that she was going to tell on him if he did something to her, and he was growling like a madman.

He caught her at the bottom of the stairs. She wriggled deliciously in his grasp and he pulled her to him and proclaimed his right for revenge and she pouted and told him that he was meant to be helping her strip the living room wallpaper, not falling asleep … to which he pointed out, mildly as he held her close, that it was her fault for finding alternative physical activity the moment Luke had been wheeled from the house by Danny's mother not an hour before …

Phantoms.

As Danny stared at the spot at the bottom of the stairs where he and Ellie had kissed, where they had more than kissed, the memory-ghosts faded. They didn't do so voluntarily, but by a conscious effort of will. He ignored their keenness to return as he walked upstairs with the vague notion of brushing his teeth because it seemed like a nice and normal night-time thing to do.

The police had been … well, they'd been professional, which was as much as could be expected. They had asked him to describe the events of the day several times, and then, very nicely and very calmly, they had asked him some follow-up questions – details of friends and relatives, their favourite places to go, that sort of thing.

They'd asked him for bank account details and the credit card numbers, where Ellie could collect any benefits they were on, but they were moral, or dopey, enough not to be claiming any, save the usual family tax credit and child benefit, and those went straight into the bank account.

And then the questions and information-gathering had switched from this track to a parallel track, so subtly that he had to applaud the smoothness of the transition, but it didn't fool him for a second. How had they put it? – *events that could be linked with the disappearance.*

How're things between you and your family, Danny? Feeling particularly happy with life recently, Danny? How about Ellie? Any history of depression there? Under any stress, Danny?

'Stress,' he echoed.

Yes, stress. We all know how things get on top of us sometimes, eh? Financially? What do you work at, Danny?

'I work for Lircom.'

Wow, Lircom. They're going well, aren't they? Saw them on the news there tonight. I'm a customer myself. Don't suppose you could get me a discount – ha ha, just my little joke there. Do you like it there?

'I did,' he said, and then realised he'd just dug himself in a little deeper.

'I'm being let go,' he said. 'I found out today.'

He saw the glance the police exchanged.

And behind every one of their questions, he felt the weight of the one they didn't ask. *Did you have anything to do with this?*

He had dialled Ellie's number and made everyone, including the police, listen to the electronic squeal. He was disappointed by the police's lack of interest in it, though; they seemed simply to put it down to the mobile being switched off or some network problem. Even Steve had, gently, agreed with this and tried to move Danny away from the subject.

Truthfully Danny couldn't provide any concrete reason for believing that the squeal was some Rosetta Stone clue to all of this, but every time it rang out, he felt the blood chilling in his veins. Maybe it was just because it sounded so much like someone crying out in pain, although he seemed to be the only one who heard it like that.

'We'll put their descriptions on the national database,' the officer had told him, as reassuringly as he could.

When the police had asked for permission to go through the house and have a look around, he had said yes, of course, and then had been faced with the dilemma of whether to sit and wait for them to finish or to follow them around as they went – he'd been conflicted as to which would seem … well, the more natural, and then he'd flinched inwardly to even find himself thinking in those terms.

They wanted a recent picture of Ellie and Luke. He hadn't immediately responded with *what for?* He'd simply nodded and gone to the cupboard in the spare bedroom to lift one of the Winnie the Pooh albums Ellie sat and patiently filled with pictures at a rate of what seemed like one every other day. He'd once remarked to her that if all their photos of Luke had been stacked in chronological order, his entire life could have been seen again as a flawless flick book.

It was the little things like this that hit him. How in the world could anyone decide which photo to use for something like this? And at the back of his mind the thought popped in, unbidden – *I'd better pick one where she looks good or she'll kill me.* Almost as soon as he thought it his eyes filled with tears and he was forced to sit there, holding the albums, wondering if walking down with red-rimmed eyes would turn down the intensity of the officers' stares a few watts.

Fuck.

And the whole time he was upstairs getting the photos with the officer having a look around, he could hear Michael Quinn's low voice, as he talked to the second officer in the living room. His ma and da were outside smoking – he caught a whiff of it in the air through the open window of the spare bedroom as it wafted upward from the front porch. His ma was looking worse as time wore on, and seeing the police had made the whole thing horrifically official.

Michael Quinn was talking about him. He knew he was. Had he pressed his ear to the floorboards, perhaps he could have made out what he was saying. He wasn't tempted to do so in the slightest.

The worst was yet to come, though.

'You want a what?' he said dumbly.

The officer had the decency to look pained, knowing how difficult this would be for anyone to hear. 'We like to have a DNA sample of every person reported as missing.'

Danny didn't ask why. Unfortunately the officer assumed his silence was as good as asking.

'For any … forensics that we might need to do. Might,' he emphasised. 'It's just a precaution.'

Danny nodded slowly. Finding the photo had been painful, but being asked this made it look like a day trip to the beach. 'Um,' he looked around, his mind a blank, 'I d-d-don't know what …'

'A toothbrush is usually good.'

He went and retrieved Ellie's. It was pink and girly and, though he didn't touch the bristles, he knew they would have been slightly damp, having seen use that morning. He handed it to the officer and watched him place it in a plastic bag and seal it.

'Can I get it back?' he heard himself say. The officer looked at him. 'If she … well it's her only one and … she' – he paused, and collected himself – 'she likes to brush.'

'I'm sure we can arrange that, yeah.'

Or you could just get another one. He saw it in the officer's eyes, even if it didn't reach his mouth.

I don't *want* to buy a new one, he thought.

'What about the …'

It hit him then. Luke was too young for a toothbrush. Too young for a *toothbrush* and he was out there, somewhere, and

Danny hadn't a clue if he was safe. His stomach lurched. He took a moment to bring himself back under control and think. He emerged from the bedroom with something clutched between his fingers. It was a dummy. It was Luke's favourite. Danny had considered for a second selecting one of Luke's lesser-used dummies, and then had thought *what if they can't get what they need because it's not used enough?*

'Perfect!' said the officer as he took it, and though Danny knew what he meant he felt like smashing his face in.

The police had departed with platitudes and promises which he understood but which didn't reassure him one iota. *Give it a few days*, they said. *Seems like the wee fella has his mother with him, after all. We're sure they'll turn up soon. If needs be, we'll go down the media appeal route. Would you be okay with that, Danny? Going on television?*

Danny had nodded someone else's head and said that it would be okay through someone else's lips.

Her ones had gone not long thereafter, to his immense relief. His parents and Steve had gone, at his insistence – he practically had to dislodge Steve from the doorframe with a crowbar – but having them stay over would have been odd, and he'd had enough of odd.

He paused at the top of the stairs, and glanced in at their bedroom. At the cot.

He could almost see himself, a ghost of a memory, sitting on the edge of his and Ellie's bed, his arm crooked over the side of the cot holding a bottle of milk in place for Luke to guzzle. The surface of the mattress was low enough that, after a while of leaning your arm in, resting it painfully against the wood of the cot, you began to lose all feeling in your fingers and started to hope that little kicking and punching sleep-suited bundle closed his eyes before permanent nerve damage set in.

But here came Ellie, with a small towel. She wrapped it up on itself and motioned for Danny to lift his arm, which he did for a second, allowing her to slip the towel onto the part of the cot where he was leaning his arm. She winked at him and tapped the side of her head and flashed him that smile of hers before climbing over him and getting into bed.

Danny walked into the bedroom, once again forcing the phantoms to leave. He sat on the bed and listened to the silence of the house around him, and he cried. He cried until there was nothing left, and the phantoms came back, though this time he did nothing to send them away and soon he was surrounded by them, surrounded by Ellies and Lukes.

Sleep escaped him, though that didn't come as a shock. Despite the chronic tiredness he'd been feeling since this all started, he knew it wasn't a desire to sleep, merely a desire to have the world go away for a while. Truth be told, he was afraid to sleep, in case it somehow signalled that he wasn't taking this as seriously as he should be.

At 2.14 a.m., he descended the stairs and headed purposefully for the kitchen. He'd felt an urge and knew it had to be obeyed. Ellie never kept bottles overnight. She made a fresh batch every morning. And so he found himself pouring out the bottles of milk he had made earlier.

The formula milk *glug-glugged* its way down the plughole. He rubbed at his eyes as he waited for the kettle to boil, knowing they would be red and puffy, knowing he must look a fuckin' mess. He had deliberately avoided looking in mirrors for the last few hours. When the kettle boiled, when the steriliser *dinged*, he lined the bottles up in a neat little row and he took the scoop from the tin. His vision was blurring.

He spilled the powder. Missed the bottleneck entirely and it tumbled onto the draining board, instantly congealing as it touched the wet surface. He set the scoop down and realised that it too was now not sterile. Not safe.

He was a bad father.

Luke had not been planned and he had thought it was enough to do the decent thing and stick by Ellie and make sure the wee fella had a da who *stayed around and didn't fuck off.*

But it wasn't, was it? He was half-arsed. He paid lip-service to it all.

His father's words rose unbidden in his mind.

I can't go on pretending to be happy with the life that has become mine. For years we thought that having a son would make our lives complete. I thought that I could be an amazing father. But the truth is, I'm a fraud. All I do is pretend; pretend that everything is fine, pretend that this life makes me content, pretend that I'm thrilled to be coming home when I have spent time away from you both.

Having a family is just … it's too much for me. I had to escape.

And I'm glad I did.

He closed his eyes and he could visualise each word on that tattered piece of notepaper – a letter that no longer existed. He could practically feel the heat of the flames had that destroyed it.

He was no better. No better than his father. Ellie had seen through it, seen his façade for what it was, and she'd decided she'd had enough of it. She'd gone and taken his son with–

Thu-crakkk.

He started violently at the noise, thinking for a second that someone was shooting at him, but the noise hadn't come from a bullet; as he turned, he saw the window at the far end of the kitchen now had a large chip. As he moved towards it, another object arced into view; a rock, hurled from the alley. It impacted against the window and another report sounded, causing the chip to grow in size and little spiderweb filaments to begin to bloom from it.

Laughter. He heard it, faint but clear, high-pitched.

Coming from the alley.

His hand curled around the hilt of the largest of the kitchen knives jutting from the wooden block – the big one that was far too large to be used for anything practical except instilling a distinct feeling of badassery in anyone who wielded it, and by fuckin' Christ he was wielding it now. He unlocked the back door and strode out into the yard. *His* yard.

'Right, you wee bastards …' he said, loudly enough for them to hear.

Knife in one hand, he unlocked the alleyway door and it felt as though the darkness, eager to have been shown an entrance, rushed at him, swallowed him. Even with his girlfriend and son close, he'd hated going out into that place in the dead of night. How much had happened since he'd last stepped out here, wheelie bin in tow?

The wee hoody bastards thought they ruled the night. When he was a kid there would have been a few teenagers hanging round the offie, asking anyone going in to get them a carry-out, slabberin' a wee bit if they were refused. It had been rascally, but it hadn't seemed threatening.

Now they hung about in packs of fifteen or more, and they went deathly silent when you passed.

The alleyway was still littered with bins; many of the residents didn't bother bringing them back in after collection until the day or so after. He could see the big metal gates, looking like a portcullis, at the far end of the alley. They looked huge, imposing, but he knew they wouldn't stop the more determined breed of fuckwit.

His hand tightened around the knife. He was amazed how empowered he felt. Danny had been in one fight in his entire life, when he was nine years old, and he had staggered home afterward and celebrated his triumph by throwing up spectacularly and having a heroic cry to himself. But now … maybe it was the fact that his stomach had no churning left in it.

'I know you're out here! Ya fuckin' wee cunts!' he yelled.

There was no reply, but he saw flickers of movement further on down the alley. Something knocked against one of the bins; he saw its outline rock from side to side.

He sprang forward, some ancient part of his brain crying *charge!* and the rest of him, for a wonder, following its lead. The Danny who had cowered down this same alley only a few nights ago was gone. The knife blade flashed in the dark.

A shadow loomed ahead of him.

Something stood up.

Danny reacted instinctively, shouting something suitably fear-inspiring and incoherent, diving forward, throwing his free hand out and getting a solid grip of the shape's throat, applying his entire weight to knock the fucker over onto its back so they both hit the alley floor with a solid *thump*.

Lights went on in some of the houses in Regent Street, no doubt in reaction to Danny's screamed challenge, dotting the alleyway's former blackness with patches of semi-illumination. One such pool of light was thrown across the area where he and his quarry had fallen ...

Teeth.

Eyes.

Hands scrabbling at his throat, hands with sharp ends ...

'Jesus!'

Danny threw himself backwards, landing on his arse in the shadows, scrabbling away until he felt his back hit solid wood. The knife clattered somewhere, lost amidst the shadows.

And it came for him. It came on arms too long, on legs too short, scuttling like an insect across the alleyway, moving too quickly to be illuminated properly. He couldn't move any further backwards and now here was the terror, here was the fear he had marvelled at not feeling before, multiplied tenfold ...

A shriek rang out, assaulting his ears; a shriek that even in his dumbstruck horror he found somehow familiar, as the thing scuttling towards him closed the final few feet to where he–

Suddenly the alleyway door behind him opened. He tumbled

arse over shite, ending up in an undignified heap.

'Close the door!' he screamed. 'Close the fuckin' door!'

A hand reached down to help him up. As he clasped it, he saw it was old, spotted with age. He looked up into the face of his saviour.

'Hello love,' said Bea, and smiled a semi-toothless smile down at him. 'Cup o' tea?'

Bea's tea was so substantial you could have dammed fjords with it. He felt like upending his cup, letting it *sloooop* out and eating it with a knife and fork. How – *teeth, eyes, claws* – many fuckin' teabags had she used anyway?

A shiver went through him that seemed to start in his bones and shake his entire body. All doubts about the tea sitting in front of him fled and he took a long draught, feeling it hit the back of his throat and begin to burn its way down, bringing back some much-needed sensation to his nervous system, even if it was in the form of possibly permanent tannin-induced nerve damage.

Bea sat at the other end of the tiny table in her kitchen. She had her own cup but had not yet touched it; she was too busy studying the young man before her with eyes that, now he saw them up close, were as keen as they were old.

'How're ya feeling, son?'

He was about to answer when another mini-flashback to that fucking thing shot through him and brought his teeth together with a *clack*. He closed his eyes for a second and forced himself to take a breath and exhale. 'All right,' he managed. 'Thanks for the tea.'

She waved a hand. 'Ach, don't be daft. Least I could do. I wasn't sleepin' and I saw you go out after I heard your window crack,' and there was that stare again. 'You must be worried sick, I'm guessin'.'

He nodded, still trying to process what had happened. In the harsh artificial light of an old woman's kitchen, with its floral tea towels and bag of cat food propped up in the corner, it suddenly seemed absurd in the extreme. He tried to conjure up the sequence of events in a more controlled way, to slow down the memory and study it, but every time his mind approached it a flush of the fear that had swept through him out there went right through him once more.

What should he do? Should he ring the police and report the damage to his window? It wasn't exactly a bazooka attack and it wasn't as if there had been a note attached to a brick telling him to go to a telephone box and bring fifty thousand in unmarked bills, though he fervently wished there had been; at least that would have been *something*. And what would he say when the police asked him, as they inevitably would, if he had got a look at his would-be assailant? They'd think he was a fuckin' lunatic, and that would do wonders for improving the looks he was already getting from them.

Had he imagined it? He had always been terrified of that alley – he had no problem admitting it to himself, not at this precise moment anyway. Had he walked out there with his head fucked from the events of the day, spooked some wee spidey bastard into having a go at him and mentally superimposed some nightmarish visage on him? It didn't sound good for his own sanity, but what was the alternative explanation? That things that went brick in the night were real? No. Bollocks. Bollocks to that.

'I just hope they're okay,' he finally replied.

Bea nodded sympathetically. 'God love ye,' she said. 'It's terrible, so it is. Terrible. I can't believe these things happen – isn't it enough to make ye question what's wrong with this world? Jesus, love, I don't know. If it's not hoods in the back alley, it's people going missin' …'

Danny felt his mind begin to wander. He'd had enough of the 'God love ye' school of crisis management from his ma earlier. 'Yeah …' he said, distractedly. His nose twitched and he noticed that the musty smell that he'd put down to Bea's advanced years was in fact coming from a fruit bowl on the kitchen countertop. Every single piece of fruit within was in a terrible state – the bananas were blackened, the peaches rotten. For a wee woman who kept the rest of her house immaculate, it seemed oddly out of place.

Bea wasn't finished yet. 'I know your wee mummy and daddy must be beside themselves – and you, like I say, such a nice wee family! I've always said to wee Jackie down the street "they keep themselves to themselves and don't bother nobody, and that chile's always lovely turned out, and their garden's always just beautiful!"'

Danny felt himself come around, as if someone had just waved smelling salts under his nose. 'What?' he asked. 'What was that?'

'The chile?' Bea replied. 'Ach he's always gorgeous …'

'No.' He shook his head, and stared into space for a second before standing up, his mind made up. Christ it felt good just to decide to do something. He glanced down at the cup, feeling vaguely obligated, and downed the remainder of its contents.

Between Bea's tea and Lircom's sandwiches, there was a good possibility all of this would turn out to be a hallucination brought on by exotic substances.

'Thanks for the tea, Mrs O'Malley,' he said, walking out of her kitchen. She rose to her feet and followed him, wincing slightly and clutching at her hip as she stood. 'And for the rescue. But I really have to go. You keep your doors locked now, won't ye?'

'Certainly, son, certainly,' she nodded vigorously. 'Any of them wee bastards tries anything on me and I'll cut their fuckin' balls off.'

Danny blinked. 'Good,' he said.

Bea's face softened and crumpled into her default expression of well-meaning wizened old crone. 'You try and get some sleep now, God love ye!' she told him and patted his cheek, unlatching the front door for him as she did so.

He made some sort of perfunctory goodbye in her direction, was inside his own house in moments, and outside of it again moments later.

Lamplight glinted off the metallic edge of his spade. Danny looked down at the small mound of earth that he'd flattened only the previous night and which, somehow, had returned during the same time period in which the two people he shared his life with had vanished without trace.

The police had asked him if he had anything else to tell them and he'd told them about the electronic squeal of the phone. But he hadn't mentioned the hump of earth, because it seemed so left-field he wasn't sure how to explain it. Steve hadn't even noticed its return until Danny had pointed it out to him just as he was leaving. His friend had suggested that maybe Ellie had had a change of heart or maybe there was some sort of subsidence, or fuck, maybe he had gophers.

'Do we have gophers in Ireland?'

'Fucked if I know. What's a gopher?' Danny had asked.

'Dunno. Beaver on benefits? Was there not one fuckin' about in *Happy Gilmore*?' Steve had wondered aloud. At any other time, this would have prompted a long, happy meandering conversation between the two mates – top five furry animals in movies (Sharon Stone's gee in *Basic Instinct* would have won), if Adam Sandler would get his balls knocked in if he dandered into a Belfast pub, that sort of thing. Not tonight.

The spade bit into the ground beneath him. He felt the shudder of resistance go up his arm and shoulder, and a wave of memories of doing this only last night with Steve washed over him, a wave that threatened to destabilise his newfound determination, since bound up within it were companion memories of Ellie bringing out beers and watching the stars. He sidestepped them and stuck to his task. He had dug this mound out last night before his life had gone to shit. He had dug it out for Ellie. By Christ he was going to make sure it stayed done.

Up the street, curtains twitched in a front room, and a pair of rheumy eyes watched him work silently under the orange glow of the streetlamps.

The eyes crinkled at the corners, and the curtains closed.

The Helper

'Jesus holy Christ of Almighty.'

The words reached into the mists of Danny's slumber and slapped him across the face. The world built itself up again, reality's Lego bricks slotting back into place, as he went through the stages of waking up. He wasn't in his bed, so that explained the lower back pain. He was lying on a hard floor, his lips about an inch from a dust bunny the size of Greenland that he mistook, initially, for a massive great spider–

'Shitfugacunye!' was the closest translation of the word that escaped Danny's lips as he got to his feet in the quickest way possible. Ellie had been the designated spider-killer of their house. Danny had a tacit agreement with anything that had more than two legs and two eyes: outside the confines of his little kingdom, if they wanted to scuttle and – an involuntary spasm rippled through his muscles even at the thought – lurk, fine. Violate his borders, though, and he would hunt them down mercilessly.

Or, you know, get his girlfriend to squish them with a rolled-up copy of *Take a Break* while he tried to look cool somewhere off to the side. Whatevs.

Steve, emitter of the colourful blasphemy that had pulled Danny from his sleep, was standing in the living room doorway. He was looking at Danny with some sympathy but mostly trepidation, as if he was approaching a cylindrical object with tailfins that he'd discovered in a hole in his basement and it had just begun emitting a *tick tick tick* noise.

'Mornin', lad,' he said, producing a key. 'Let meself in, that all right?'

'Course,' Danny mumbled, wondering why Steve hadn't bothered to shower before he'd come over. Holy fuck, the smell was unbelievable.

His eyes settled on the spade that was lying on the hearth, the blade covered in earth and muck and bits of grass, as were, he noted, his clothes which he'd slept in all night after doing some hard graft …

Ah.

Well, that explained Steve's wrinkled nose.

'Um,' Steve said. 'Take it there's no word?'

'No,' Danny replied. Water. He needed water. He moved past Steve, who retreated *well* out of his way to allow him to pass and get to the kitchen. As he filled a glass with water, little incidentals occurred to him; the missing knife in the block. The back gate to the alley, still open. The chip in the window. He gulped the water down gratefully.

'Jesus! What happened to yer window, lad?'

Danny set the glass back in the sink. He didn't even look up at Steve for a second. Even a few moments after the incident, it had already seemed ridiculous. Now, in the cold light of day, he burned with embarrassment just recalling it.

Some fuckin' protector he was. Some fuckin' man of the house. Scared shitless by some wee hood until he'd almost pissed his fuckin' knickers in terror. And him heading out with the big knife and all like a hard man. Ha. That was a laugh. Not five minutes ago he'd laid an egg of terror at the sight of some bellybutton fluff and skin particles about to sink its fangs into him.

He'd been prepared to let Ellie bring the blue bin out for the extra collection too, hadn't he?

'Jesus Christ! It's bringin' a bin out to an alley! I'll do it if it bothers ye that much!'

'Righto. Seeing as how I did your night feed last night, yeah?'

He looked up at Steve, who was reaching out a finger to explore the spider web of cracks that had spread from the initial point of impact. 'Some wee hood durin' the night,' he said, as casually as he could. 'Probably hadn't a clue what house he was aimin' for and didn't care.'

'Wee cunts,' Steve said hotly. 'Knew I shoulda stayed last night. Told ye.'

'Forget about it,' Danny said. 'I chased them anyway,' he added, which was broadly true, there had been some chasing and knife-brandishing … before the cowering in fear. Of all that he said nothing. There were limits to what he was willing to disclose.

Amazingly, he found himself phoning work. Of all the things to remember to do at a time like this, some part of him had still flagged the fact that he'd need to let Lircom know he wouldn't be coming in today.

'Hello?' Thomas' voice sounded on the duty mobile. He

carried that fuckin' thing about on an honest-to-Christ utility belt whenever he was in the building.

'Thomas, it's Danny. I won't be in today.'

'Well Danny' – and he could *hear* the bastard checking his watch – 'it's past the usual time for informing the duty manager of an unplanned absence. You are required–'

He couldn't let him go on any further, lest he say something truly monumentally stupid and force Danny to take the time out of his day to track him down and give him a good murdering.

'Ellie and Luke have gone missing, Thomas. I've been up all night. The police have been. So …' and he trailed off, trying to think of a way to finish that sentence that didn't include any variations of the phrase *fuck you* and failed, so he left it at that.

There was a pause. He found it all too easy to picture Thomas' face at that moment processing what he'd just been told – 90 per cent of the time, calls to the duty mobile to announce an unscheduled absence were accompanied by excuses weaker than a bubble-gum elevator cable. Thomas was in uncharted waters here. Plainly he was trying to get back on track.

'Um. Ellie. Your … partner, Ellie … and … I'm sorry, not sure I caught the second …?'

'Luke. My baby son.'

'Oh …' and now there was genuine puzzlement in the fucker's voice. Somehow, Danny wasn't surprised. Thomas had stalked the office floor enough times when he and Cal and Alice had been chatting across the desks, and since Luke had been born, Danny had been entertaining the other two with horrific tales of sleepless nights, but to Thomas, all of this would have been so much white noise; all he was interested in was that where there *should* have been constructive work-related conversation, there was idle banter.

'Right. Okay. Um. If they come back before lunch, will you be in this afternoon, d'you–'

Click.

When he'd taken several deep breaths to steady himself and quell the murderous urges, he found Steve standing in front of him, hopping from one foot to the other and clapping his hands in what was probably supposed to be a decisive gesture, but only made him seem psychotic.

'Right,' he said. 'I've brought the car. We're going out.'

'Out?' Danny echoed. He understood the word but not the concept.

'Out. Out lookin'. Have a wee drive round. Maybe if you're out and about you'll think of a few places you forgot to tell the police about.'

'I don't want to leave the house. Just in case there's a call or …'

Steve rolled his eyes. 'Come on, lad. You'll feel more useful gettin' out and about and fuckin' *doin'* somethin' other than sittin' here on your hole feelin' – what was it? – useless? Ready to tear yourself apart?'

He had a point, Danny had to admit. These four walls were so stuffed full of memories that every time he entered and re-entered a room he felt a fresh jab of pain go right through him. He was tired of it. That was partly why it had been so fuckin' therapeutic to get out of the place last night and flatten that garden once more.

'Sure if you're worried about the home phone goin', ring your ma and get her to house-sit,' Steve suggested, when Danny had, in theory at least, assented to the out and about plan.

In more jovial times Danny might have been tempted to ask this helpful person before him, chock full of good ideas, who he was and what he had done with his best friend. As it was he simply nodded. He grabbed his coat but as he went to put it on he caught Steve's expression.

'What?'

'Look, mate, not that I'm questioning your particular method of stress relief in a crisis,' Steve said, holding his hands up to ward off any comebacks, 'but um … d'you think you might go up and have a wee shower before we head off …?'

Steve drove like Steve talked – quickly, a little aimlessly, and pausing every so often to emit a loud *fuck* in someone's general direction. Danny couldn't be too harsh, though, because at least his friend *could* drive; he'd been all set to start his first driving lessons, had even started saving a few quid here and there with an eye on acquiring himself a wee runabout, and then … well, a blue line had appeared, or not appeared, or appeared twice (he could never remember which) and driving had … gone away, along with a lot of other things.

His ma had waved them off not five minutes ago, promising to ring if any news came through. Christ, she'd looked haggard. Danny guessed, correctly, that she hadn't had a wink of sleep the previous night. He'd had a flash of guilt about not asking her to stay over the night before, but he knew rightly what would have ensued – the two of them sitting in the living room, glancing at the telephone, trying to talk about anything but Ellie and Luke and eventually crumbling and engaging in a long sob-fest.

He couldn't have handled that. Besides, it would have deprived him of his nervous breakdown in the middle of the night with a side order of hallucination. Wouldn't that have been a tragedy?

She'd stopped talking about Luke altogether, he noticed. This morning, she had made reference to Ellie only. He didn't comment on it. No doubt she was just working from the assumption that news about Ellie was news about Luke. Danny's own mind shied away from any other eventuality like a scalded cat.

They slid to a stop at a red light only a few streets away from Regent Street. The hazy plan was to crisscross the estate and its surrounding estates, on the off chance (and it was an extremely off chance) that one of them would spot something. Quite what the fuck that 'something' was meant to be, Danny hadn't a clue, but he had to admit, just being in a car moving along wasn't completely horrible. A moving car implied an end destination.

'So,' Steve said, and Danny sighed, for he knew immediately that this was The Talk.

'So?'

'Um ... how were things with you and–'

'My da already tried this with me, lad.' Danny cut him off neatly, making a show of looking out the window as if for the mystic clue they were seeking. 'Don't make me use the same language on you that I used on him. I like you.'

'Fella in work a few weeks back was telling me about his cousin – came home one day and his wife had taken off with some fucker she met on the internet. Moved to Belleek. Belleek, fuck's sake!

129

You'd think it'd at least be somewhere like New York.'

I can't go on pretending to be happy with the life that has become mine. All I do is pretend; pretend that everything is fine, pretend that this life makes me content, pretend that I'm thrilled to be coming home when I have spent time away from you both.

They weren't Danny's words, but they sprang up like a fucking gag reflex, regular as clockwork. He pressed his fingers to his temples and said nothing. The lights turned to green, and the car moved forward. Steve licked his lips, knowing full well he was skidding on a razorblade and about to use his balls for brakes, but feeling compelled to continue.

'Apparently,' he went on, 'she'd been chatting to this twat for six months. Decided to go and buck him instead of her husband. Mental. Cunt musta used a nice font or something.'

Danny glared at Steve. 'Am I talkin' to my fuckin' self here?' he said.

Steve shrugged in a don't-shoot-the-messenger way. 'I dunno … women … I'm just sayin'…'

'It's Ellie, Steve. Not women. Ellie.' The car seemed suddenly claustrophobic and he cursed himself for being so stupid as to think Steve had taken him out on this drive for any reason other than to have The Talk. And he probably could have left it there and Steve would have, maybe, caught the warning tone in his voice and let it be. But he didn't. He was angry and pissed off and he didn't.

'That's your fuckin' problem, you know? You got fucked about and you can't tell the difference between women and a woman anymore. Did you ever think that maybe, just maybe, you backed the wrong horse? Or that maybe you can be a bit of a fuckin' big eejit yourself, lad? Don't start talkin' about me and Ellie just because you fucked things up with Maggie, all right?'

The silence was thunderous. For a while as the car glided through the streets, Danny simply stared out the window, his heart thudding in his chest, somewhat stunned that the car was still moving forward and that he hadn't been fucked out on his ear.

'I'd hate to hear what you said to your da,' Steve said quietly.

Danny closed his eyes, skewered by the hot stab of guilt he suddenly felt. When he'd marinated in the burn for long enough, he looked at his friend just as Steve did the same. A look born of many years of friendship passed between the two, a look that pretty much said, only because it's you.

'I'm sorry, that was outta line,' Danny said, but then his face hardened a little. 'But, lad, I did warn ya not to talk that balls to me. Think about it for one minute would ye? I'd fucking love to believe you. Right now finding out Ellie and the wee fella are in Antarctica shacked up with the New Zealand rugby team would be far better than the sort of alternatives that are running through my mind. But I know, *I know*, that she didn't leave me. How do you think that makes me feel?'

Steve frowned. 'The wee fella?' he echoed.

Danny wasn't paying attention, though; a thought had come to him, unbidden, out of left-field, but intriguing. He reached into his pocket and pulled out his mobile. 'Cover your ears,' he told Steve.

'Aw, fuck, no …' Steve said, realising what was about to happen. The electronic squeal lasted until Danny pressed the end call button.

'Thanks for that, lad,' Steve said, his voice strained. 'I know you don't drive and all that, but one thing you'll notice about people who do is that they have to keep their hands on the fuckin' wheel. So covering ears can be quite fuckin' difficult.'

Danny was staring down at the phone. 'It's not as loud,' he said. He'd listened to that squeal enough times, like picking at some sort of aural scab, that now knew every nuance of it. The synaesthesia helped with that too; sometimes sounds could form a sort of map in his mind, and the pattern of that squeal was different than it had been before. He was fucked if he knew how, though.

'If you say so,' Steve said, shaking his head as if to restart his brain. 'There's definitely something weird about it, lad. You said to the police about it like, didn't ye?'

Danny rolled his eyes. 'For all the good it did, aye. I don't think they're gonna do anything, though. I think they're much more interested in me.'

'In you?'

He couldn't help but be touched by the level of Steve's naivety. 'Jesus, you've seen enough of this on TV. It's always someone close to the family. Didn't you see the way they looked at each other when I told them I'd got the sack yesterday?'

Steve drove on, not replying immediately. 'What are you gonna do about that?' he asked eventually. 'I mean' – and he forced lightness into his tone – 'obviously this oul ballix will all clear itself up sooner rather than later and Ellie will turn up safe and sound. But you'll still be unemployed, man.'

'I can't think about that right now,' Danny said, forcing down annoyance that Steve too had decided to talk as if it were only

Ellie who was missing. Biting his friend's head off for the second time in as many minutes, stressful time or not, might be pushing it.

'I could maybe see about getting you somethin'…'

Danny shifted in his seat. More pity. He knew Steve meant no harm but the only work Steve could get him would be clerical stuff in the IT company he worked for. At least Lircom had involved a bullshit eight-week course on the ins and outs of technical support so that he would be qualified to take people through the minefield of switching it off and on again. That had bumped his wage packet up a bit – not a lot, Christ knew, but a bit. It had also stopped him feeling like a complete numpty.

To go from that to delivering the post or doing the filing would be yet another redefinition of 'bottom scraping' in the Big Danny Morrigan Book of Barrels. On the other hand, what were his alternatives? The worry about Ellie and Luke was so all-consuming that Steve was correct; he had more or less forgotten about his impending unemployment, as though finding them would bring some sort of cash reward. It wouldn't work like that. Pushing a cart about would keep a roof over their heads.

'We'll see,' was all he said. 'Like I said, it's not really my priority now, all right?'

'Course, lad. Course …'

After that they lapsed into silence. Danny's mind went back to the phone signal oddity, and somewhere, finally, something sparked into life in his mind. Could he …? Yes. Yes, why not? They were doing fuck-all good circling the estates here, and now that they'd had The Talk, he could see Steve's interest in this exercise had waned. Another ten minutes and he'd start throwing hints about dropping by the nearest KFC.

'Get onto the main road,' he said.

Steve complied. 'Where we going, boss?' he asked. 'I was thinkin' we might grab a–'

'Queen's,' Danny said firmly, doing a drive-by on the drive-thru suggestion. 'I'm gonna visit an oul mate of mine …'

The place smelled of new paint, very old books and carpet that hadn't seen a hoovering since the days of the Ming dynasty. Turning up feeling like a rock star on his first day of Queen's University, Danny had been blown away by the design of the main Lanyon Building. It looked like a cathedral spreading its wings, all Tudor-Gothic splendour, and walking inside it for the first time, he had almost felt his brain kick into gear, his appetite for learning increase. I've come home, he had thought.

Of course, about six minutes later at the Freshers' registration desk, an extremely bearded man had told him he'd be spending almost all his time in 1–3 University Square, the nondescript terraced street across the road, and he wouldn't be near the Lanyon Building again. In fairness, though, he had thrown up almost an entire Jägerbomb inside it three months later. By that stage his insatiable eagerness for learning had been supplanted by other types of eagerness.

His initial disappointment in the School of English and its location hadn't lasted long. There was something right about going into that wee row of houses, all antiquated as fuck, with their big white banisters and maze-like winding hallways and landings. It felt like you were hanging out at your uncle's big house in the country. All memories of secondary school with its sterile corridors and row after row of wee desks and chairs were banished. This was grown-up shit you were into now.

It all washed over him as he stepped inside. This was the only time the synaesthesia felt like a disability, and even now, it wasn't its fault; it was simply doing what it did best – connecting dots in his head that stretched across the five senses. Coming back for the first time in over a year, to a place where he'd seen some good times, a place he missed, he was almost overcome by the onslaught of the smells and tastes and memories. To Danny, nostalgia could sometimes be so overpowering that it bordered on time travel.

He and Steve made their way up to the third floor. Steve was looking around nervously, as if he might be ambushed at any moment by a paramilitary metaphor. He wasn't comfortable around big words. Medium words made him think twice. Put him in front of a computer that was spitting out gibberish and he could have it singing sweetly in an eye blink, but ask him what the difference between a colon and a semi-colon was and you stood a good chance of seeing a grown man cry.

They heard the lab before they saw it, and felt it before they heard it – a faint vibration in the floorboards which grew in intensity as they approached.

'It's the subwoofer powering up,' Danny explained.

'Powering up? You mean that's what it does before it's even on?'

Danny shrugged. 'It's a big one,' he offered. He knocked on

the door. 'Doc?'

'Big speaker? *Doc?*' Steve snorted. 'What's next? A DeLorean?'

Danny ignored him. He was already planning what he would do if someone else opened the door, some assistant or other that might have been employed recently and not know him. Bluff, seduce, or failing that, a surgical blow to the back of the head were all valid options.

As it turned out, he needn't have worried. The door opened, revealing a bearded middle-aged avuncular little man whose expression changed from irritation at being disturbed to a broad beaming grin when he saw who stood at his door. Although to call Doc Hammond bearded would be doing him a kindness – since Danny had first known him and kindled an instant kinship with him in first year Linguistics, he had been trying his best to grow what he probably thought was a beard with suitable academic gravitas, but which looked perpetually scruffy and ragged, the face-fuzz of a man not supposed to have anything more than a five (maybe six, tops) o'clock shadow.

'Danny! Come in, come in!' he cried. Danny inclined his head in thanks and walked in, flinching inwardly at yet another assault of memories as he did so.

He'd taken a girl he'd been going out with here one afternoon to show her the equipment. She'd been a bit dubious about the fun factor of it, but he'd finally managed to persuade her into coming along. He didn't tell her that Doc Hammond had taken delivery of the big subwoofer only the day before and had arranged to test out the new baby, with Danny and a few of his other favourite students, by hooking in a Playstation and a copy of *Guitar Hero*.

Five minutes after arriving, the shredding had begun in earnest, and nary an eardrum was safe.

Danny's rendition of 'All Along the Watchtower' had been heard as far away as Cookstown. Seismologists' needles had trembled in the face of his plastic guitar's fury. *And* he'd successfully nailed a blowjob for his troubles later that evening. Star Power indeed …

'Can you analyse something for me?' he asked.

Doc put a hand on his shoulder. 'Danny, I heard,' he said gravely. 'You must be out of your mind with worry. I'm surprised to see you here, to be honest, welcome though you are.'

'You heard?' Danny said. 'Who told you?'

Doc held up his phone. 'Maggie sent a text yesterday evening. I don't have your number so I couldn't–'

Danny goggled. 'Maggie? Maggie texted you? Who told her?'

Steve raised a hand. 'That'd be me,' he said. And on seeing the look that Danny gave him, he shrugged. 'What? I told ye I was gonna send texts to everyone askin' them had they seen or heard anything, didn't I?'

'Aye, but …' Danny started to reply, and then sighed. Steve was right: everyone was everyone, although the chances that Ellie would have chosen Maggie to confide in about her plan to abscond were so miniscule as to be laughable. The last few times the girls had been within spitting distance of each other, Danny had thought they were about to give the truth to that cliché. Not surprising given the history between the two, and Danny himself, but that didn't make it any easier.

And for Steve to text her … Danny couldn't help but be touched. He might not know much about the break-up between the two, but he did know that since it had happened they hadn't been in touch.

'Forget it,' he said. He proceeded to fill Doc in on the events of the day before, highlighting in particular the weird phone interference and the police's lack of interest in it. He rang Ellie's number at Doc's request – this time Steve *was* able to put his fingers safely in his ears – and allowed the sound to blast out.

As he'd hoped, Doc was intrigued. 'Let's give it a go,' he said, and began buzzing about the machines.

'Cheers, Doc.'

'Least I can do. Least I can do. As you say, relying on the police for progress would be like asking Slyvia Plath to man a shift on the Samaritans.'

He and Danny chuckled knowingly at this. Steve rolled his eyes, but he seemed captivated enough by the technology not to mind the book-geek talk too much.

'Doc, this is Steve, a friend of mine,' Danny said, realising that he hadn't introduced his friend to his old mentor.

'Delighted to meet you, Stephen. I'm–'

'Dr Hammond,' Steve said dryly. 'Yeah, I know. I think I've listened to Danny here recount every single lecture you ever gave.'

Doc beamed in his direction as he finished hooking the landline into the computer. 'And yet our Plath reference was lost on you? Surely you must know something about the finer points of literary tradition, my boy!'

Steve shrugged. 'Think so, wouldn't ye?' he said. He seemed impressed despite this gruffness. 'You're pretty good with the computers,' he said, grudgingly. 'I didn't think …'

'… anyone over fifty knew their USB from their ASCII,' Doc finished for him. He winked. 'Life's full of surprises. I discovered that the day your friend here enrolled in my tutorials.'

Danny coloured as Steve looked at him sceptically. 'Why, what'd he do? Fart in the middle of the lecture? He did that in one of my IT ones. The dirty bastard. Jesus. I felt like Wilfred fuckin' Owen in the trenches choking on mustard gas. See?' he said triumphantly. 'A literary reference!'

Doc looked affronted. 'Studying Danny's synaesthesia brought our understanding of how linguistics can interact with human senses forward in leaps and bounds,' he elaborated. 'Danny has an incredible gift. If we could bottle it and reproduce it, people would be queuing up to get it, believe me.'

'What, to smell colours and hear tastes?' Steve snorted. 'Aye, sounds like a right fuckin' laugh. Fuck only knows why there isn't Synaesthesia Man in the X-Men. Missin' a trick there' – and he struck a dramatic pose and sniffed – 'what's this?! I can smell the Bat Signal! Ho! Away to the Tastes of Wednesday Cave!'

'Synaesthesia is not a superpower, young man!' Doc thundered, twisting *superpower* in his mouth in the way only someone over fifty can. 'And it is more than simply a rewiring of the brain. Research has proven that the sense of smell, for example, does not even need to go through the brain in the same way as the other senses to be perceived – so how can our friend Danny smell colours? Clearly, more is going on–'

Realising Doc was about to launch into an impassioned defence of the fascinating mysteries of his brain, Danny decided to intervene. He had other things on his mind.

'Doc, are we ready to go?' he said, pointing to the equipment.

'Yes' – Doc tore himself away from the juicy argument looming before him like a dog letting go of a steak – 'all hooked in. We can dial the number and record,' and the sound of someone dialling a long string of numbers on a touch-tone keypad was amplified through the lab. Steve's eyes widened as he saw Doc turn the volume up. He slammed his hands over his ears. Danny did the same.

He was never quite sure what happened next. If his eardrums had been made human, it would have been as if someone had picked them up by the throat, shaken them violently, and slammed them to the ground. The room rumbled with the bass reverb even as the *eeeeeeeeEEEEEEEEEeeeeeeee* squealed at the higher pitch.

He felt the strength go from his legs, and saw through fast failing peripheral vision that Steve and Doc had collapsed too, their balance shot to fuck by the sound waves crashing through their heads. His cheeks were wet with tears brought on by the pain. He wanted to reach inside his brain and rip out the hearing part ... even if it meant being deaf, it was better than this, Jesus Christ *anything* was better than this–

Purple.

He tasted purple on the air, for a moment, just a moment. The same purple he tasted every time he kissed Ellie. *How? Why now?* he managed to think, but thoughts were a luxury at this moment, and the floor was rushing up toward him.

It stopped.

There was a half-second of silence.

'*The other person has hung up,*' a prim electronic voice announced, albeit at a ridiculous volume.

It took the three of them a few minutes to find the strength – and the balance – to stand up. Steve was first to manage it and Doc last; Steve and Danny had to hook a hand each under his armpits and pull him up. He kept trying to open his eyes, wincing and clutching a hand to his temple, and then closing them again. They plonked him down on the lab's comfy little two-seater couch and each sat on one of its arms. For a while the only sound was that of their elevated breathing.

'What the holy fuck was that?'

Danny and Doc looked at Steve. His words had come through bloopily, as if he were shouting at them underwater.

'Some sort of …' Doc began, and then stopped and stared into space for a moment. They waited patiently. Eventually, he simply shrugged. 'Fucked if I know!'

Doc fished out some painkillers and they took them hungrily with a glass of water, even as the professor sat down at his workstation and began to tap gingerly at the spectrographic program before him.

'Just tell me you're not gonna call that number again,' Steve said. 'Please?'

'No intention of it, never fear. Ah … the program was able to analyse the feedback – excellent!'

Danny hauled a spare swivel chair over and sat beside Hammond. Steve, after some searching, managed to do the same. 'Well?' Danny asked, when he tired of seeing Doc flick through graph after graph. He'd been no slouch at Linguistics, but it had been at an undergraduate level; the stuff Doc was flicking through now was light-years beyond his ken. 'Doc, what was that?' he said again, trying to bring him out of his reverie.

This time it worked. 'There are seven distinct layers of sound. The first – the loudest – layer seems to be electronic – that's the … the screech we heard. Unfortunately it seemed to react with the amplifier at a frequency painful to human hearing … although how that happened I haven't a clue, because it should be impossible …'

'Doc,' Danny said pointedly.

'Yes, well, the point is,' Doc said, 'spectrographically, it's rather similar to what you'd get from a large electromagnetic pulse. Which again, is impossible: the only thing to produce an EMP burst like that would be, well, a nuclear detonation.'

Danny sighed. 'Doc … please. Much as these layers might seem fascinating to me at another time, what's causin' it? What is it?'

His old professor turned to look at him. 'I think it's a message,' he said.

Strange. In a way that was what Danny had longed to hear. His worst-case scenario had been to come here and have Doc tell him that it was just Ellie's phone, wherever it was, having a technical fault. To have his one avenue of exploration shut in his face. Doc was saying the opposite, was saying that there *was* something to this. And yet Danny didn't feel relieved. Didn't feel determined, or vindicated. He felt cold.

'A message?' he repeated.

Doc nodded. 'There are voices.'

'Voices? More than one?' – this came from Steve.

'Whose voices?' Danny said. 'What are they saying? Let me hear.'

Doc was back at his computer now, flying through open windows like a mosquito. 'They're barely discernible,' he said, frustrated. 'I'm not sure how audible they're going to …'

'Let me hear them!' Danny burst out. It was the first time he'd ever raised his voice to Doc Hammond, but the older man didn't seem angry to be the target of the blast. He simply nodded and with a few clicks, had a media player open on screen. Danny watched him hit play.

The central speaker on the sound system crackled and hissed into life. Danny leaned forward in his chair. The silence in the room was somehow just as unbearable as the sound avalanche they had experienced. His hands were trembling. He interlaced his fingers together to try to steady them. And then it started.

And then it stopped.

'That was it?' Danny asked.

Hammond nodded.

'Play it again. Turn it up!' He'd heard … something, yes. A voice, certainly. But as to what it had said – he hadn't a clue.

Doc played the message again. He'd increased the volume (although it was still barely audible compared to the wall of sound that had erupted before), but even though Danny leaned in close and concentrated as hard as he could, he still couldn't tell what was being said. Worse, the words didn't even fire off any synaesthetic flashes.

'Play it again. Louder,' he said.

Doc sighed. 'Danny …' he began.

'Wouldn't do ye any good, lad,' Steve said.

'Oh aye?' Danny said, sensing a meltdown brewing but feeling in no mood to put a stop to it. 'And why would that be, Mr Fuckin' Expert?'

'Sounds like Irish,' Steve said conversationally, while trying his best not to look smug about this sudden role reversal.

'So what's it say in Irish then?' Danny asked.

Steve shrugged. 'Dunno.'

'You don't know? How can you know it's Irish and not know what it's sayin'? Do you speak Irish or don't ye?'

'I speak it grand, lad, as you know,' Steve shot back. 'But I speak English too and if you asked me to read Shakespeare, I wouldn't have a fuckin' clue what he was on about.'

'Some dialect of ancient Gaelic?' Doc mused. 'Incredible.'

'Spectacular,' Danny spat. 'Fuckin' wonderful. If there was room in here I'd do a cartwheel or two. What the fuck is ancient Gaelic doing comin' out of my girlfriend's phone? Ellie wouldn't know Irish from Swahili. And how are we supposed to know what they're sayin'?'

'Danny, we're in a university in Ireland! This place'll be fuckin' stuffed with brainy bastards who could translate that no bother. Am I right?' Steve asked Hammond. 'I bet you know the fella for the job.'

'I do,' Hammond said.

'There you go!' Steve said triumphantly. 'See? Where's he at? Somewhere along University Square? What number?'

'Alaska.'

Steve's smile wilted. 'Alaska!' he thundered, outraged. 'What's a

Gaelic expert doin' in Alaska?'

'Kayaking, I believe.'

On seeing Danny throw up his hands in despair and Steve, somewhat wisely, decide to quit while he was ahead, Hammond sought to reassure them. 'Not to worry. Professor Blackwell's the best we have at the minute, but there was another fellow, rumoured to be just as good if not better. He was Blackwell's predecessor here. I never knew him, but by all accounts he was fully immersed in all aspects of ancient Celtic civilisation.'

'Where can we find him?'

Hammond pursed his lips. 'You probably couldn't,' he admitted. 'But I can put in a call to the School admin team and get his last known address. I'll tell them it's a potential consultation for a research paper or something. A minor misuse of privileges, of course, but' – he looked at Danny – 'all in a very good cause.'

'Thanks, Doc,' Danny said. He didn't need to embellish it. The linguistics expert would doubtlessly pick up on his tone, his body language, and know the depth of his gratitude for all that he'd done for them.

Fifteen minutes later, they exited the School of English, Danny clutching an address and an amplified recording of the whispering recorded onto a digital Dictaphone. Hammond had insisted they 'borrow' the Dictaphone, on the proviso Danny returned it personally. When the time came, of course.

Danny looked at the scrap of paper on which the name and address had been scribbled. Dermot Scully. The letters of 'Dermot' coloured and triggered a flash; he'd heard that name before.

'Uncle Dermot? How's he doing?' Ellie had asked of her father, her eyes flashing with defiance as they had sat around the dinner table. And Michael Quinn had deflated.

'Scully … '

Another flash: Ellie, applying for a loan, the phone pressed to her ear. They'd been trying to get some things for the house – a new suite, a new fridge. Money was so fuckin' tight and with his wages … and they'd said no. But there she'd been, trying so hard – he could see her now, answering those endless fuckin' questions from some idiot in a call centre – *Here go easy on the call centre monkeys, love* – and setting her password: Scully.

He got into Steve's car, fearing that if he didn't the world would simply spin away from underneath him like a fairground ride gone nitro. What the fuck was going on? First the disappearance, then the phone thing – an ancient Irish message which only one person in the country could hope to decipher, and that person just so happened to be Ellie's family's black sheep?

'What's all this about your Uncle Dermot?' he had asked her once, as they painted skirting boards. They had been in the house for over two months but this was the first chance they'd had to get some decorating done. Danny's mum had taken Luke for the day so he was fervently hoping the skirting-board painting would be peppered with sex – if not, considering how much he was already beginning to loathe painting, he was beginning to seriously warm to suicide as a lifestyle choice.

Ellie had looked pained. 'He was … he is … well,' and she'd sighed. 'He used to mind me when I was younger sometimes, when Mummy and Daddy wanted to go out for a night.'

Danny had pushed away the image of Michael and Christina Quinn 'out for the night' – he had visualised them in 1920s garb doing the Charleston whilst manic Big Band music played in the background. They just seemed the sort.

'Aye?' he said aloud, and cursed under his breath as he noticed that he'd failed to spread enough newspaper to cover the floor properly. Piss. Fuck. Now she'd see it. Balls.

'He used to tell me the best bedtime stories,' Ellie said. 'I liked him. It was hard to believe he was my da's brother sometimes. They were so unlike each other. He was spontaneous and he was funny and … well. You get the picture.'

'Do I?' he'd said as innocently as he could.

'Yes, you do,' she shot back with a half-smile. 'And then, about five years ago, he had a bit of a breakdown. Daddy's really embarrassed about it.'

Bit of a breakdown. Bit of a breakdown. Like one of those old Windows 95 screensaver animations, the four words bounced around inside his mind.

And again, there was no sense of a puzzle coming into focus, no pride or achievement or feeling of usefulness; only the sense that the tear in the accepted reality he'd constructed around his tidy, if not exactly ideal, little life was growing. Where was it going to end?

For the first time that afternoon, his mind wandered to last night's encounter with the … the whatever-the-fuck it was in the alleyway. He'd convinced himself so completely that it had been a person going for him that he'd almost started to whitewash over the incident in his mind. But now he forced himself to remember the thing that had loomed in front of him – the shape of it, the sheer fucking *wrongness* of it. And the shriek.

He looked at the Dictaphone he held in his lap like a talisman. The shriek in the alley – the one the shape had emitted even as it scrabbled and scampered and skipped toward him – it was the same kind of shriek that had come from Ellie's number …

'Lad?'

Bit of a breakdown.

They were moving, he realised. 'Yes?' he said.

'Do you not think we should' – Steve shifted uncomfortably in his seat – '… well, is this not something the police could be doin'? It's sorta their job to look for a missing person, like, isn't it? That's all I'm sayin'.'

'You wanted me to feel useful, didn't you?' Danny replied, knowing there was more to how he felt than that, but not wanting to involve Steve to that extent. Not yet. For all his faults, Steve was a good lad through and through, but he wouldn't be able to cope with the thoughts currently going through Danny's mind. Christ, he wasn't sure he was really coping with them.

Steve seemed to accept this and they kept driving, heading for the north of the city, where Dermot apparently lived. Something was bothering Danny, though, and after a moment's thought he figured out what it was.

'And it's missing *people*, lad. I know the wee fella is only small and I know Ellie is with him' – *at least I fuckin' hope she is* – 'but he counts too, like.'

Steve frowned at him. 'There you go with that again,' he said.

'Again?'

'That *wee fella* business. That's twice now. You said it earlier on too.'

'Sorry, do you want me to call him Luke or somethin'? Does my use of nicknames offend you?'

And then Steve said the three words that ripped Danny's world asunder. Not just because of what they meant, but because when he said them, it was without a trace of deception. Steve had only genuine puzzlement in his voice.

'Luke?' he said. 'Who's Luke?'

The Rabbit Hole

'Ellie? Who's Ellie?'

He kissed the top of her head as it lay on his chest. It was a good weight. He liked that weight. His other hand held his mobile phone, which had just beeped with an incoming text message, apparently from Ellie.

'Very funny,' he said. 'Girl was your best friend once upon a time.'

Maggie made a face. 'Once upon a time is right.'

'Don't start …'

'Aw, come on,' she said impatiently. 'I roomed with her for a year. I thought we were friends. Best friends, as you say. Huh. Didn't take much to offend her, did it?'

'Just me,' he said cheerfully.

'Huh!' she said again. 'You'd broken up. You'd been broken up for near a month before we started going out. And she told me she was fine with it!'

'Really?' he said, curious. 'She said that?'

'Well' – Maggie shrugged – 'that's the impression I got.'

'Ah,' he replied, in a carefully neutral tone. He rolled his eyes but he was grinning as he did so.

He opened the message, and felt the room spin around him.

Whatever he'd been expecting – some daft joke, or some dopey chain-text (she was prone to sending both) – it hadn't been this. He closed the message and placed the phone back on the bedside table.

They lay together for another few moments. And then it came, as he knew it would. 'What did she want?'

He thought about lying. Lying would be good right now. Lying was fantastic.

Maggie lifted her head from his chest and looked at him, right into his eyes, and he felt the ability to lie melt away. 'Jesus,' she said softly, 'your heart's goin' a dinger all of a sudden. What's wrong, Danny? She okay?'

'She's pregnant.'

He could see it impact like it was a physical thing; could see it reach in behind her eyes and splat itself on her mind. She pushed herself up on her palms so her body came away from his and opened her mouth and then closed it again. He simply stared back at her. They stayed like that for a few moments, and he could hear some small part of him saying *reach out, reach out and touch her*. He couldn't even begin to comply, couldn't visualise the sequence of events and commands. His body was a slammed door.

She swung her legs over the end of the bed and sat, semi-turned from him, so the eye contact was broken. When she spoke now it was directed at the bedroom wall, in a voice that seemed so distant as to be coming from next door.

'It's yours?'

'She says it has to be.'

'I thought,' she said, and the words came out harshly, so she took a steadying breath and started again, and this time they came out more softly, 'I thought you used–'

'We did,' he said, through lips that didn't seem to want to function properly. 'We did.'

'All the time?'

He didn't reply.

'Is she keepin' it?'

He flinched at the question. Since absorbing the text message and what it meant, all that been running through his mind was a purely selfish stream of *oh shit oh fuck oh balls oh Christ Almighty*. But while what he was feeling was stomach-churning, at least it was his own life he was weighing up. The truth was, his life wasn't the only one on the line here.

'I don't know.'

'Do you want her to?'

'I don't know. Jesus, Maggie, I've just been hit with this! You can't expect me to toss a coin and decide.'

Maggie nodded, and reached for the dressing gown draped across the bottom of the bed. 'I assume she's asked to meet you?' she said matter-of-factly as she threw it on.

'What are you doing? Are you going? Where are you going?' he asked dumbly.

She flashed him a look, seemed about to launch into a rant and then retreated from the idea. 'I don't know,' she confessed, and sat down heavily on the bed. There was another long pause before she raised her hands and covered her eyes. He couldn't blame her for the tears, but he couldn't comfort her either. So he sat, naked, until her shoulders stopped shaking and she stood up, composing herself as best she could.

'Go. Don't go. Do what you need to do,' she said, not looking at him. 'You know where I am. But I won't be there forever.'

He watched her walk out of the room and shut the door. His body twitched suddenly, as if it was making the first move to get out of the bed, perhaps to follow her … and then he froze.

After a few seconds he lifted his mobile, read and reread that text.

Call button.

'Hello?'

'Ellie, it's Danny.'

'Oh.'

'I got your message.'

'Okay.'

Long pause. He didn't know what to say.

'Well, I wasn't sure how to tell you. I'm sorry if it was–'

He shook his head. 'It doesn't matter. Look,' he said, licking suddenly dry lips, 'we need to talk.'

BELFAST, NOW

Steve had pulled over. It was easier than trying to drive and argue with Danny at the same time. Danny, for his part, was only a hair's breadth from attacking Steve.

'You were at his fucking christening!'

Steve, who had started off thinking that this whole thing was a bit of a gag, was now genuinely concerned for his friend. He shook his head, speaking quietly and softly so as not to provoke Danny further, 'I don't know what to tell ye. I wasn't at a christening. Are you sure this– '

But no amount of speaking quietly and softly was going to calm Danny. 'Why? Why the fuck are you doing this?' Danny yelled, each sentence getting progressively louder and his face going a shade further into the crimson spectrum. 'Have you gone fuckin' mental or are you hopin' to drive me fuckin' mental? What, what is it, what's the fuckin' plan? Eh? Is there some fuckin' joke that I'm not fuckin' in on?'

At this point there were people outside, walking past the car, who had stopped and were looking inside to see what the racket was. Steve felt their eyes on him, as well as the laser-intense glare of his best friend, who looked as if he were about to launch himself at him and tear his throat out at any second. Steve wasn't accustomed to fearing Danny, but as well as being afraid for his friend, he realised he was afraid of him.

'Maybe we should head back to yours,' he said. The last thing he wanted to do now was to go to some random guy's house with Danny in this form; he was liable to say the wrong thing and be on the receiving end of a forehead.

'Yeah,' Danny said, to his immense relief. 'Yeah, we should. Let's fuckin' do that.'

They passed the journey in silence, Steve not daring to talk, Danny trying not to hyperventilate, his mind racing. He could have phoned ahead, told his ma they were coming back, but he didn't. He felt like phoning the police, telling them there was a fuckin' conspiracy going on, but again he simply couldn't face the thought of it. Steve was no more a conspirator than he was the Dalai Lama.

The car pulled up outside his house and he was out of it in a flash, throwing open the gate and the front door within seconds. As he moved into the house he could see his ma in the kitchen, getting herself a cuppa by the looks of it. She frowned when she saw the expression on his face but he ignored her for the moment and ran into the living room.

No blankets. No changing mat. No wee bucket of supplies. The emergency nappy was gone from the second shelf of the bookcase in the corner. Ellie's big book of child health she'd got from Bargain Books for £3 was missing too.

'Danny, what's–'

He pushed past her and into the kitchen, threw open the fridge. No bottles in the door. No steriliser in the microwave. No baby rice in the cupboard. Each fresh discovery seemed to reduce him a little, as though he were shedding parts of himself.

'Will you just tell me what's–'

Again, he pushed past her. The time would come when he would have to talk to her, but not just yet. He ran for the stairs and climbed them two at a time and was inside his bedroom in a heartbeat.

Where the cot had been, there was nothing. He dropped to his hands and knees and ran his hands over the carpet. There weren't even four depressions where its legs had pressed into the floor.

He threw up, suddenly and violently, his stomach convulsing and unable to cope with the panic that was pulsing through him in great waves.

A shadow fell across him from the doorway. He looked up into the concerned eyes of his mother, and he knew the time had come. Steve lacked a reason to lie. Linda Morrigan lacked the capacity. Whatever she told him, he knew she would believe it as the truth.

'Where is he?' he croaked. 'Ma, where's my wee boy? Where's my Luke?'

If there was some conspiracy going on, some sick joke, it might have claimed his best friend. Might even have resulted in someone clearing his house of any baby paraphernalia. But there was not, and there would never be, a power on this Earth capable of making his mother forget about the little grandchild that she adored more than anything else in the world.

Before she answered, he saw the look in her eyes. He knew what she was going to say.

'Luke?' she asked. Danny felt as though time had slowed to a feeble crawl. His eyes were fixed on his mother's lips as she shaped the words.

'My son,' was all he had left to say.

He saw her recoil at that, surprise fighting with concern. 'Son,' she said, each word a lifetime, 'I don't know what you're talking about.'

Steve and Linda had to carry him downstairs. They sat him on the sofa, and talked to him, but he simply stared back, not bothering to reply to their questions. He had been through too much.

When they retreated to the hallway to talk, leaving the way to the front door unguarded, Danny was past them and outside the house in an eye blink.

'Danny!' Steve called desperately, chasing him down the garden path. 'Danny!'

His friend vaulted the front gate and made for the far end of the street, his arms and legs pumping. Steve considered doing the same but knew he'd end up with a fucked ankle. By the time he was outside the garden, Danny was rounding the corner at the top end of the street.

'Danny!' he called. His friend was already gone.

'Let him go,' said Linda, coming up behind him.

'Did he ask you? About some baby?' Steve said.

She nodded, dabbing at the corner of one of her eyes with a tissue. 'I think it's all too much for him,' she said quietly, staring up at the end of the street. 'Ellie goin' missing like this ... he's starting to think what might have been.'

Steve frowned. Something about the way she'd said that.

'What do ya mean?'

She looked at him and her lip trembled a little. 'Ellie had a miscarriage,' she said, and was about to say more when emotion got the better of her and she was forced to walk back inside the house to hide her tears. Steve watched her go and stood there for a moment longer, debating whether or not to jump in the car and chase after his friend.

Eventually his shoulders slumped and he walked toward the door, but not before something caught his eye, something in the garden beside him.

The mound had returned. Perfectly circular, raised and unblemished. Steve stared at it, a frown on his face.

In another moment the frown passed, the crease in his brow

smoothed, and he turned and followed Danny's mother back inside without a backward glance.

'Are you all right?' Ellie asked for the hundredth time.

He looked at her, lying on a hospital bed, wearing some flimsy hospital-issue nightie, not a scrap of make-up on her, forehead covered in sweat, with a large midwife between her legs.

'Uh ... yeah, not too bad,' he answered.

'Right, when I tell you to push, you push!' the midwife ordered.

Ellie looked up at him. Her eyes were very blue and very clear and very sincere. 'I,' she said in a reasonable tone, 'am going to murder her.'

Danny patted her shoulder. It seemed the least hazardous course of action. He flinched as she let loose with a god-awful yowl of agony, but it wasn't his touch that was causing the pain.

'Push! Push, Ellie!'

Ellie arched her back and howled like a wild beast and Danny felt his other hand, which she was squeezing, begin to occupy far less space than should have been possible. He bit his lip, fucked if he was going to howl in pain over someone pressing his fingers together while she was trying to squeeze a human being out of ...

Out of...

I'm not fuckin' all right. Not in the slightest.

Jesus, why was everyone so relentlessly casual about this sorta thing? At one of those interminable antenatal classes, they'd been subjected to the sort of nudge-nudge wink-wink school of patronising explanation: the 'women have been doing this for millennia – do you really wanna be the big girls' blouse?' theory. And then they asked the men if they were gonna be there for the birth and, as one, all the fellas had glanced at each other and then at their wives and the nurses taking the classes and realised it was one of those female multiple-choice questions that ran something along the lines of:

Are you going to do this for me?
A) Yes
or
B) Yes

Successful completion of this initial question would lead to the sub-question:

But are you doing it because you want to do it, or because I made you do it?
A) Cos I want to, love, Jesus Christ of course, why wouldn't I?
or
B) Why – because you made me do it, of course! Now, I grow weary of existence – give me the shotgun.

This was horrific. And worst of all, because Ellie's bump was blocking her view and, y'know, because she was in tremendous pain, every time there was a new milestone, she asked Danny to go down there and confirm it.

'I can see hair!' the midwife exclaimed.

Ellie let out a sort of half-laugh, half-cry. 'What colour is it? What's it like?'

He rotated around on his axis, hand still attached to hers, and brought his eyes to bear on the target. He was instantly put in mind of the half-second shot of Ben Stiller's balls caught in his zipper in *There's Something About Mary*. There was a heavy element of 'oh fuck, I didn't just see what I thought I saw, did I?' It was at times like this that having synaesthesia really did seem like a fucking disability; each new sight wasn't just experienced by the eyes alone, but flashed across to a sound, a smell, a taste …

'Mmmm, black,' he said, and moved back as quickly as he could, without losing his dignity, to where her head was. It was all proving too much for even the fixtures and fittings in the delivery room; the clock fell off the wall with a crash that didn't faze Ellie or the midwife in the slightest, but that made Danny almost jump out of his skin.

'Are you all right?' she asked again.

'Never better,' Danny said with brittle brightness.

'Here he comes!' the midwife announced. 'Get ready, Mummy! One final push!'

Ellie let loose such a shriek of intent that Danny was amazed her internal organs didn't follow orders and march out as well, along with the baby. And there was a noise, a wet sort of *pllllhhf* noise, and something slid out of her like a wet fish and into the midwife's arms.

His sense of causality was a little fuzzy after that. He remembered washing, and a little plaintive cry, and Ellie's body slumping back to the bed even as her neck and shoulders tried, tried as best they could, to raise themselves up. And the midwife was asking – nay, *ordering* him – to come forward. So forward he came, and something was put into his arms, something small and red and squawking.

'Say hello to your son, Daddy,' he was told.

As he heard the words, he felt an immense coldness go through him and he panicked. All he'd heard about this moment was that you were meant to bond instantly with the little bundle in your arms, how everything was meant to make sense. Instead, he felt as if someone had thrown a bucket of freezing water at him from point-blank range.

He looked down at the scrunched-up little face, all nose and eyes – well, eye at any rate, since the right one was caked over with some substance or other. He could feel heat radiating off the little thing, but it shook, it shook with fear and anger and sheer shock at this crazy new place it had found itself in, and outrage at being placed in the arms of so clueless and inadequate a protector as that to which it found itself entrusted now.

Looking down at this outraged little lifeform he had created, he expected to be overwhelmed with the feelings of numbness he'd experienced only moments before. Instead, he felt the coldness ebb from him, a fading heartbeat of anxiety, less prevalent with each passing second he locked eyes with the tiny being in his embrace.

He felt … he felt as if someone had reached inside him and whispered, *It's going to be all right.*

'Daddy,' it was the midwife talking, gently but no less patronisingly for it, 'put the baby on Mummy and let her see him.'

How? How was he meant to do something like that? He couldn't do one side of a fuckin' Rubik's cube, and now he was supposed to place a little entity, not three minutes old, onto Ellie's chest without causing injury or distress? You had to get a licence to drive a fuckin' forklift, and here they were, these medical professionals, entrusting a newborn to the sort of imbecile who'd once stuck a frozen beer can in the microwave to 'thaw it out'.

'Let me see our son,' Ellie said softly.

He did it. He stepped towards her and he did it even before he'd realised it, turning the little fella over in his hands and lowering him onto his ma. The internal script in Danny's head said that this was meant somehow to reassure Luke that everything was okay, and that he hadn't, say, after thirty-nine weeks of gloopy serenity, been squeezed down a tube way too small for him and forced to use a respiratory system for the first time.

Luke was clearly an ad-libber, because he fuckin' screamed.

'There, there. It's all right, wee man. It's all right. Sssssh.'

He was about to compliment Ellie on her innate grasp of reassuring baby-talk when he realised that it was he who had spoken. The words had come forth from his mouth without needing such trivialities as conscious input. And little Luke, all 7lb 1oz of red angry baby, squirmed and flailed and then went silent so quickly it was eerie.

Ellie's hand found his again and, though she didn't squeeze it nearly as tightly as she had done in the throes of labour, it felt more intense.

'I'm a da,' he said, not meaning to sound surprised but feeling it anyway. He looked around the room. The midwife was exhausted but exhilarated. Ellie was a sweaty, red-cheeked, utterly spent mess. The clock had fallen off the wall and the stool he'd sat on was lying somewhere by the window on its side. He must have knocked it over in the final moments. Jesus knew what he himself looked like.

'You're a da. No mistaking it,' she answered him.

BELFAST, NOW

'There must be some mistake,' Danny said weakly. 'There must be.'

Father Mackle looked at him with probably as much kindness as he was able to summon, having been all but dragged to the parish offices in the pastoral house next to St Bridget's and forced to go through the records. 'Even if there was a mistake with the computer system and the books, you said yourself that I did the christening. I'm sorry, Danny. I have no memory of that.'

Father Mackle watched as the young man before him crumpled. Danny drew his knees up to his chin and cried. After a moment's indecision, the priest got up from the chair in front of the computer and sat down beside his young parishioner and waited for a while. You had to learn to be a good listener in this game, and a huge part of that was waiting.

'I think I'm going round the fuckin' bend, Father.'

Given Danny's mental state, he decided to overlook the language. 'Have you been under stress lately, Danny?'

Danny's head was still between his knees. 'Yeah,' he said, his voice slightly muffled. 'Yeah, I have. I' – and he was wracked with fresh sobs for a few moments that Father Mackle let pass – 'I was gonna say how difficult it had been with the wee man, but ...'

'Children are a big responsibility. Maybe ... maybe you are afraid of that responsibility and you ... were confused, especially with Ellie's disappearance.'

Danny lifted his head. 'I'm not making him up, Father,' he said. 'Because if I was, if I had dreamed a son for the last eight months, people would have noticed before now, wouldn't they? Why would I suddenly come out with all this Luke stuff now and not before?'

'I don't know,' the priest replied truthfully. He sighed. 'Danny, I've known you since you were only small yourself. I remember what it was like for your mother when your father left. Have you considered that this Luke thing may be your way of imagining what it would be like to let someone down who was depending on you? As a reaction to how you feel about Ellie being missing?'

Danny absorbed this. 'No, I hadn't,' he said. He seemed to mull this over for a few moments, and then unfolded himself from his seated position. Father Mackle did the same.

'I'd better go,' Danny said, and turned to do just that.

'Danny, if you need to talk–' Father Mackle started to say, but the young man was already gone, walking out of the reception area and into the afternoon air.

Danny felt that if he stayed still for too long, dwelt on any aspect of this for too long, he would begin to unravel completely – Christ knew the conversation he'd had with his ma and Steve had brought him close enough to a breakdown: it had taken every ounce of mental strength he possessed to get up and run out of the house after that one.

His first thought had been to go to the police, but on his way to the nearest station, he had detoured to St Bridget's church instead, to see if whatever was going on had affected baptism records. Apparently it had.

He knew he wasn't crazy. Knew it as surely as he knew Wednesdays tasted of strawberries. Whatever madness had affected his ma and Steve and now, it seemed, the world at large, it hadn't reached him yet. But that wasn't a comfort in any way – far from it. He knew he wasn't insane, so the only option left was that, over the course of the last twenty-four hours, two people he cared about had had their memories rewritten and all evidence of him ever having a son erased.

There had to be a reason for all of this. Your perception of the rigidity of reality didn't evaporate on a whim, he fuckin' knew that much. So he had to think. He owed it to Luke, owed it to every time he had received an entirely unexpected gurgle of delight midway through a nappy change, every time he'd blown belly kisses on that tiny wee stomach and felt those limbs go nuts and that giggle escape.

That was when he saw Michael Quinn enter St Bridget's.

He was after him instantly. Just as the older man reached the altar and knelt down, Danny was upon him, hauling him to his feet and shoving him against the nearest pillar.

'What's the meaning–'

'Dermot Scully. Your wee brother,' Danny snapped, ignoring the surprise that crossed Michael Quinn's face at the mention of the name.

'What … what about him?'

'Anything I should know?'

'About Dermot?' Michael said.

'About anything. How about we start with Luke? You gonna go along with everyone else on all this shit that he never existed, are ya?'

The older man squirmed under his grip. 'I don't know what you're–'

'Danny!'

It was Father Mackle, hurrying toward them, his cassock whirling. 'Danny, what do you think you're doing? Let Mr Quinn go, or I'll have to call the police!'

Danny released his grip. Truth be told, he'd been overcome with anger so quickly and so completely that he hadn't even realised he had manhandled the bastard in the first place; he'd merely wanted to get his attention. It seemed as if it had worked, too: Michael kept his eyes on Danny, even as Father Mackle leant in to check if the older man was all right.

'I don't know what you're talking about,' Michael repeated. 'I'm here to light a candle for what I've lost and pray for a safe return.'

'I think you'd better go, Danny, don't you?' said Father Mackle.

Danny accepted the dismissal. 'I've got people to see anyway,' he said, and walked away without looking back. Michael and the priest watched him go.

'Sorry about that, Michael,' Father Mackle began. 'My thoughts are with you at this difficult time, obviously. Is there anything I can do?'

Michael shook his head. 'I'm just here to …' he said, and indicated the candles. Father Mackle spread his hands and nodded sympathetically before moving away to give the man his privacy.

He spent a few moments quelling the fears of a few elderly parishioners who had been distinctly troubled to see the altercation and by the time he'd finished reassuring them, Michael Quinn was already striding out of the church.

By the altar, two newly lit candles flickered and burned.

There was something wrong with Dermot Scully's house.

Okay, the street was working class, but so was Regent Street. Okay, he'd had to slalom past dogshit just to get to the front gate, but this was Belfast, dog turd Mecca. And the house itself, although mid-terrace, was actually a little bigger than the one he, Ellie and Luke – *keep thinking his name, keep remembering him, don't forget him* – had called home.

Nonetheless, there were clues that all was not well. The path had cracked and never been repaired. The garden was overgrown to the point where grass and jaggy nettles lounged luxuriously in their triumph. And he spotted several footballs lying amidst the greenery. You could always tell the creepy houses by the fact that the kids would rather just slink off and buy a new ball than risk clambering over the fence and retrieving the one that had just strayed into the wrong place, even if it rested tantalisingly in plain sight, as these did.

He was suffering badly, he knew that, was still self-aware enough to know that. The initial shock of Ellie and Luke's disappearance had been bad enough, bad beyond his wildest nightmares. But at least it had been graspable, in a horrific sort of way; at least he had some frames of reference, even if they sprang from the realms of the terrible and the unthinkable. These sorts of things had happened before.

But he had nothing to compare this to. How was he supposed to deal with the fact that memories of his son had been deleted from the minds of those closest to him? He had been clutching at straws by examining the church records, he knew that – if it was possible to reach into a person's mind and rewire it, taking a trip down to the local parish church and tippexing out a name in a baptism record wouldn't prove too much of a challenge.

In a way, though, his trip to St Bridget's hadn't really been about checking the records. Danny wasn't religious. In fact, something about the whole organised religion thing just plain bothered him – this concept of trooping off to a big building to chant, inhale some incense and offer up a sacrifice.

It had always seemed such a primitive practice – civilised paganism varnished with a veneer of respectability. But really religion seemed to serve only one purpose: comforting the old, the infirm, the tortured souls, to reassure them that life wasn't just a collection of randomised events, a human Brownian motion with an ultimate destiny of becoming worm food, with an inch-and-a-half every anniversary in the *Irish News* until your remaining relatives ran out of interest; that somewhere out there in the eldritch world of mysticism, some great big bearded man in the sky had a purpose for the sheer madness that was existence.

In saying that, though, getting Luke christened had been a quick and easy way to pocket more than three hundred notes from friends and family. He remembered looking longingly at a big shiny flat screen TV in Curry's the next day on his lunch break, but they'd eventually plumped for a large home heating oil delivery, enough to see them through the coming winter. Yay. Oh the rollercoaster thrill ride of excitement that was adult responsibility.

However, when your partner and child vanished into thin air, you encountered strange creatures in your back alley, you received voicemails in an ancient dead language, and everyone around you started suffering from collective amnesia, religion suddenly took on a whole new light. That was why he'd gone to the church – he'd had some crazy notion that Father Mackle, man of the cloth, would be immune to this madness and would lead the fight back. Seemingly not.

Danny could feel his mind slipping every so often, and wasn't quite sure what he could do about it. Unconsciously he was doing a sort of mental fire-walking; he needed to keep going over the hot coals and not look down, because if he faltered, or if he realised what he was doing, he was fucked. So he couldn't think too much about the impossibilities spiralling around him, because if he did, he'd be catatonic and then Ellie and little Luke – little pudgy, punchy Luke, who last week had decided that Danny blowing raspberries was Officially The Funniest Thing In The Entire World, Ever – would be gone without anyone even to mourn them.

What if I forget?

It kept going through his mind. That was why, even though it hurt like a bastard, he kept bringing to mind little anecdotes about his son, lest he try to recall something about him and have it slip through his fingers like water, like a dream gone by the time he tasted the toothpaste the next morning.

That was why he was here right now, standing in front of this grim, grey house, with footballs in the garden and decay hanging over it like a bad smell. Every synaesthesia-affected sense in his body was throwing equally unpleasant sensations and sights and sounds at him.

'I'll show ye a *bit of a breakdown*,' Danny said softly, and opened the garden gate.

He felt something then; something that a few days ago, back when the universe made sense, he would have dismissed as simply a warm breeze carrying the waft of an unpleasant aroma. Now, attuned and on the lookout for such oddness, he experienced it as a feeling akin to passing through a hanging bead curtain; some resistance was offered, but he was able to push through without undue fuss.

In a few long strides he was at the front door. Jesus, this place was a fuckin' mess. Now that he was closer to the windows, he could see that every one of them had the blinds pulled shut and such a layer of dirt and dust lying on the outside that it looked as if they hadn't been opened in years.

The door itself – he had a brief flash to standing at the front door of the Quinns only two nights previously – was similarly old and battered, lacking even a house number, its frosted glass panels offering no clue to what lay within. The only adornment of any note was, of all things – and Danny's eyes narrowed on seeing it – a horseshoe, nailed to the centre of the door as if it were the most natural thing in the world.

Seeing it, Danny felt a twist in his stomach as he realised he was essentially here with no means to defend himself. What if this Dermot character turned out to be a fuckin' loony?

A shadow moved within. Danny's hands balled into fists. He might not be armed, but, by fuck, he was itching to hit something.

'Dermot Scully?' he called, when the shadow showed no signs of opening the door. 'It's Danny. Danny Morrigan. I'm Ellie's partner. Ellie Quinn, your niece?'

Nothing.

'Ellie Quinn your *missing* niece?'

Nothing.

'I've got something I need your help with,' Danny said, shifting tack slightly. He still had the Dictaphone that Doc had given him back at Queen's. He pulled it out of his back pocket, thumbed the volume dial up to maximum, and hit play. The whispering hissing voice rang out.

That got results.

The door opened and Danny found himself looking at a man who wasn't a kick in the arse off sixty. He was barely over five foot tall, and hunched over with it, making him seem even smaller. The little hair that remained on his head was white and wispy. His skin was weather-beaten and the colour of old footballs, and he was dressed in clothes that, judging from the odour emanating from them, he had slept in for quite a number of nights running.

Dermot glanced furtively up at the six-footer on his doorstep, and despite his supposed fragile mental state his gimlet eyes shone with what Danny judged to be a keen intelligence. Intelligence … and barely concealed panic.

'Are you mad?!' he hissed. 'Don't play that! Not here! Never here!'

'I'm coming in,' Danny said. He hadn't meant to sound so forceful; he'd meant to ask could he come in, but somehow he wasn't in the mood for asking anymore. He moved forward, and Dermot slammed the door in his face. Danny's mood darkened with a terrible swiftness.

'Listen to me, you oul bastard. I've had a really bad fuckin' day, so you open this fuckin' door right now,' he growled.

'I can't,' the answer came. 'I'm sorry but I can't. Go away or I'll call the police.'

Danny felt rage descend on him. He slid the Dictaphone back into his pocket and advanced until his forehead was pressed up against the dirty, frosted glass. He could see the warped outline of Dermot within, watching him. He wanted to smash the door down, but he forced himself to hang on to some semblance of reason.

'Do you know what it says? The message?'

'Yes. "Consider it granted."'

Danny's mouth opened and closed. 'Con ... consider it granted?' he repeated dumbly. Of all the things he'd imagined that message to say, of all the ransom demands or the cryptic clues or the fuck knew what, *consider it granted* wouldn't have been on that list. 'What the fuck does that mean?'

'Someone got their wish, I'd say,' Dermot said.

Danny felt his anger ratchet up another notch at the man's insouciance. 'Do you know why my girlfriend and son have vanished? Why no one can remember my son?'

'Yes.'

Danny closed his eyes and felt a shiver go through his entire body, a shiver that was part relief and part forcing back a tide of sweltering emotion that threatened to unbalance him completely. He felt as though he were clinging desperately to sanity, and his fingers were slipping by the moment, but he wouldn't give in, not now, not when an answer was finally within reach.

'Open this door,' he said, quietly and insistently, each word a dark promise of what non-compliance might bring. 'Open this door and give me some answers or, so fuckin' help me, by the time the police get here, there'll be nothin' left of you.'

The door opened a few seconds later and Danny had to fight the urge to leap across the threshold and wrap his hands around that scrawny little neck. Instead he stepped inside and watched as Dermot Scully slammed the door behind him and threw across at least five different locks at five different heights. This house was a fortress, it seemed. What was he so paranoid about keeping out?

Or keeping in …

'Where are they?' he asked, his voice close to cracking. His hands were trembling, he knew. He didn't care.

Dermot didn't reply, he merely walked into his living room and sat down on an ancient armchair, which threw up a cloud of dust. Danny followed close behind, aware of the filth of the place but managing to ignore it. Dirt didn't matter. Nothing mattered except answers.

'You're Danny Morrigan?' Dermot said, regarding Danny with something approaching awe. He reached for a tumbler of water with shaking hands, and dropped at least four tablets into it. They fizzed angrily.

'I asked where they are,' Danny said warningly. 'Don't fuck me about. If you know–'

'Answer the fuckin' question!'

Danny blinked. He wouldn't have believed Dermot had it in him, but there had been a flash of something there in that anger; something beyond the nervous, cowed facade the man had projected thus far. 'Yes, that's me.'

'Look at you, all grown up. Last time I saw you …' he trailed off, unable to finish the thought. 'You look like your da, you know that?'

Dermot was talking in a croak; his throat sounded as if had dried up completely. He knocked the tablet mixture back and immediately hunched over as if it had caused him more pain.

'How do you know my da? What's he got to do with all this?'

Dermot laughed hollowly. 'That's right. He wasn't around to tell ye, was he? All part of the arrangement. Sorry, I'd forgotten.'

'What the fuck are you on about?' he snapped. '*Consider it granted*? What wish? Whose wish? What does any of this have to do with Ellie? With Luke? With this?' and he fished out the Dictaphone again and hit play.

'Noooo!' Dermot screamed, diving headlong at Danny, rugby-tackling him off his feet and knocking the digital recorder from his grasp so that it bounced into the hallway and beyond their grasping hands. The message hissed out in its entirety.

Danny, the shock of the attack wearing off, threw Dermot off easily, leapt to his feet and grabbed the older man by the filthy collar of his shirt, bringing his own face level with the leathery features of the crazy old bastard.

'What are–'

'You let them in! You let them into my house!' Dermot screamed at him. 'Get out! Get out, get out, get out, get out!'

The house around them began to creak. Danny glanced to the corner of the room from where one such *creeeeeeauuuchhhh* had emitted. He'd been in better houses than this that had been infested with all sorts, so no doubt there were rats and mice all over the joint, but that hadn't sounded like a noise made by a rodent's tiny little feet.

The creak came again. Not just from the corner, but from upstairs, moving across the landing, moving towards the top of the stairs.

Dermot ripped himself free from Danny's grasp and made for the kitchen. He was faster than Danny expected and managed to evade Danny's attempts to re-grab him and, with a final twist, he disappeared through a door in the back of the kitchen, a door that revealed a staircase leading down to some sort of basement. Danny had a brief overpowering whiff of stale air and sensed an incredible undercurrent of something that defied classification, something foul, and then the door slammed shut behind him and he heard a *clunk, clunk, thunk* of multiple locks being slammed across.

'Open this fuckin' door!' Danny bellowed, wrapping his hands around the handle and pulling for all he was worth. It didn't budge an inch. He heaved again – and then stopped.

Some *thing* was coming from upstairs.

He could hear it breathing, could hear it moving, and he knew in that moment that it was the same type of thing that he'd encountered last night in the alleyway. It was coming down unevenly, as if the regularity of the stairs was too much for it to process, a *thump … thump … thumpthumpthump* that reached into his very soul and dragged fingernails across it, filling him with the sort of certain dread that Horrible Things were About to Happen he hadn't felt since childhood.

Or since last night …

And now it had finished its descent. He could hear it in the hallway. He couldn't go back through the living room. His eyes settled on the back door, locked with bolts. He drew them back.

It was in the living room now.

He pushed at the back door. It refused to open.

Eeeeeeee? the shriek asked him. He blinked, and felt his eyelids move over his eyes. Time had grown lazy once more. The sound was so familiar now, almost reassuring. A part of him wanted to see what was making it and surely, surely it wouldn't be so bad … ?

The smell of purple flooded his nostrils, breaking the lull, accelerating time to its proper speed. Danny had only seconds before the thing made its way to the kitchen and he now knew with an awful certainty that if it got into in the room, he would be compelled to look at it, and that when he did so, he would be lost completely.

Danny battered at the back door with his foot until it buckled a little. He did it again, panic giving him strength if not finesse, and the door bent and broke free of its moorings, pitching outward at a crooked angle, affording him a chance to escape.

He took it, gathering himself up into a ball and leading with his shoulder, punting through the rest of the door and out into Dermot Scully's back yard, another overgrown jungle of grass and weeds rippling in the afternoon wind. Then he heard the thing again, as it discovered its quarry had escaped.

Something moved in the grass under his feet. A tug at his ankle almost destabilised him, came close to knocking him onto his ass even as he made for the waist-high hedge. He screamed, in terror and in challenge and in determination, and made a leap for the hedge and was over it and back into the city once more.

He kept running, sprinting past a few confused people, until he no longer felt like he was being chased. He slowed down and risked casting a glance behind him – the glance he'd so dreaded back in the kitchen.

There was nothing there. Nothing was stalking him.

He found himself coming to a bus shelter, so he stopped reached for the bus stop pole beside him and doubled over, expelling and sucking in air in huge gulps, feeling his entire body spasm with exertion and waves of fear.

A *ssssssh-pliss* beside him caused him to start – he stood and brought up his hands as if to defend himself. He found himself looking at the face of a disaffected bus driver. Not that there was any other type.

'You goin' somewhere or what?' the driver asked.

Danny swallowed and got on board. Right now there was only one place to go, and one person to see.

The Refusal Of The Call

'What d'you mean, *gone?*'

His ma blinked at him with eyes that had obviously been full of tears not long previously. Danny could see Steve scowl at him for the harshness of his questioning, but right now he couldn't care about that. 'He's gone,' Linda Morrigan repeated. 'I thought he'd just gone out this morning, but I've been trying his mobile … and I went back to the house, and his stuff is …'

She broke down then, taking herself into the kitchen where she could cry in private. Danny watched her go, knowing that he should follow her, comfort her. Tony Morrigan had vanished from her life – from their lives – *again* and it must be bringing back all-too-painful memories. But how could he comfort her? How the fuck could he do that right now, in the middle of all this?

'Lad, you need to–'

'Shut up,' he snarled at Steve, moving past him and into the kitchen. His ma was turned away from him, her shoulders shaking. He remembered seeing her like this so many times when he'd been a kid – when his da had left them and he hadn't known what to do, only that a hug was as likely to make things worse as better.

'Mummy,' he said, deliberately using the term to try and snap her out of it. It seemed to work. She straightened her shoulders and glanced back at him, wiping her nose, her eyes full of heartbreak.

'Is there somethin' you're not telling me?' he said, being careful to keep any trace of accusation out of his voice.

She blinked, confused, as if she did not understand. 'You what? About what?'

'About him. About why he left us.'

'Oh, Danny,' she said, and dissolved into tears once more.

'Jesus Christ, lad, what the fuck are you playin' at?' Steve demanded from behind him. 'Can you not see your ma's in bits?'

Danny turned to his friend, his eyes flashing dangerously. 'Butt out,' he snapped.

'No I fuckin' won't,' Steve shot back. 'Look, I know Ellie's missing – Jesus we're all worried – but all this today about chasing down fuckin' phone messages and babies that never fuckin' existed in the first–'

That was as far as he got.

The next thing either of them knew, Steve was on his arse on the floor, raising his hand almost in slow-motion to his bloody nose, and Danny's fist was aching from the impact. It was only when Steve saw that his fingers were covered in blood that he realised what had happened, and by that time Linda Morrigan had positioned herself between the two young men, her own breakdown forgotten in the face of a more pressing crisis.

'We're going,' she said firmly, clamping her hand on Steve's arm. 'We're going. He needs time.'

Steve, on his feet now, seemed to be cycling through anger, humiliation and sympathy before going back to anger again. He and Danny locked eyes for a long moment.

'Don't you ever tell me my son never existed,' Danny said.

Steve thought about replying, but shrugged it off. He turned his attention to Mrs Morrigan instead. 'You're right, Mrs M,' he said, walking to the front door. 'Let's get the fuck outta here, eh?'

He waited outside. Danny couldn't even watch him leave, turning his back and glaring at the wall instead. But Linda grabbed his arm and forced him to face her, placing her hand on his cheek and staring into his eyes with deep concern.

'It'll all turn out right, son,' she said. 'I promise.'

He was going to throw it back at her, to come up with some smart comment or ask how in the name of Jesus she could possibly know that, but instead, he toppled forward into his mother's arms and cried, heaving with huge anguished sobs as she held him.

For the first time he worried that maybe he was going mad, that everyone else was correct and that little … little …

The name slipped between his fingers, pouring through them like grains of sand. He grabbed desperately and couldn't, couldn't get a hold …

He pushed away from his mother, eyes wide, as if she were the one responsible for all of this. 'Luke!' he screamed at her. 'Luke! His name is Luke!'

Not wanting to hear any more, he ushered his mother from the house and slammed the door closed behind her. This done, with them gone, he slid slowly down his front door until he was sitting on the cold floor.

And he cried until the tears wouldn't come.

BELFAST, 7 MONTHS EARLIER

Smmmm-chluck.

'What's this?' he said, holding a piece of paper in his hand as if it were a timer fuse.

Smmmm-chluck.

Ellie looked up at him with eyes so full of exhaustion that it was a wonder her cheeks weren't charging her excess baggage allowance. Her eyes flitted to the piece of paper he was brandishing at her, and she exhaled lightly, seemingly lacking even the energy to sigh properly.

Smmmm-chluck.

'Mmmmmsssssaaa,' Luke moaned in his sleep.

'I was gonna say to you.'

'Were ye? When was this?' he said, trying not to crumple the paper in his hand as he held it. 'When I checked the fuckin' balance and seen it? Is that when?'

Smmmm-chluck. Ellie was wincing.

'I told ye,' he carried on. 'I told ye to get it paid. And now look. Look at this. Fuckin' £30 late payment charge. Thirty fuckin' quid that has pushed us over-fuckin'-drawn, so we got a fuckin' charge for that an all – a daily charge – and now we're poorer to the tune of fuckin' sixty-eight notes. Sixty-eight!'

Smmmm-chluck.

She didn't reply, except to glance at Luke and make sure he was still asleep in the Moses basket. He was three weeks old and

Danny was starting to think all he did was sleep, eat and shit – rinse and repeat. He was also starting to think that all *he'd* ever do was wake up knackered, fuck off to work knackered, listen to a menagerie of mentally-challenged morons moaning about their upstream speed knackered, come home to a baby and a merry-go-round of chores knackered, and go to bed knackered.

All while watching Steve and Maggie – Officially The World's Greatest Couple™ – parade themselves around, so happy and carefree. Steve kept inviting him on nights out – *Bring Ellie along! Get the wee fella minded!* It was all so easy, wasn't it? – and his ma would have probably offered to mind the wee man now and again, but unless the city centre's drinking establishments had started an IOU system, what exactly were they going to spend?

They were skint. They were more skint than Danny had ever thought it possible to be. His ma hadn't exactly been rollin' in it when he was growing up – *especially compared to Ellie's ones* – but he'd never really sensed they were living hand-to-mouth. Bills had been paid and his ma had held down a wee job here and there working in shoe shops and bars – they'd been all right.

Smmmm-chluck.

But even if they hadn't been skint, what exactly were he and Ellie supposed to do on a night out that included Steve and Maggie, anyway?

To give him credit, Steve had been almost hilariously nervous about confessing to Danny that he and Maggie had 'a thing'. He'd offered to stop it immediately if Danny had the slightest objection and Danny had sensed his friend had meant it, but he'd also sensed that Steve was growing to like Maggie at a rate of knots.

So he'd waved it away, said no, don't be silly. All ancient history. Besides, ha ha ha, it was me told you to go to her that time and check she was all right, wasn't it? *Can't remember telling you to check her that thoroughly, mind …*

Smmmm-chluck.

The household expenses he didn't mind. Christ knew they had to eat, and Luke had to have nappies, even if the wee man did seem determined to break some sort of Guinness World Record on that score. But this, this sixty-eight quid he was waving in front of her nose right now, this was avoidable. This was downright fuckin' stupidity, and he burned to think of each and every penny in those sixty-eight pounds. That was over a day's wages for him, well over. Poured down the fuckin' toilet because she'd been too dozy to make a phone-call.

So he told her. He told her it was stupid and she was stupid and she needed to wake up and be more alert, wanting her to rant right back at him, needing some way to vent all of the crap that was bouncing around inside of him.

She didn't. She simply reached down and removed the breast-pump from her right breast, and began to cry, and it was then that he noticed that the bottle attached to it had only the thinnest skin of whiteness across the bottom, despite the fact that the fuckin' thing had been *smmmm-chlucking* for the best part of the last hour. He saw her nipple, distended and red and looking more like an open wound than something that had once sent him into a happy little tizzy every time he caught a glimpse.

'I'm supposed to feed him,' she sobbed. 'I'm supposed to be able to, and I can't. And I'm so, so tired. He was up five times last night,' and he blinked at that, having only been semi-awake for one of those feeds.

'I want,' she said, in almost a whisper, 'to call my daddy and ask him to get me out of here.'

It hit him like a hammer blow. Not just the thought of that cunt coming here and taking his girlfriend and son away to a big ole house and lifting and laying them, and not just the look of triumph he'd inevitably give Danny as he did so.

What hit him was knowing that all the feelings of inadequacy he had right now – the fear that he was a failure as a parent, as a provider – were probably the exact same feelings Ellie was having.

He knelt by her and pulled her head to his and she didn't resist, didn't pull back. They didn't kiss; it wasn't the right moment for that. He simply held her and she held him and Luke slept on, oblivious to it all.

Danny found himself wishing, not for the first time, not for the last, that things didn't have to be like this.

BELFAST, NOW

Night fell on Regent Street once more. The lights began to go out in front rooms one by one as their inhabitants got their fix of police procedurals or reality TV (or in the case of Number 47, some distinctly odd pornography). It was another gloriously clear night, quite warm for the time of year.

The faint sound of cars on the main road going into the city centre was the only noise to disturb the peace; that is, if you discounted the incessant barking of Number 12's dog in its back garden (which the residents of Regent Street had long since learned to do, since the alternative was to obtain a shotgun and become proactive about the problem).

But the lights of one house in the street remained on. Danny sat in his living room, watching a DVD he had found on the bookshelf. He was doing so with some astonishment, because what he was seeing on screen was an utter impossibility.

It was a home movie – he and Ellie cavorted on screen, larking around, as Maggie filmed them on their first day in the new house. But as he watched he knew that the scene unfolding before him had never actually happened.

When he'd first started dating Ellie, it was clear that he would need to impress Maggie, her best friend, and earn the girl's approval, lest he be deemed not good enough for 'her' Ellie, and be unceremoniously dumped.

But he'd done it – he'd successfully impressed Maggie, and he and Ellie had been together. Then, after a while, they hadn't. It didn't end with some blazing argument or one of them cheating or anything like that; it just … ended. Danny had been a bit nonplussed by it, but at that stage in his life, going through uni, he quite liked the prospect of drifting along, finding attachments here and there. Nothing serious. Nothing too heavy. He had the impression this was fine with Ellie too. Certainly she had made no effort to stop whatever they had dissolving into nothingness. One thing ends, move onto the next.

As life would have it, 'the next' had been Maggie …

When Ellie had sent that text, the one telling him she was pregnant, he'd gone to see her. She'd told him she couldn't have an abortion. She just couldn't. He'd thought about it for a day or two, and then asked her did she want to give it another go. She'd said yes. Just like that, they were back together.

Too cowardly to break the news to Maggie, he'd asked Steve to do it for him. Less than a month later, she and Steve were a couple. Life was so strange sometimes.

Yet on this video footage, here she was, on a day he knew she hadn't been here, filming him and Ellie as they explored their new domain. Danny watched himself talking to cam, saying things that weren't true and that hadn't happened.

In the course of a lifetime of voracious reading he had, of course, come across Sherlock Holmes' famous mantra that when studying a problem, if you eliminate the impossible, whatever remains, however improbable, must be the truth.

He remembered having a son. The rest of the world did not remember this, and the rest of the world wasn't afraid to bring in ample evidence to back up its stance. So either the rest of the world had decided that a human life should be wiped from existence, and had rewritten reality to accomplish this – including falsifying memories, faking DVDs, erasing records – or ...

... or there was something wrong with him.

Because, you know, generally people who saw monsters in dark alleys and had panic attacks in houses upon hearing footsteps down a staircase weren't generally exalted as prime specimens of sanity.

Okay. He could do this logically. Think for a moment. After the shock of Ellie's disappearance he had imagined Luke – *keep thinking the name, keep remembering it* – into existence. Presumably he had also imagined the happenings in the alley and at Dermot

Scully's house, or at least exaggerated them into the realms of the supernatural.

Why?

Father Mackle had suggested it was because he felt guilty about Ellie going missing. He could see a certain logic in that, admittedly. It would explain why every time a memory of his former life with Ellie and Luke surfaced, it wasn't exactly an idyllic scene of domestic bliss; more as though he was inventing new ways to punish himself.

Except … what about the phone message? How had it knocked him, Steve and Doc to the floor so effortlessly? Why was it in ancient Irish?

Why had Dermot Scully told him he knew what was going on? Why was Dermot fucking Scully the sole person in the last twenty-four hours that hadn't said *who?* when he'd mentioned his son?

Who kept rebuilding that mound in his front garden?

When the DVD finished – actually, that was a lie; he had pressed the power off button long before it was over – he was up and at the window and looking out at his tiny little insignificant garden, all twelve foot by eight foot of it, and the defiant raised hump in its centre which put him in mind of Dermot's stoop …

A face appeared at the window, wrinkled and hideous.

He jerked back, almost toppling over the coffee table, arms pin-wheeling desperately as he tried to stay upright. He steadied himself and looked again.

Dear God. Cast against the harsh light of the lamp, lit by streetlight from the back, it was even more grotesque.

'Can I come in, love?' Bea asked brightly.

He walked to the front door and opened it. She was standing on the doorstep. He'd been so engrossed in staring at that fuckin' thing in his garden he hadn't even noticed the elderly woman limp up his path. His cheeks flushed. 'Bea?' he said, checking his watch. 'Bea, it's near midnight.'

'I was invited,' she replied mildly. 'I had an appointment to come and do some tea leaves. I fell a wee sleep earlier or I'd have come round then.'

'Bea, that was Ellie wanted you to do her tea leaves. And she's missin', remember? Plus, um … it's near midnight?' he repeated, putting extra stress on the words this time, in the hope they would sink in.

Sink in, fat chance. Bea was like that fuckin' steak pie she'd sent round as a housewarming present – impossible to penetrate with anything short of a nuke.

'Son,' she said in a kindly tone, 'I'm an oul woman and I'm standing here freezin' my arse off on your doorstep. Let me in or I'll start tellin' everyone in the street I caught you sniffing a pair of my knickers when you came in to put up that shelf for me.'

And it happened.

Danny laughed. He laughed 'til his sides were sore, and by the time he was done wiping his tears away, he had long since waved Bea inside and he was just putting the finishing touches to their cups of tea. Whether consciously or not, he even made them using the box of tea leaves Ellie had bought in preparation for having hers read.

Bea winked at him as he handed hers over – on their least distressed china, no less – and he sat on the other side of the room.

Since the impossibilities had began stacking up he'd wondered when he'd reach the point of laughter. It seemed he just had. Where was he to go from there? Madness?

Bea sipped her tea and made a face.

'Somethin' wrong?'

'Ach no, son, I'm just a creature of habit, ignore me. The only person who can make my tea right is me. Don't feel bad about it.'

'I'll try not to let it keep me up nights.'

For a few moments they sat at opposite ends of the room, sipping away. Danny had the mad thought that, should one of the neighbours walk past his front window at this time of the night – unlikely, yes – the sight of him sitting drinking tea with crazy oul Bea from up the street would cause them severe neck trauma from the violent double-take.

'What's ticklin' ye?' Bea asked, seeing him smile. He told her. She grinned gummily. 'I don't doubt it. Never thought you had much time for the oul fogeys, Danny.'

'Ach I wouldn't–'

She held up a hand. 'Please, son. I like ye. I do. So don't be spoilin' that with wee lies now. Anyway, it's only right in my book – I am an oul fogey. Not denyin' it. And you were always respectful' – and he bit his lip at this, recalling a bedtime conversation with Ellie about Davros and the Fat Controller – 'and that's what matters. I always thought to myself, seein' you and that wee girl pushing the wee fella up the street, them three are a lovely wee family.'

She said this just as he was raising the cup to his lips.

He let the remains of the cup lie where they had shattered on the floor, and ignored the burning sensation of the hot tea settling on his T-shirt.

'Family?' he managed.

'Family,' she repeated, and she didn't seem to think it odd that his fingers had lost motor control, that he'd dropped his cup, or that he was looking at her so intensely now.

'Please tell me,' he begged her. 'Please tell me I'm not crazy.'

She set her tea down on the little table beside the sofa and looked at him with such kindness and pity that for a moment he was reminded of Thomas telling him he was a liability at Lircom. But unlike then, he felt no surge of humiliation or anger at receiving such a look from Bea.

'Son,' she said softly. 'There's so much you have to learn …'

'I'm not going anywhere.'

She sighed. 'Don't be so sure,' she told him, but before he could ask what she meant by that, she went on. 'Indulge me for a minute or two first. Let me tell you about my wee brother, Colm.

'Fifty-eight years ago it was, out in the sticks, my da worked as a foreman to a team of labourers. He and a team of his men were sent out to clear land to make way for a new motorway the government wanted to construct.'

She lifted her cup to her mouth and Danny saw her hand was shaking, but he couldn't decide if it was due to age, or to the memories she was relating, or both. Though every part of him burned to know more about Ellie and Luke, to know whatever it was she knew, he found himself waiting for her to carry on without comment.

'My da,' Bea said, 'was a big proud fella. Strong as an ox, but as thick and as stubborn as one too. The route for the motorway went right through a rath.'

The word rang a bell. He saw it, coloured in his mind, and felt his synaesthesia spin it off in its different directions; he smelled cinders, tasted lavender. It was a red word, fiery. He struggled to compute all of this at once into a coherent impression, and Bea seemed to notice his discomfort. She looked curious.

'You've heard of them?'

'It's ... like a ring. A fort?'

Bea looked impressed. 'Good,' she said. 'And it was well known that any man who dared to disturb the rath, even trim the plants that grew within its borders, would suffer for it. But my da ... he fancied himself a progressive modern man. He called the fellas workin' for him a bunch of superstitious oul Ginny Anns, and he took the tools and he dug up the rath himself, thinkin' they'd be willing enough to get back to work so long as he was responsible for that.'

The old woman was gone now, lost in the memory. 'It was a warm oul mornin'. My ma was three months gone with my wee sister Annie. And she sent me and Colm up to my da with his lunch – up over the fields and onto the new road site. I didn't want to take Colm because I was near sixteen at the time and I fancied myself a bit of a looker, and Colm had only seven years on him – I was afraid he'd embarrass me in front of my da's crew. But my ma wanted him out from underfoot as she was terrible bad with morning sickness. And so off we went, sure as God.'

She finished the last of the tea in one gulp before continuing, still making that grimace as it passed her lips. 'My da was a sight to behold,' she said. 'The sweat drippin' off him. In one day, and all by himself, he'd done work that woulda took three men three days to do. His fellas were standin' round, feelin' a bit ashamed of themselves, and my da had half the rath dug up already and was startin' on the second half.

'Colm took him his lunch – lovely big bit of bacon, I remember that plain as day – and my da ruffles his hair and shows him off to the lads and says, this is my big lad, this is my heir. And wee Colm as proud as anything, and me a bit jealous but not mindin' too much because a lovely wee fella from the town over had winked at me. Without my da seein', thank God.'

She put the cup back on the saucer. It rattled with the trembling of her hands, which Danny could see now was definitely not attributable to age. Bea's eyes were moist and she rubbed one with her palm, taking a long steadying breath. 'It was the next day,' she said. 'I remember wakenin' and the house quiet, and that was unusual in itself because the wee fella was a terrible one for early risin'. He'd my ma distracted with it and oftentime she'd have sent him into me to get up and make him somethin' to keep his gob occupied.

'But it was quiet, and it was because Colm was nowhere to be found. And we searched, dear Jesus, we searched high and low and in all directions of the compass. My da asked his lads to help in the lookin' but they'd each and every one of them walked away on the spot, sure as God.

'And then,' Bea said, her voice cracking, 'three days after my da had touched the rath, I'd gone back to it thinkin' maybe, maybe wee Colm had gone there because he'd loved being shown off so much by my da. And it was back. Back as good as new. And I went home thinkin' that the lads had rebuilt it for fear they'd be touched too. I worried over what I would tell my da, and then wondered that maybe it had been my da who had done it, trying to make up for what he'd done, because such an awful change had come over him, dear bless us, you wouldn'ta thought it was the same man at all. Not at all, son. Not at all.'

She looked at Danny now, right at him in a way that went down into the very depths of his soul. 'But when I got home …' she began, and found herself unable to continue.

She didn't have to.

'… no one knew who your brother was.' Danny completed the sentence for her.

She nodded, rocking back and forth slightly in the chair with the pain of recollection. 'And they called me all sorts, Jesus God they did. Called me all sorts of liars and lunatics for makin' up such a ridiculous thing that I'd had a wee brother, sure did I not remember that my poor mother had lost him not four months into carryin' him.

'And the boys didn't wink at me no more. No, no they didn't. Because I wouldn't give it up, son, you see. I kept on remembering and I kept on talking about him. Because I' – and she sobbed – 'I kept thinking, thinking of me and him walking with that lunch to my da, and me with my head full of boys and him with a mind full of mischief, and I'd thought … I'd thought, *why doesn't he just go away?*'

Danny's eyes widened as the implication of what she was saying settled on him.

She reached across, surprisingly quickly, and showed him the teacup and the leaves at the bottom. 'This?' she said, making no attempt to hide her disgust. 'This brings in a few quid and gets me a bit of a standin' in the street, son. I know it's a lot of oul shite, believe me. But up here' – and she tapped her head – 'I have it up here. The gift. You do too. You know it. And you know what I'm tellin' you right now is the truth, and why I'm tellin' you it.'

He looked out the front window, to the garden beyond. To the mound.

'It's a rath …?'

'If I'd known, son,' Bea said ruefully. 'Jesus, if I'd only known. Oul Mr Gaynor lived here before ye and he kept that garden immaculate – I just thought it was a wee feature.'

'So you're saying,' Danny said slowly, 'that because I dug up my garden, the … the faeries have come and kidnapped my girlfriend and son and taken them away.'

Bea met his gaze unflinchingly. 'That's what I'm sayin'.'

'The faeries,' he said again.

'I call them the Low Folk,' Bea replied. 'You say faeries to anyone and they start thinking of wee girls messin' about with photographs and Tinkerbell. Trust me, son, they're not like that. No, they're not like that one bloody bit.'

Danny absorbed this. He felt close to laughter again, except this time it wouldn't be on the cathartic side of madness, it would be on the psychotic side. His T-shirt was soaked with tea – ha! – and it was damp and uncomfortable against his skin. He was tempted to stand up and take it off, ensuring that his mystery spy looking through the window now saw him start a striptease routine for his elderly guest. Ha. Ha ha.

And yet–

'Ancient Gaelic,' he said, almost involuntarily. Seeing Bea's expression, he told her about the phone signal and the buried voicemail within.

'You have a recording?' she said eagerly, her eyes gleaming in the lamplight. 'Let me hear it.'

Danny shook his head. 'Sorry. I dropped it in Dermot Scully's house when the Stair Monster tried to come down and eat me.' Ha ha ha ha ha. Stair Monster. Hey. This was fun.

'Danny,' Bea said, in a 'snap out of it' tone that only made her seem funnier, 'Danny, I know this is a lot to deal with–'

'Fuck you,' he said quietly and calmly. 'Fuck you and your fuckin' stories, all right?'

He went to the front door and opened it. A warm breeze wafted in, despite it being long past midnight. 'Out,' he called to her. 'Out. Out to fuck, go on.'

She emerged from the front room, nothing but disappointment in her eyes as she glanced at him. She walked past and paused on the threshold. 'Keep remembering,' she told him. 'That's your power, Danny. Assuming' – and she cast that laser-intensity glare at him, the one that only old ladies could fully master – 'assuming you want to.'

'Get out,' he snarled. 'And take yer fuckin' faeries with ye.'

She replied with words that chilled him to the core. The same words he'd heard whispered on the phone message. Words in ancient Irish that she couldn't possibly have known. And seeing his reaction, his shock, Beatrice O'Malley smiled thinly. 'It means the same to you as it did to me all those years ago.'

She leaned in close. He made no move to stop her. 'Consider it granted,' she whispered.

Not waiting for a response, she walked away, without so much as a backward glance. He watched her go, fighting the twin urges to call her back and to call her an oul fucker.

Why had he rejected her story so vehemently? Why had he told her to go? Because what she was saying was impossible – *but was it any more impossible than losing a son in the same way you'd lose a pound coin between two cushions?* – there were no such things as faeries. No such thing as magic. The world was mundane. The world was full of stinky nappies and oil bills and inadequate parenting, not mystic swords and stolen children and epic quests. He knew this for a fact. He'd been up to his fuckin' ears in reality this last year.

He went back inside, though the house was the last place he wanted to be right now. Where else could he go? Who could he talk to? The only two people who didn't think he was crazy were a post-nervous-breakdown academic eccentric and the crazy woman from up the street whose specialist subject was tall dark handsome strangers and Messages From Beyond the Tetley.

Without quite knowing why, he got out his phone and accessed his saved messages. He'd kept that first message from Ellie, the one she'd sent when he'd been wrapped up in Maggie's arms, the one that had told him about the pregnancy and had sent his life off in a different direction. Of course, it would be gone now too …

Except … except it wasn't.

He felt his heart leap in his chest as he read and reread it, afraid to stop looking in case when he looked again, it would have evaporated into the ether. Somewhere at the back of his mind the irony occurred that this was the polar opposite of the reaction he'd had the first time he'd read it.

Sitting down on unsteady legs, he began to read through all his messages, and as he did so he felt that glimmer of hope twist in his gut once again. A message, dated three months later, asking him was his phone switched off, could he come to the hospital as quickly as he could. A message from his mother asking if there was any update on Ellie. Another from Steve, asking the same thing. A day later, a message from Maggie, of all people, saying that Steve had just told her. Passing on her condolences.

So. The universe wasn't going to erase Luke completely, it seemed. He was just never going to make it out of Ellie's womb alive. For a horrendous moment, Danny wished that whatever cosmic whitewashing was going on here would complete the fucking job. It was so complete – christening records, memories, camcorder videos, now text messages. Who was he to fight against all this? He was Danny Morrigan, monumental fuckup, reluctant partner, last-resort father.

You were there. You saw the message, got to the hospital, held her hand as they kept passing that scanner over her belly, searching for a heartbeat that refused to come.

No. She'd squeezed his hand and the clock had fallen off the wall with a thump and he'd had to go and check out the colour of the baby's hair and the midwife had said …

'I'm sorry,' the obstetrician had said, after more fruitless searching. 'I'm truly very sorry … ' and Ellie had let loose with a wailing, terrible moan that had rent the air in the room …

They'd placed little Luke in his arms …

They'd told him the procedure to remove the baby from Ellie would only take a few hours …

He was a father. Oh God.

He wasn't a father. Thank God.

Danny was suddenly outside, gasping. He had no memory of opening the front door, but here he was, on his knees in his front garden. For a wonder his eyes were dry. He had nothing left to give, even tears. He looked up at the stars, each one a soul going to heaven, each one a furnace of nuclear fusion.

The night was as clear as it had been when he'd stood out there with Ellie and Steve, drinking beer and looking up at the stars. The first night he'd destroyed the rath and incurred the wrath of the – what had Bea called them? – Low Folk.

In one smooth collection of movements, almost on autopilot, he was up and off his arse. Ducking back inside, he grabbed the spade which had been propped against the hearth since he'd abandoned it last night. The night was chilly now, but as he looked down at that little circular patch of earth beneath him he didn't feel the cold one bit. He was still very far from believing what Bea had told him to be true, but he knew one thing; if this was to be his Sisyphean task – if he had to come out here and flatten this fucker every fuckin' night, and if by doing so he would come one single inch closer to any answers – he would do it gladly.

'What have I left to lose?' he cried to the world at large. Almost immediately, as it had done that first night, the rain seemed to come from nowhere and everywhere. Danny couldn't have given two shits. He worked until his back and legs ached and burned and until the earth was flat and the mound destroyed, and only then did he stagger inside, stinking and exhausted, and, shedding filthy clothes as he went, he managed to collapse onto his bed, naked, asleep almost before his body hit the mattress.

The Looking Glass

'Danny?'

'Mmm?' he grunted sleepily. A hand touched his shoulder and shook him gently, which interfered with the dream he was having about mile-high waterspouts and salt and vinegar crisps. He rolled out of reach of the hand and buried his face in the lovely cool unslept-on part of the mattress, allowing the coldness to seep in and soothe him back to a deeper realm of sleep.

'Danny,' the voice said again, more insistently.

He opened his eyes, wincing as light bounced off his pupils at what was frankly a ridiculous speed. What was light's fuckin' hurry anyway? Couldn't it be a bit more sedate, like sound, or a bit sexier, like taste?

'Mmmwhat,' he mumbled, face still half buried in mattress.

'You're gonna be late for work, love,' Maggie told him. 'It's near eight.'

He moaned at this. Shitting work. Bastarding job. Wanky Lircom. Fuck buckets, the lot of them. But his body, as though his house lacked a roof and he were being operated by a gargantuan puppeteer looming above, pivoted around until his legs dangled over the edge of the bed. He reached up and rubbed the sleep out of his eyes and, while he was doing so, felt a succession of kisses being planted on his forehead.

'I've gotta run,' Maggie whispered. 'Early morning meeting. My taxi will be here in five minutes.'

'You should have wakened me earlier,' he said a shade reproachfully, opening his eyes properly to confirm that yes, damn, she really was fully dressed in her work clothes and even had her jacket on.

She punched him on the shoulder. 'You're a fuckin' laugh you are, Danny Morrigan,' she said. 'What do you think I've been tryin' to do for the last forty minutes? I was shoutin' and everythin'.'

He stood up. 'I keep tellin' you,' he said. 'Don't shout. Go to the far end of the house and whisper, *fancy a blowjob?* and you'll hear my wee footsteps thumpin' across the land– ow!'

'You're a pervert.'

'I'm a pervert?' he said, offended, rubbing the spot on his shoulder where she had just punched him. 'Dear heart, I'm a fella. I'm supposed to like that ... that filthy degrading act. That's the role that society has assigned to me. Whereas, you? You're a lady. You're meant to abhor it, are you not? So who's the real pervert here, I ask you?'

'Well maybe I should start hating it, you're right,' she said, eyes twinkling, drifting downward.

At that exact moment, the strangely wimpy beeping noise of a taxi horn sounded outside. A few seconds later, it went again. Immediately Danny had the driver down as overweight, impatient and, if there was any justice in the world, nursing a stomach ulcer of some description. He made a fist and shook it at the heavens. 'Curse you! Curse you, cruel god!'

She kissed him and said goodbye and that she'd see him later and that no, she didn't mind having to get a taxi, and then she was gone, leaving a trail of perfume in her wake that he followed, Pepé Le Pew style, to the bathroom. He performed his ablutions there, rinsing and wiping and spitting and excavating, pondered over the purpose of nostril hairs for a while, and when he returned to the bedroom he discovered she'd left a work outfit hanging on the back of the bedroom door for him.

The weather was glorious today; and even better, that rainstorm he'd heard battering the windows last night must have washed the humidity out of the world, for there was a fresh tang to the air and a spring in his step as he turned the key in the lock and stepped out into Kensington Avenue. The newbies at Number 2 were just emerging, he noted, marvelling at his labelling of them as newbies – that had been him and Maggie only six months ago. Hard to believe.

The clutch on the car was sticking. Fuck. He rolled his eyes. Reliable Renault? Arses. That was the last time he let Flanagan advise him on car buying. But despite this momentary clutch-related funk, as he reversed out of the driveway Danny took a second to marvel at the feel of the vehicle around him, the fact that this big machine was completely under his control.

He caught himself patting the seats as though they were a dog that had just learned a neat new trick, running his fingers over the smoothness of the dashboard. He stopped just short of smelling the steering wheel. The whole thing reeked of new car, which was ridiculous – he'd had it for months. He put it down to his good mood.

As he wound through the early-morning streets, Danny turned on the radio to listen to that prick of a DJ on the BBC, not because he liked him, but because he actively despised him and listening to him reliably got his blood nice and boiling.

The only thing Danny Morrigan liked more than liking something was despising it – if you liked a thing there tended not to be a lot more to say about it, but by hating something you could approach it from all angles of ire: really sink your teeth into a good solid loathe and discuss it at length at work with fellow-minded workmates, or better yet, argue with idiots holding the opposing viewpoint.

He had a good four or five little nuggets of irritation lined up by the time he ascended from the underground car park and nodded curtly to the receptionist. He managed to slink inside the lift just as the doors shut, much to the obvious nervousness of the two people from his floor who were already inside and who, he couldn't help but notice, hadn't exactly busted their arse to hold the doors open for him.

Balls, he thought. *What d'you call these two?*

'Cal?' he hazarded, and got a nod from the male. Emboldened by this success, he went for broke. 'Alison?'

'Alice.'

'Tch!' he rebuked himself, overly cheerily. 'Good morning!'

'Morning, Mr Morrigan,' they replied, one a half-second behind the other.

'It's *Danny*,' he said, waving away the formality as sincerely as he could, which wasn't very, to be honest. He liked the Mr Morrigan thing. Who was he fuckin' kidding, he loved the Mr Morrigan thing.

The lift insisted on stopping on every floor between ground and fourth and allowing more people to get in, which wasn't ideal for Danny in terms of timekeeping, but meant he was inside the lift long enough to learn that the two from his floor really needed to get over themselves and just get it on with each other.

Fourth floor. They walked together as far as reception in a heavy, awkward sort of silence, and he reflected on the fact that, even though he was not their direct line manager, as a member of the upper echelons of the company he probably should say something suitably motivational to them.

'Only two days to go!' he reminded them. 'Game faces on!'

This didn't go down well.

'We're all working as hard as we can,' Cal shot back instantly.

'Has someone been saying something? Has Thomas talked to you?' Alice demanded, all traces of nicety gone.

'No, no.' Danny waved his hands desperately. Fuck. This never happened in the management away-day role plays. 'You're both doing great. Um, well I don't know that for sure, because I don't know you, you know, personally, but you seem like two good workers to me. So. Er–' he searched for something to help him explain, to say that he'd just been trying to impart some of his own enthusiasm; that had been very prominent in the away-days Mr Black had sent him on. He wasn't implying anything.

Looking at them, he knew saying anything else would just make it worse. He settled for nodding and smiling in what he hoped was a 'we're all in this together' type way, before he turned and walked away to the management side of the building.

'Prick,' Cal muttered, as he and Alice walked into the telephony side, hit immediately by the dull chattering roar of customer service. '"Game faces on" – what was that meant to mean? What's he heard about me? That I'm sittin' swingin' the lead? Cheeky fucker.'

'Graduate recruits. What have they got that we don't?' Alice agreed. 'I've a degree too y'know. I went for that scheme an all.'

'Yeah?' Cal said, mildly surprised. 'You never said.'

'Well,' she paused, 'the test wasn't fair.'

'How so?'

Alice's eyes were wide as saucers with injustice. 'Well, it was really fuckin' *hard*.'

Jesus, Danny thought, as his email account roared into life and spat new emails at him, Steve still hadn't got the hang of what constituted 'Safe For Work' and insisted on sending him emails like, just for example, 'World's Hairiest Minges: The Slideshow'. Sitting just outside the chief exec's office on an open plan floor, he doubted that would be a career-enhancing presentation.

Stop sending me those things, you twat, he typed, fingers flying. And then he reconsidered, and deleted *you twat*, because after all it was Steve, and he didn't want to seem ungrateful for him keeping in touch. He knew Steve wouldn't get too much time for that these days. It was a wonder he could even look at pictures like that without thinking of …

Ew.

'Danny? Ready to go? Destiny awaits.'

For a moment, a horrible stretched-out moment, he had visions of accidentally hitting the wrong button and a sequence of huge, horrendously hirsute vulvas materialising on his monitor, despite his desperate, feverish, sacked efforts to prevent it. But a furtive glance at his screen reassured him sufficiently that he was able to swivel smoothly around and adopt a suitably sophisticated expression. 'Morning, Mr Black,' he said brightly. 'How was the golf?'

'Grand, Danny, grand,' David Black, chief executive of Lircom, said with that ever-present faint smile he wore. Danny had seen that smile vanish only twice, and, thankfully, he thought, remembering the shit-storm that had followed on those two occasions, he had never been the cause. The man had a temper that made his surname seem woefully inadequate.

'Where were you again?' Danny said, as much for something to say as out of genuine curiosity, even as he grabbed his sheaf of notes and printouts and swept around from behind his desk to stand beside Mr Black, who wasted no time in setting off toward the conference room.

Mr Black could have simply gone to the meeting without him, Danny knew, but it was a measure of the trust Mr Black had in him that the chief exec had waited for him to be by his side before making his entrance. There were whispers that he was being groomed. As long it wasn't for bum sex, any and all grooming was fine with Danny.

And even if it is for bum sex – Maggie had once said to him with that mischievous grin of hers tugging at her lips – *at what David Black earns, you can fuckin' well consider it boyo.*

'The Royal Tara. You must know it, Danny, surely?'

Danny ran the name through the extensive database of golf clubs he knew. This did not occupy a great deal of time. 'Sorry,' he said.

'It's not far from the *Dá Chich na Morrigna*,' Mr Black went on, slipping into impeccable Gaelic, as his hands rested on the conference room doors. Through the frosted glass Danny could see everyone else was already assembled. Seeing Danny's politely blank expression, his perma-smile went up a little in its intensity. 'The Breasts of the Morrigan,' he explained.

'Is that where we left them?' Danny said, not really knowing what else to come back with.

Mr Black laughed. He had a musical laugh.

The presentation went pretty well, Danny thought; reassuring their financial backers and shareholders that the network was ready to go ahead, and presenting the media strategy, which was key to ensuring that uptake was sufficient to begin to recover the setup costs of manufacturing.

The buzzwords ran through his mind and set off little sparks here and there as they were supposed to, and he made sure to take notes dutifully throughout because the Lircom Board would probably hold a less formal internal meeting later to pick the bones of this one, and his notes would form the fall-back if anyone couldn't remember the specific gist of a particular part.

All the usual suspects were here around the table; he'd met them at the Lircom annual gala dinner the previous month, which had been pretty much the most nerve-wracking night of his life. Seventy five of the industry's movers and shakers, and Danny Morrigan, three months out of university and feeling as if he didn't know which to tuck in first, his shirt or his umbilical cord.

He cast his eyes to one attendee, sitting at the far end of the table, not far from Mr Black's position at the head. He was the sole person Danny didn't recognise and, since the newbie kept shooting glances in his direction, he made a mental note to try to get Mr Black to introduce them after the meeting.

'Danny ...'

He glanced to his left, to Andy, the head of Human Resources, who had just whispered at him. Not willing to risk an answering whisper – Mr Black was in full flow, halfway through the PowerPoint – he raised his eyebrows in a questioning, *yes?*

Andy didn't say anything more, but simply nodded to the notes Danny had been writing. His record of the meeting had not exactly turned out as he thought. Oh, sure, in some places he could spy paragraphs that made sense, but they were interspersed with paragraphs of complete gibberish, stream-of-consciousness nonsense.

What if our uptake rate fails to rise above the lower level? What are our financial options for extending the credit on the loans given to Luke his name was Luke power your remember is remembering consider it granted that your power is Dermot and the thing on the stairs coming down down you let it in it's not an alleyway, it's a cat purple her lips aren't purple remember that your power is extension over the first two years at

a consistent rate of interest, which should, with the government incentives
we'll qualify for, easily cope with the risk …

He felt himself begin to sweat. Andy was looking questioningly at him in a way that said *do you need to go?* Andy had a look for everything; it was his uncanny knack for relating to people that made Danny amazed he'd ever secured a job with Human Resources.

No. He shook his head and refocused on the meeting, grasping his pen tightly, as if daring it to venture off the beaten track. He'd have a few tablets when this meeting finished, maybe lay off the rowing machine tonight and take it easy. Workplace stress, Mr Black was fond of telling his management team, was the single biggest problem in the modern office environment.

The remainder of the meeting passed off without incident; Danny kept his gaze firmly locked on his writing hand and it behaved itself.

As everyone filed out, Mr Black took the time to shake their hands and ask after partners/children/cats/fish. He had an uncanny knack for remembering little details like that, Danny had noticed. He made it look effortless, and he must have sensed Danny's attention was on him because he glanced his way and gave him a conspiratorial wink, before beckoning Danny over.

'Danny, I'd like you to meet Michael Quinn,' Mr Black said, stepping to one side to reveal the attendee whose face Danny hadn't known. 'Michael works for FormorTech, but we mustn't hold that against him now, must we?'

He laughed, as did Danny and Michael, even if Michael's laugh seemed a little clipped and artificial. Michael didn't seem to know what to make of Danny, and Danny found himself shifting his weight uneasily from one foot to the other under the wattage of the older man's glare. Mr Black had since turned his attention back to the crowd at large and was doing the handshake routine again, leaving him and Quinn alone.

'How are … uh,' Danny ventured, feeling the conversational conch had been passed to him, 'how are the negotiations going?'

Michael shot a sidelong glance at Mr Black. 'Cordially,' was all he said. His eyes swung back to Danny. 'It's … good to … meet you,' he said, sounding as if every word had been crowbarred out of him. Danny felt the ridiculous urge to crane his neck to see if there was a hand going up Michael's back, operating him like a ventriloquist's dummy.

'Yes,' was all he could think of to reply.

'Your name seems familiar,' Michael said.

Danny frowned. 'Oh … really?' he said, nonplussed. 'I can't think where from.'

'My daughter went to Queen's. Ellie.'

'Ellie?' Danny said, disbelieving. If you'd lined up a hundred guys and asked him to rank them from 1 to 100 on likelihood of contributing one half of Ellie Quinn's genetic code, the stiff in front of him would have been sitting pretty on triple figures. 'I know Ellie dead well – her partner was … *is* my best mate.'

'Yes,' Michael spat out, making the sort of face a cat makes when yakking up a particularly viscous hairball. 'Steve.'

Oh my God. This is him.

Danny tried to keep his face neutral as about a thousand emails and texts and MSN conversations and phone calls from

Steve flashed through his brain, all on the subject of 'her fuckin' ones and the pole up their holes' and how they made it perfectly obvious that they despised him. Jesus.

And worse, he'd absorbed it all with a sort of fuzzy patronising scepticism, thinking that anyone who fathered someone like Ellie couldn't have been that bad. Guilt festered within him. Between the almost-a-dismissal of him via email this morning and the vindication of his strife-ridden position with the in-laws, he was beginning to think he owed Steve a pint.

Mr Black was hovering nearby again. They were the only three people left in the conference room. He smiled faintly at Michael, who took a half-step back. Danny could only assume he'd been startled by Mr Black's soundless approach – Christ knew it had taken some getting used to at first: the man walked like a panther.

'Small world, isn't it?' he beamed. 'Couldn't help but overhear. Danny's one of our best and brightest here at Lircom. Big things ahead of him. We're very proud to have him in the family.'

'Steady on with that family stuff,' Danny replied, deadpan, his eyes wide with apparent alarm. 'Don't want you jinxing me. My life's stressful enough at the minute, thanks.'

Mr Black found this hilarious.

Michael Quinn didn't even smile.

At home that evening, Danny dialled the number he'd jotted down from an email. He'd never bothered to put it in his most recent mobile. That fact alone had caused him yet more guilt.

'Hello?' A familiar voice sounded at the other end.

'What about ye, mucker?' Danny said cheerily. Too cheerily? He'd been a little worried about how casual to seem on the phone. It had been about six months since he'd actually seen Steve in person, after all. He pushed the frets out of his head. He could worry about that later when he was half-cut, on the basis that he wouldn't worry about things like that, for the very reason that he was, in fact, half-cut.

'Ach, Danny, ya wanker ye. Fuck me, what's the craic?'

'Not bad, lad, not too bad. Busy at work, like, you know how it is. This fuckin' network thingy goin' live and all that oul guff.'

'Aye, I seen that on the news. Seen your ugly face in the background at that press conference an all. Jesus Christ Almighty. You looked a sight. What's with the half-mullet you're sportin'? Fuckin' tryin' out for a rock band are ye?'

'Aye, and yer ma's the biggest groupie. She's sucked my cock so many times she's worn a lip-groove into the shaft. Fits her mouth like a key in a fuckin' lock.'

Steve laughed long and hard at this. Danny grinned. He'd always been quicker off the mark than Steve wit-wise, but Steve had never minded a bit; when he was outmatched in a game of Yer Ma, he'd just roar with laughter.

'Anyway lad,' Danny said, 'there's a few of us headin' out tonight. It's a special occasion.'

'Oh aye? What's that?' Steve asked.

'Did you not see it? The Grand Opening?'

'Lad, I've seen fuck all,' Steve said, sounding harried. 'What Grand Opening is this?'

'Yer sister's flaps.'

'Jesus Christ!' Steve exclaimed, dutifully outraged. 'Ya dirty bastard, ye. See when I get ye, lad, I'm gonna knock yer melt in.'

'So you're comin' out, then?'

There was a slight pause.

'Um …' Steve replied, his voice suddenly a lot less confident than before.

Danny heard something in the background. Footsteps, and a small, muffled, sound. He knew it must have been Ellie, and somehow at that moment he knew also that she was holding wee Aaron in her arms.

He hadn't told Michael Quinn the full truth about him and Ellie. Somehow, by the look on the miserable fucker's face, Danny didn't think he would have appreciated hearing that he had once, however briefly, done a little more than know his daughter as a casual acquaintance – although the word casual could probably have been used in a slightly different context.

Ellie had been fun. He and Ellie had hooked up one night in The Attic, his Saturday night student haunt. And they'd gone back to her tiny little flat in the Halls and they'd done what young people are wont to do – twice, with pizza for afters. And she'd called him sweet but corny, and he'd shot right back by saying he hadn't mushroom for girls with pepper only in their personalities. And after this, they'd decided they quite liked each other and had dated, for a while.

Until Maggie happened to him.

Until Steve happened to her.

The road not taken? Nothing as dramatic as that. But more

than once he'd found himself wondering if he would have been a little more willing to go visit Steve if Steve had ended up with someone other than her; if he shied away from that house not just because he had a morbid fear of nappies and baby sick but also because he didn't want to see her as this Mummy person but as this half-naked girl reclined on a bed, matching him pun for pun, joke for joke, the first time a girl had ever done that.

And the last.

'Who is it, love?' he heard from the other end. He kept quiet, thinking he should probably tell Steve to say hello from him, but not quite able to bring himself to do so.

'It's Danny. He says hello.'

Danny blinked at the lie and also at his own surprise at hearing it. From the other end of the line the conversation started to sound indistinct, as though Steve were underwater.

His front door opened. 'Hey, love,' Maggie said easily, and then realised he was on the phone. She rolled her eyes. 'Work, again?'

'No,' Danny replied. 'Er, I'm phonin' Steve. Thought I might ask if he wants to go out.'

Why was he nervous to admit that to her? Why would she have a problem with that? And indeed, she didn't in the slightest. 'Oh, that'll be nice,' she said, pecking him on the cheek and moving into the house proper. She was carrying a few Sainsbury's bags and placed them on the kitchen counter.

'Hello? Danny?'

It was Ellie. Ellie was on the phone to him. *Ellie was speaking to him right now.*

Ridiculously, ludicrously, his mouth dried up. He opened it

to respond to her greeting, but no sound emerged. Standing at the foot of the stairs, he found his legs wobble and he sat, a trifle heavily, on the steps below him, banging his arse as he did so.

This was absurd. He'd just this minute finished legitimising Ellie in his own mind, and now confronted with her voice, he had to force down the most immense tide of relief that washed over him, as if … as if she'd been gone. Well, she had been. She'd been gone for almost two fuckin' years. Jesus. What was *wrong* with him?

'Danny?' she said again. 'Danny, hello? Are you there?'

He swallowed to moisten his throat and found himself turning away from the kitchen and from Maggie, shielding the phone with his body. 'Hey,' he said, his voice having dropped significantly in volume. 'I didn't … I … um' – and he was floundering now, *why? why? why?* – 'I didn't expect to be talking … to you. How … uh, how are you?'

'I'm fine.'

'Yeah?' he said, overjoyed beyond measure. 'You are?'

'I was wondering if you and Maggie wanted to come over,' she said. 'For dinner.'

'Yes … yes, that sounds good.'

'It's just that …' and she sighed. 'Well, Steve won't tell you this' – and her own voice dropped in volume now – 'that's why I sent him to change Aaron, but the fact is, we don't really have the money for going out. But he really misses you, Danny. The rest of them too, but especially you. It's the forlorn look in his eyes when he calls you a miserable shitstick of a dirty bastard.'

'Steve said that?' Danny replied, touched.

'Oh yeah. So it'd be nice if you could come to us. What d'you think?'

I don't know what I think. I don't know why I don't want you to stop talking to me, or why I feel like your voice is as familiar to me now as it was way back when.

'Yeah,' he said weakly. 'That'd be grand, Ellie.'

'Tomorrow night then? About seven? Suit ye okay?' she said, all business again. A noise erupted in the background. She sighed. 'Danny I'll have to run. Is that …'

'Yes,' he said, feeling a sudden panic to close the deal. 'Yes, yes, it's okay. We'll be there.'

'Great. Cheerio,' and she was gone.

'Goodbye,' he said into empty space.

'Sorry about that, lad,' Steve's voice sounded. 'Teething troubles with the wee fella. Was she sayin' to ye about dinner?'

'Yeah. Tomorrow at seven,' Danny said hollowly.

'Aye. Long as you're not expecting haute cui-fuckin'-sine like. Although speakin' as someone who was subjected to your ma's cookin' as a teenager more than a few times, you'd have a fuckin' cheek like, lad,' Steve said, sounding a bit worried.

'Yeah,' Danny replied, snapping out of his reverie. 'Yeah, sorry, lad … um …' and he tried to think of a riposte but couldn't, so his mind threw up something else instead. 'Here, I bumped into her da today at work …' which led to a tirade of graphic swear words from Steve. 'I see what you mean about him. Barrel of laughs isn't he?'

'You've no idea,' Steve said grimly. 'Normally he's enough of wanker like, but see this last few days, he's been even worse. I think he's losin' it lad. He forgot the name of his own fuckin' grandchild. Swear to fuck. And this guy's meant to be a corporate hotshot,' he snorted derisively. 'Troubleshooter, my balls. Windee licker more like.'

'What did he call him?' Danny asked. More to the point, he thought, why did he want to know? But he did. He really did.

'Ach I can't even remember now, lad. Listen, I'll have to run. See ye tomorrow. And' – Steve hesitated, obviously extending himself beyond his masculine comfort zone – 'uh, it'll be really nice to see ye both.'

He was gone a moment later. Danny hung up and sat looking at the phone for a few seconds. Hearing the lull in conversation from the hallway, Maggie poked her head out from around the kitchen door. 'Can you give us a hand with starting the dinner?' she called.

He got up and walked to her, smiling sheepishly so that she looked at him with suddenly narrowing eyes. 'Speaking of dinner,' he began, and filled her in on the plans he'd made, again steeling himself for protests or for objections.

'Hey, sounds like fun,' she said, and then winked at him. 'Be nice to coo over the wee chicken and how cute he is and then at the end of the night go – right we're off, see ya!'

She kissed him and laughed. He didn't.

Her lips tasted of – and this was crazy, this was insane, but he had the oddest sensation that they tasted of – *red*? But how could anything taste like a colour? It bothered him, itched at him, but not nearly as much the thought that came hard on its heels.

Why did red taste wrong?

Her lips aren't purple. He'd written that in the minutes during

217

his little mental walkabout at the meeting this morning.

'What's up, babe?' she said, pausing to look at him. 'You're miles away.'

With an effort he pulled himself back. 'Sorry, I'm just thinking about tomorrow night. Just hoping it goes well.'

She grinned easily, confidently. 'It will, don't you worry. Wait and see.'

He turned away and busied himself with making dinner, telling himself it was to cement his role as fellow housework doer and all-round modern man. And definitely not, for talk's sake, because she had looked for a moment like she was going to come over to him and kiss him again and he wanted to avoid that.

They had eaten dinner, and Danny was just closing the cupboard after sliding the last plate back into place. He stared at the closed cupboard door for a moment and then reopened it and regarded his crockery collection. Generally speaking he didn't think of himself as a fan of kitchenware, so this was in itself a fairly remarkable act.

It was so clean. So orderly. He lifted one of the saucers from the top of the pile and examined it for a few seconds. He'd bought this as part of a set in Debenhams, when they'd been moving into this place. They'd been so excited, running around CastleCourt like two idiots, dissolving into paroxysms of glee at having to decide whether getting an apple corer and a juicer were necessary expenses.

Something made him sniff the freshly-washed saucer. It

smelled of not smelling of almond and coconut. *That doesn't even make sense. What the hell is wrong with me?* He sighed, replacing the plate with a chink.

'What's wrong?'

Her hands wrapped around his upper chest from behind. The instinct to drop his jaw and plant a kiss on them was neck-and-neck with the instinct to take a step sideways and break contact.

'Nothing,' he half-lied. After all, what was he supposed to say? The dishes were giving off a smell they didn't smell of? 'Just wondering what you fancy doing tonight.'

'We-ee-ee-ll,' she said, and gently spun him around so his back was against the countertop and she could move closer to him. She was pursing her lips and giving his question some intense consideration. Her breasts were squashing themselves into his torso. 'I don't know,' she concluded eventually. 'We can go out and catch a movie if you feel like it. Go for a drive maybe. Go have a few drinks. Normally I'd say we could stretch to hitting a club after the drinks but, what with going to Steve and Ellie's tomorrow night and with the hangovers you get, we might be better off limiting ourselves.'

'Limiting ourselves?' he echoed. 'You call that limiting ourselves? We're coming down with choices, Maggie. It's a big old choices smorgasbord and everybody's invited.'

He couldn't get over it. Somehow the plethora of options seemed astonishing. So much freedom. He felt almost guilty – *why?* – just thinking about it.

'And I wasn't even finished yet,' she said, looking up at him with sparkling eyes. 'Those are just the ones that involve going out. There's plenty of things we could do right here at home.'

She stood on tiptoe and kissed him, softly, on the lips.

'How about some quiet time with a DVD and our big comfy sofa?' she said softly.

'You'll just pick a rom-com.'

'However could I sweeten the deal?'

'However indeed …'

Thus it was that a short time later they found themselves ensconced on the large, full-backed, luxurious leather sofa, one so soft that you didn't so much sit on as sit in the damn thing. Maggie's head rested on Danny's chest. The DVD they'd picked – some oul bollocks about Gywneth Paltrow missing a train, or not missing a train, and being somehow split in two because of it, passed by mostly unnoticed. Try as he might – and he wasn't – he couldn't focus on it because of two things.

The first was the feel of Maggie's head on his chest. It was intimate, casual, the sort of thing couples did without even thinking. It didn't feel uncomfortable, it didn't feel unwelcome … but the one impression he couldn't shake no matter how he tried was that it felt, well, *new* somehow. As if her chin hadn't worn a groove in his chest so that it fitted like a gun in a holster.

His mind went back to driving the Renault that morning, the almost overpowering smell of new car. That was it. The smell of Maggie's head reminded him of new car. Somehow, he doubted it was a new type of shampoo.

And now that his mind had made that connection, it felt like a switch had been jammed on, and he could sense newness everywhere – the sofa, the TV, the entire fucking house, they all gave him that new car sensation.

The second was the quiet.

Oh the movie made noise, of course; the surround sound system he'd paid some guy a few quid to install when they'd been outfitting this place (one of his wee treats to himself after landing the graduate job at Lircom) was working its usual magic and thanks to that he could now hear Pepper Potts snivelling in full 5.1. Marvellous.

It wasn't enough that his sense of smell was going off the deep end. Now he wasn't hearing noises that he felt somehow he should be hearing. Nothing dramatic, no, he was certain of that. Not a big noise. A soft noise. Rhythmic …

… and then, to his astonishment, he heard the missing noise, coming from right beside him.

'Maggie?'

'Bunh?' she murmured, starting only slightly before snuggling back into his chest and immediately drifting off again.

He listened to the sound of her sleeping, realising with each passing inhale/exhale that, no, it wasn't the exact noise he'd been listening out for, but in a way he couldn't explain, even the semi-familiarity of it was strangely comforting, comforting in a way that very few things had been these few hours. He clung to it.

'How long have I been out?' Maggie eventually said, yawning as she slowly extricated herself from his chest. 'Sorry – didn't realise I was tired.'

'Don't worry about it. You've only been out a few minutes.'

She glanced at the clock and raised an eyebrow. 'A few minutes?' she repeated, and glanced at him. 'Try two and a half hours, Danny. It's almost 1 a.m.'

'What? It can't be.'

It was.

'I'd always meant to watch that movie,' Maggie was saying as they climbed the stairs moments later to go to bed. 'We really should give it back to Lisa. She loaned it to us yonks ago.'

'Yeah,' he replied absently.

'How'd it finish anyway?'

He stopped at the top of the staircase and looked at her expectant face. For a moment he contemplated coming clean, telling her the truth, that he'd fallen into some sort of half-trance listening to the sound of her soft sleep-breathing and hadn't an earthly how the movie ended. It sounded romantic, after all. It'd probably get him brownie points.

'I … she … um, she got yer man.'

'Which one?'

'Um. The nice one?' he hazarded.

'No, I mean which version of her?'

Having paid zero attention during most of the movie, Danny was now completely lost. 'Both of her?' he ventured.

'Oh,' Maggie said. She shrugged. 'I like happy endings.'

'Yeah. Me too.'

Danny found himself in a twilight world, in the countryside, with nary a sight of civilisation in all directions, and had been tempted to start looking for the clubhouse as, being a city boy his entire life, he imagined the countryside as one overlapping golf course after another. Despite the abruptness of his arrival here he'd kinda accepted it in the casual way you do when sleep claims you and, with some relief, you realise that the world doesn't have to make sense anymore.

'Son.'

His da was standing beside him. He was wearing the same faded blue jeans and red tracksuit top he'd worn on the day he'd taken off down the garden path and hadn't reappeared for ten years.

'Da,' he returned.

Oh, so he was having *that* dream, the one where his da told him in exacting detail how disappointing he'd been as a son. Okay, sometimes he did it riding a seahorse while it rained tiny little ghosts from *Pac-Man* all around them, but generally the theme was the same. Danny glanced around. The scenery was new, at least.

'Where the fuck's this meant to represent in my subconscious?' he asked, wondering when his long and fruitless dreamtime quest for the Land of Porn would come to fruition.

'This isn't your mind, Danny,' his da told him, and Danny saw a blood-red tint seep into the colour palette of the vista around him, as if someone had just thrown a crimson veil over his head. He looked at his da with his eyebrows arched, and his da nodded upward, and Danny looked to see that the moon, emerging from a cloudbank, had become bored of being blotchy white and decided to plump for a slutty shade of red.

It was at that moment Danny noted, with the lack of surprise that one only finds in a dream, that his da's shoulders spasmed and without fuss, sprouted a magnificent jet-black set of wings.

'Nice wings.'

'Thanks.'

Danny huffed out a breath. Generally his dreams didn't take this long to get going. He supposed he'd better get the ball rolling.

'So why'd you fuck off? Why'd you leave us?' Danny asked. He'd get through this and then ask the follow-ups about why his da came back. Same old shit.

'It's complicated,' was the reply. That brought Danny up short. Normally at this stage his da was taking great delight at listing his flaws as a son. Disquieted now for the first time, despite the blood-red moon and the fact his da was apparently a giant crow, Danny shifted from side to side. He didn't like it when nightmares didn't behave themselves.

'I read your letter. Didn't seem that complicated.'

'*My* letter?' his da laughed shortly. 'You'd be surprised, son.'

'You couldn't hack it, could you?'

'No. I couldn't.'

'Being a father.'

'No,' Tony replied, steel in his voice. 'Not that.'

'So what was it? The paint scheme in the hall? My ma burnin' the chips? What? Somethin' must have caused you to go "fuck this". So what was it, Da?'

'Now's not the time.'

Danny sighed. 'This is one of them cryptic fuckin' dreams then,' he said.

'Life is cryptic. Why should dreams be any different?'

'Thanks, Big Bird.'

His da didn't rise to it. He was more concerned with the countryside around them, which was, Danny had to admit, a fair bit creepier given the red tint. Rustles and crackles reached his ears, which was also a bit strange, given that there was fuck-all wind. But then, he imagined the laws of physics applied only loosely in imaginary places.

'I tried to get to you, Danny,' his da told him, his voice going up a little, as if he were worried and wanted to get the words out as quickly as possible. 'I felt it. I felt it all change. Your ma never even flinched. I couldn't believe that. I had no idea they could do that, not on that scale. I should have warned you when they went missing ... should have told you everything then, but how do you even start? They found me. I had to go, had to get out. I knew you'd be safe, for now.'

Danny simply stared. 'Could you cryptic that up for me a little more?' he replied acidly. 'I think a part of the third sentence was almost coherent. Here, d'you want a crayon to write REDRUM on a fuckin' wall?'

'It's changed,' his da went on, as if Danny hadn't spoken. 'It's all changed. And it'll change again before the end of all this. But you – you'll remember. That's what your power is, Danny. The sword can change the rest of us. It can change the whole world. But not you. Not for long.'

Rrrrrooooooo.

'Was that,' Danny said, very slowly, his shoulders stiff as a board, 'a wolf?'

'No. It wasn't.'

His da stopped scanning the surrounding hills and moved to stand right in front of him, placing his hands on his shoulders so he could look into Danny's eyes. Danny realised he was taller than his da by a good four inches. Huh. How about that?

'You don't understand, Danny. You think I didn't want you? I wanted you more than anything. That's what got me into this fuckin' mess in the first place. That's what gave him his in with me. I made the deal. But he fucked me over. Just like they always do. They hate us and they want everything we have, everything they say we took away.'

The moon was obscured then by another cloudbank. The red retreated around them, and the menace of the landscape seemed to seep away with it. Danny, who had been spellbound by his dream-father's words, found himself pulling away from his grasp.

'Well, that was informative,' he said bitterly. 'Glad we had this chat. Feel free to stop by my other dreams. I'd love to see you in the one about the big pair of brown trunks chasin' me down the city centre.'

'Remembering is your power,' his da said, and then his face hardened and Danny realised it was the first time he'd ever seen his da annoyed at him. 'Assuming that you want to remember ...'

Something sprang at Danny then, before he could respond, and the words choked in his throat. For all the world it seemed as if the thing had sprung directly from the flash of anger he'd felt at that final accusation. He was thrown away from his da as the thing knocked him flat to the ground. It was big, it was misshapen. That was all he was able to glean from his terrified vantage point on the grass.

His da was screaming. Not in terror, but in challenge. Danny watched him roll and twist and throw the thing off him, sending it scrabbling for purchase on the surface until it was able to get back on its feet, its back low, its teeth bared. He could see some wolf in it, but only in the sense that you could see some goldfish in a Great White.

Its head, hanging too low on a neck too long, turned from his da – currently struggling to get to his feet – to him, and that was when the clouds hiding the moon moved. The scene was bathed in scarlet rays, making the thing even more horrific than it had been in the darkness.

He'd like to wake up now, he decided. Very much.

And then, as if things couldn't get any stranger, the misshapen monstrosity decided to speak. He never really saw its maw move, or saw a tongue – though how the thing could expect to accommodate a tongue amidst that sea of teeth it displayed, he wasn't sure.

'*Connnnnnnssssssider it grannnnnnnnnnted,*' it somehow said, and emitted a series of nails-on-chalkboard squeals that were rhythmical enough to sound like laughter.

It sprang for him, but never got there, barrelling into the body of his father instead, who had thrown himself into the path of the onslaught. He watched as the thing and his da rolled crazily on the grass, over and over, his da's wide wingspan seeming to increase in size as the brightness of the moon overhead kept growing.

The light was so bright that Danny could see his bones through his hands. He screamed, long and loud and again and again as it began to burn his flesh, his skin blistering all over, bubbling, smelling of cooking meat … and then, black wings, black wings covering everything, turning off the inferno, soothing the pain so he couldn't help but throw himself into the feathers.

'Remember,' a voice whispered. And as the dream imploded around him, his last thought was that the voice was not his father's.

'That was some nightmare you had last night,' Maggie was saying, between strokes of the toothbrush. She was obsessed with brushing those fuckers. If he spent as much time in her mouth as that brush did, he'd be the luckiest guy alive.

In the midst of vigorously rubbing his head dry with a towel, Danny paused, his head still enveloped so that he looked like a low-budget *Doctor Who* monster circa 1976. 'Was it?' he said.

'You clung to me for about an hour after you came out of it,' she said, sounding amused. 'Don't worry, by the way – I won't be tellin' Steve that tonight. What was it about, anyway?'

He poked his head out, the towel draped around his shoulders. 'Something about a bird and a golf course,' he said vaguely, feeling the details of the dream evaporate into mist the harder he tried to make them solidify. 'One of them oul weird ones.'

'My poor baby,' she cooed, cupping his face with her hand and kissing him on the lips, tasting of toothpaste. And of red. The sensation passed across his tongue and he must not have been able to disguise it because she frowned and pulled away. 'What's the matter? Is that brand not that nice?'

'No,' he reassured her. 'It's just … well I haven't brushed yet. Bit self-conscious.'

'Such a gentleman,' she cooed.

'One of a kind,' he replied, starting to brush. When he'd finished, she was nowhere to be found. Assuming she was combing her hair in the mirror, he walked back into the bedroom.

'Hey.'

He started slightly. She was there, on the bed. The bra and panties she'd worn in the bathroom had been discarded. She was looking at him with a raised eyebrow and a smile of intent. She beckoned him to her.

'All minty fresh?' she said, and, although the words were absurd, somehow she twisted them in her mouth so that they seemed sensuous.

He knelt on the bed and dipped his mouth to hers by way of reply, and as their lips met and he felt her tongue slip into his mouth, he felt some of that tension melt away. She pushed forward, kneeling upright herself, so that they could continue to kiss even as she arched her back sufficiently to be able to slide off his boxers.

'We probably won't get a chance tonight,' she said breathily, as they finally broke the kiss.

She had a point and she put it to good use, he had to admit. And looking down, it seemed like he had a point too.

He slid forward, she fell backward, landing softly on the mattress so that, suddenly, her legs were on either side of his hips, wrapping around his back. He put his hands on either side of her head and lowered his face down for another kiss, dropping his lips to her neck and planting soft little rows of lip-tracers in a line from her shoulder to her ear. She moaned underneath him. It was time.

In a few motions he was inside of her, feeling her warmth and her wetness and losing himself in the glory of that sensation …

'Uh, Danny?'

Her voice wasn't dripping with passion anymore. He looked down and saw confusion on her face as she stared up at him and then dropped her eyes to where they were currently joined together.

'Aren't you forgetting something?' she said.

Her eyes flitted to the right, to the bedside table, where a few silver-foil-wrapped packages sat beside the mobile phones and the books.

'Can't we just …?' he asked. 'You're on the Pill, aren't you?'

A wrinkle formed in her brow and she wriggled upward, so that he slipped out. She propped herself up on an elbow and looked at him with something approaching bafflement. 'No,' she said, patiently and in a tone that brooked no argument. 'No, Danny, I can't "just". Jesus, I thought you understood that.'

'I do,' he replied, angry at himself, angry at her, grabbing for one of the foil packages, knowing full well that it was too late. The moment had passed.

He drove her to work and dropped her off. The car radio did the talking.

Danny sighed when the meeting reminder popped up. He'd been over the moon to land this graduate job. During the first two years of his degree he'd signed up with recruitment agencies over the summer break and taken whatever shitty job they threw his way.

One summer they'd sent him to the Parole Board HQ in the city centre and he'd turned up all cheerful and full of the joys to work as a receptionist.

'Good morning, sir,' he'd said to his first member of the public in a chipper and chirpy tone, the summer stretching out before him and the prospect of no-fuss money for drinking a warm and fuzzy one. 'What can I help you with?'

'Sex Offender registration.'

After that, and after a few other such bottom-of-the-rung positions, the middle management opportunities presented to him by Lircom's graduate scheme had seemed heaven-sent. Responsibility. Promotion opportunities. Decent salary. Company-subsidised bloody car! He felt as if a giant hand had reached down from on high and said, here ye are, Danny, always knew you weren't a bad lad.

As ever, though, it hadn't quite turned out the way he'd expected it to. And meetings like this were part of that small print he hadn't anticipated. He walked into the small meeting room and saw the other man had already arrived. Of course he had.

'Good morning, sir,' said Thomas.

'Morning, Tom,' he said briskly. 'How's the–' and he paused, and wished not for the first time that he had Mr Black's effortless knack, for he knew absolutely nothing about this man's private life, and wasn't sure he wanted to know. 'How's tricks?' he managed.

Thomas laughed nervously. Everything he did around Danny was done nervously. He looked as if he were permanently caught in the final few seconds of a Bond movie and didn't know whether to cut the red or the blue wire. Invariably in Danny's experience he could be relied upon to cut the fucking annoying wire. 'Tricks are grand, sir. Grand.'

'Good.'

'Well,' Thomas amended. 'I say grand, but I bought a car last week and the previous owner must have been a bit of a cat fanatic.'

Knowing he just shouldn't, but unable to stop himself, as if it were a scab that he had to pick at, Danny asked, 'Why's that, Tom?'

'Whole car smells of cat piss,' Thomas admitted freely. 'Embarrassing when I have passengers. I always make sure to tell them it's cat and not human, though.'

'That must reassure them,' Danny said faintly. He cleared his throat, staring down at the papers he'd brought into the room and fighting the urge to throw his arms around them and cling to them like they were a life-raft in choppy waters. 'You're wondering why I've called you in here,' he said.

'If it's to discuss Cal and Alice,' Thomas said, 'I'm on top of it. I'm going to tell them there's a strict policy on workplace relationships, don't worry.'

Danny frowned. 'No, that's not it, and what policy are you talking about?'

Thomas looked confused. 'The ban on office romance,' he said.

'I'm pretty sure a ban would be illegal, Tom,' Danny said. And because he could practically see what Thomas' next question would be, he felt compelled to add, 'I'm not talking about actual physical relations, so to speak, within the building. That's off-limits.'

'But the disabled toilet …'

'Those are just rumours, Tom. We've all heard them.'

'If we need proof, we could install a camera.'

'No we couldn't, Tom!'

There was silence for a moment in the room. Danny fancied that outside he could see a few heads pop up from cubicles like curious meerkats. Thomas looked cowed.

'As I was saying,' Danny said, ignoring the junior manager's hangdog expression, 'I've called you in here today to … well, this isn't easy, Tom …'

Thomas' face fell even further at those words, and didn't pick up for the five minutes it took Danny to lay it on the line. He had graphs. He had reviews. He had supporting evidence coming out of his fucking ears. He paraded it in front of Thomas' poor stunned little face until he realised he could have been showing him hardcore pornography and the other man wouldn't have batted an eyelid, such was his state of shock.

They left the room and Thomas trundled off to the workfloor to begin collecting his things. Theoretically he should have had to work the rest of this and next week, but Danny had told him he could go and he'd be fully paid up to his proper leave date. He'd square it with Mr Black. He'd told Thomas this and hadn't been sure if he'd get thanks, and sure enough no thanks had been forthcoming. But he couldn't exactly blame him.

He sat down on his chair and stared balefully at his screen. He'd just fucked a man's day, a man's week, probably his month, possibly his entire year. Delivering the news hadn't even been the hardest part. Just as it had been within his power to grant Thomas those extra days' pay, if he'd really pushed for it, he knew he could have argued for the man to be given another chance. He could have arranged for further leadership courses for him, called him in for a few chats about his managerial style.

But he'd done none of these things. Because he knew Thomas was a hopeless case. The man couldn't motivate Goths to look depressed. He was universally despised by his staff, about as effective as a Magic Tree in a sewage works.

His work phone rang. Internal number. 'Lircom, Danny Morrigan speaking.'

'Danny, it's Sarah. Mr Black is wanting a chat with you. He's on the line.'

Danny sat straighter in his chair and flicked his mouse so that the screensaver died and something that looked like work popped up on the screen. 'Yes, go ahead. Put him through.'

'Okay. Hold for a sec.'

The line clicked for a moment and then a smooth voice cut in. It sounded like the recorded voice guy who said 'Cashier number four please' at the post office.

'*In a final battle with the Formorians,*' cashier guy said in his pleasant little Oirish lilting voice, '*Nuada grew arrogant when he saw his forces marching toward victory, and refused to use his silver sword, preferring instead to attack Formorians with his bare hands. His pride caused him to lose his arm to a well-placed Formorian blow, and despite claiming victory on the battlefield that day, the Tuatha Dé rejected Nuada as king, since his disfigurement meant that their ruler, and thus their representative, would not be deemed perfect. Nuada was exiled to the countryside and his silver sword was taken from him ...*'

Danny started drumming his fingers on the desk. He moved his chair back a foot or so and stretched his neck to look inside Mr Black's office to see what he was doing and why it was taking so long, but the blinds were drawn. The voice droned on.

'The Morrigan,' cashier guy said, and Danny blinked in surprise to hear his own surname thrown out, and started to pay marginally more attention, '*fiercely loyal to Nuada, was furious at this decision, and went into exile herself. But not before taking the Spear of Destiny and shattering it into ten thousand pieces. The Tuatha eventually installed a new king, Bres, of half-Tuatha and half-Formorian descent. Bres was struck with fury when the Stone of Destiny refused to cry out beneath him, but he was able to use the sword of Nuada to re-shape the memories of everyone present so that they heard the stone cry out clearly.*'

Re-shaping memories. Wow. Some sword.

'*Only the Morrigan, watching from a distance, escaped the sword's influence and saw clearly that what she had suspected was true – Bres was no king.*'

Click.

'Danny?'

'Mr Black,' Danny said, momentarily off-guard. 'Sorry, I was …'

Laughter came down the phone line. 'I see my little trick worked. No need to apologise. Come into my office – I want to show you something.'

Danny nodded to Sarah as he passed. She smiled at him. Danny wondered, not for the first time, if the girl actually had legs; she was here every morning when he arrived and still here every evening when he went home, even when he pulled some late-nighters, and in all the time he'd worked here he had never *once* seen her away from the desk. Whatever Mr Black was paying her, clearly it wasn't nearly enough.

'Come in,' Mr Black said, as Danny opened his office door. It was a chief executive's office through and through and though he'd been inside many times before, it struck him now as if it were the first time – floor-to-ceiling windows covering one side opening out to a very grand view of Belfast's harbour estate while another wall incorporated one of those massive deluxe fish tanks in which a myriad of aquatic creatures large and small ducked and dived over and under each other in a ceaseless ballet.

There was a large and immaculate conference table with chic minimalist office chairs stationed around it, a modest but fully-stocked little bar in the far corner, and of course Mr Black's desk itself, which was three-pronged and had nary a ninety-degree angle in sight. If a woman had possessed the curves of that desk she'd have provoked erections at a hundred yards. Someday he'd sit between the legs of a desk like that, Danny promised himself. Someday …

Mr Black was sitting in his chair, which was, in Danny's opinion, not nearly throne-like enough. He'd decided if he ever climbed to the dizzy heights of chief exec he'd get a chair with bloody great flowing spike arrangements coming out its arse, like an evil Emperor, and he'd have a button on the armrest that would play a suitably *dum dum dum DUM de DUMMMM* theme tune every time he wanted someone to come in and be terrified in his presence.

Come to think of it, though, David Black didn't need a theme tune for things like that. He just needed a faint half-smile and the threat of its removal. He was in his early forties, of average height and average build, with a darker-than-normal complexion which Danny rather enviously put down to many expensive holidays abroad. He did possess striking green eyes – Danny had personally witnessed their spellbinding a fair few power-suited members of the fairer sex across the conference table.

'Sit,' he said, and Danny sat. He was holding a remote control and pointing it in the direction of a wall-set LCD TV.

'First things first,' he said. 'Did you get a chance to speak to Thomas?'

Danny nodded, very, very extremely glad indeed that he hadn't succumbed to temptation and put it off until this afternoon. 'Yes, I did.'

Mr Black inclined his head approvingly. 'Good. We can't afford to hang on to those who hold us back, Danny, unfortunate business though it may be to break bad news.'

'I know,' Danny said, and steeled himself, 'I, uh … I told him he could–'

'Go home now and still get paid until his final day?'

'Yes.' Danny winced.

Mr Black smiled. 'I thought you might. Why did you do it, can I ask?'

'Because I thought it was a nice thing to do.'

'For Thomas?' Mr Black asked mildly.

Danny frowned. 'Yes,' he said. 'I don't see who else …'

Mr Black met his gaze with the same mild detachment. 'Thomas lived and breathed this job, undoubtedly bad at it though he was. If you'd let him work until his final day, I'd bet you ten to one that by this afternoon he would have concocted a story for his staff that he'd been offered a better job somewhere else. He'd have squeezed every last drop of enjoyment out of his position before he left. By letting him go now, by telling him to go now, you took that away from him and made it seem – to his thinking – as if we couldn't wait to get shot of him. So tell me, Danny, was it really for Thomas, or was it because you felt bad about telling a man he'd lost his job, and wanted to do something to make yourself feel better?'

Danny opened then quickly closed his mouth. He wanted to deny it, but no matter which way he turned it over in his mind, Mr Black was right. 'Myself,' he admitted, and waited for the tirade to continue.

'And it's that human factor that gives you such potential,' Mr Black said, to Danny's surprise, without a trace of rebuke in his voice. 'I'm not interested in people who take pleasure from delivering bad news to my staff. But those who'll do it when it's necessary and try to empathise and soften the blow – even if they don't empathise quite right – they're the kind of leaders I'm interested in. Kudos, Danny. Kudos.'

Danny stared for a second, as if he was still waiting for the trap door to open beneath his feet. 'Thank you, sir,' he said eventually. 'You, um … you wanted to see me about something?'

'Yes!' Mr Black boomed, waving the remote. 'You've already heard some of it – a little joke on my part. I hope you didn't mind holding the line.'

Danny pieced it together. 'You're … replacing the hold music?' he asked.

'Absolutely! God how I loathe that pan pipes shit! Doesn't everyone, I ask you? How many times have you been on hold with the bank or the telephone company and thought – if I hear a fucking pan pipes version of 'Orinoco Flow' one more time in my life I shall take a sawn-off shotgun to the nearest public place and begin firing indiscriminately into the crowds?'

'Too many to count,' Danny said without a second's hesitation.

'So I thought, we've got some of the richest mythology in the world right here in Ireland. Why not relate some of it to our callers when we're unfortunately too busy to get to their valuable calls right away, rather than subject them to mental torture?'

Danny nodded. It actually wasn't a bad idea – it appealed to him, but then he was a literary buff. 'Like Cú Chulainn and all that?' he began.

'Danny!' Mr Black scowled at him, to his surprise. 'Don't tell me you're like everyone else. The moment anyone starts talking about Irish myth, everyone automatically trots out the name of that awful man and his boring tales. Imagine if the only Bond anyone ever talked about was George Lazenby …'

'That's true,' he said, frantically dredging up every scrap of knowledge about Irish mythology he'd ever half-assedly absorbed through his studies – which wasn't much. 'Thought I heard my namesake get a mention …'

'You were just getting to the good part – I baited the hook well!' Mr Black said delightedly. He hit the play button on the remote control and immediately the cashier guy voice played over the embedded 6.1 surround sound system, seeming to come from

239

all six speakers at once. Just hearing it, Danny felt naked without a parcel in his hand.

'*Rejected by the Stone of Destiny, Bres in secret decided to embrace instead his Formorian ancestry. He undermined the Tuatha and built up the strength of the Formorians, culminating in a huge battle between the two races for mastery of Ireland.*'

'It's good stuff. Very dramat–' Danny said, but was silenced by a single raised finger from Mr Black.

'*The Tuatha won the battle decisively. So it was that Bres, beaten and humiliated, sent a message to Athens, where the sorceress Carman lived with her three monstrous sons; Dub, Dother and Dian. Long had she desired the treasures of the Tuatha, particularly the Cauldron of the Dagda, and she quickly saw Bres as the weak-minded fool who would prove to be her way into Ireland to get them.*'

Mr Black stopped the story with the push of a button. He looked questioningly at Danny who judged it was now safe to speak. 'It's really good,' Danny said, and to his surprise found that he wasn't entirely blowing smoke. 'I can imagine people being quite disappointed to have to speak to one of our staff. They'll probably want to go back on hold to hear the end of the story.'

'Do you really think so?' Mr Black said, leaning across the desk. The eagerness in his voice surprised Danny a little; he hadn't expected the chief executive to care so much about Danny's opinion.

'Um, yeah,' Danny nodded. 'Absolutely,' and because he was a little freaked out by the way his boss was looking at him, he searched for a sideways move in the conversation. 'How did you come up with the idea?'

Mr Black rose from his seat and strode over to the window, spreading his arms out to encompass the magnificent view of Belfast. 'This city, Danny,' he said. 'Look at it. Do you have any idea how amazing it is? Do you have any idea how long humans lived in mud huts, eking a living from the land, lurching from crisis to crisis? Time was when a bad winter or a crop failure would have destroyed an entire community. But now, look at humanity. Living in gleaming cities of stone and metal, impregnable to all but the most extreme disasters to such a degree that new ones have to be invented so that fear does not become a meaningless concept.'

'So you're not one of these people who thinks everything was better in the old days, I'm guessing?' Danny said, rising from his own chair to stand six feet or so to the left of Mr Black, not to toady by mirroring the man's physical gestures but simply because he loved this view, loved seeing so much of his home town stretched out before him. 'I thought, with the myths and legends stuff, you were going down a nostalgic route, y'know, a more innocent age and all that.'

Mr Black stared at him searchingly. 'A more innocent age?' he said, sounding amused. 'That's not quite how I think of it. If anything, this is the innocent age, Danny. Comfort has made mankind complacent and soft. The closest thing we have to a male rite of passage now is constructing a flat-pack sideboard from Ikea. Correct?'

'Mmm,' Danny said, looking at the floor, remembering a certain effort of his own that had ended up being an eclectic, if temporary, addition to the wheelie bin.

'I simply think it might be interesting for us to reconnect with our history. Revisit an age when magic existed and when you couldn't explain everything fantastical with the three letters CGI. Have you heard of a Black Swan Event?'

Danny struggled to keep up. 'Black Swan?'

'Europeans once believed through the evidence they had available to them that all swans where white. And so the phrase 'black swan' came into use as the embodiment of the impossible. Until someone went to Australia and discovered – tah dah! – black swans swimming happily, unaware that they were meant to be impossibilities. The term Black Swan Event has come to mean something thought to be impossible which later rears up to bite you in the arse. Or break your fucking arm.'

Danny had rarely heard Mr Black speak so passionately. 'I see,' he said.

Mr Black stared out over the city. 'Beware the Black Swan Event, Danny,' he said softly. 'Beware it, but don't avoid it, for you'll find it's as laden with opportunities as it is fraught with dangers.'

'I'll bear that in mind.'

Mr Black seemed to snap out of it. The half-smile returned and he turned to Danny, all business once more. 'Now,' he said, 'back to the grind. Enjoy your dinner tonight, by the way. And when tomorrow hits, Danny …'

Danny felt compelled to finish the thought: '… it's going to be a big challenge.'

'The biggest,' Mr Black said gravely, looking him straight in the eye. 'It's going to change Ireland forever, Danny.'

That was a bit much. Despite all the hype and the PR, when you got right down to it, the Hypernet was going to give Irish people the chance to download porn quicker than anyone else. Of course, Danny would rather have gargled nails than expressed anything close to that view out loud.

'Absolutely,' was all he said.

As Danny left the office, he frowned. He must have mentioned his dinner plans to someone in the office in passing before his meeting with Thomas. News travelled fast in this place – even news as relatively mundane as his evening engagement apparently reached the chief exec. He supposed he should feel honoured.

The office doors swung shut, and Danny left Mr Black standing facing the city, looking for all the world like a ruler surveying his kingdom.

Maggie showed no sign of bringing up this morning's incident, and Danny was glad of that. They had bustled around doing various little domestic things since arriving back from work. It was just after six, and he was waiting at the front door.

'What do you think?' she said, descending the stairs and indicating her outfit, a modest knee-length fitted purple dress.

It's not your colour.

He caught himself before the words came out. 'It's lovely,' he said instead, as they locked the front door and made for the car. 'You do know we're only going to their house don't you though? I just hope the baby-drool will wash out.'

Opening the driver's door, he was surprised when she stepped across him. 'I'll drive,' she offered. 'I'm sure Steve is hoping you'll have a few beers with him tonight. Catch up.'

She was right, although it would only be a few, what with the launch tomorrow. Go-live day was shaping up to be a whirlwind of press conferences and television spots, and Mr Black had already indicated he wanted Danny to come with him.

The journey passed pleasantly enough; she had some irritating customer or other in work who wasn't quite playing ball and she chatted to him about that. He nodded and clucked in sympathy in the right places, but his heart just wasn't in it. The destination they were approaching loomed larger and larger in his mind until her voice was just a drone in the background to be responded to politely.

'Next left. Continue one hundred yards,' the satnav said.

Belfast got progressively less and less leafy as the car moved from one side of the city to the other. He could almost see the areas change from middle- to working-class; his ma still lived on this side of the city and, though he despaired to see the wee smicks and spides hanging around in shop entrances, and women young and old tramping around in public in their Primark pyjamas, he had a sense of guilt at his own snobbery in doing so. This was his home.

In Mr Black's office, when he'd stared out for a few long moments over the city, he hadn't been looking towards Kensington Avenue. He had been looking here.

'In two hundred yards, turn right.'

They swung into the estate Steve and Ellie had moved into; all terraced houses and footballs sailing this way and that. As they did so, Danny felt the detachment he'd been experiencing evaporate and he began to feel distinctly strange; claustrophobic inside the car, which was ridiculous. This car was spacious. He could have held his wedding reception in the back seats.

He scanned the houses they were cruising past. Maggie, who was still harping on about the injustices of being a legal trainee and how unreasonable customers could be, was keeping the speed at barely 20 mph so he had time to look, but he could see nothing remarkable; a succession of little houses, a few people in their front rooms moving past their windows …

'If you look to your left,' the satnav said, in a voice that was not quite its own, 'you will see a faerie rath.'

A chill ran through his body. 'What?' he said urgently. 'What did it say?'

Maggie gave him a puzzled look. 'What are you on about?' she said, a mite testily. 'Were you even listening to what–'

'It said something!' he blurted, tapping the satnav's screen accusingly. 'Something about wrath or looking and seeing! Didn't you hear it? Where the fuck are we anyway?'

He glanced at the street name. Regent Street. It seemed to resonate within him, as if he were a symphony, and this street one of its movements.

'We're here,' he said. 'Stop.'

Maggie sighed. 'Is this one of your gags?' she said. 'Because I have to tell you, I'm not really in the mood. We're not here. You told me Steve and Ellie lived in Fitzwilliam Street; it's at the far end of the estate.'

By this time they had reached the end of Regent Street and were turning left onto the main avenue connecting the other streets. Danny twisted in his seat, before looking over at Maggie. 'Turn around,' he said.

'Do what?'

'Turn us around. Take us back down. I just want to … want to hear if it happens again.'

She let loose with an epic sigh, shrugged, and pulled down the next street to the right, so that they reached the main road again. Once on it, she dutifully turned right and headed up Regent Street once more. Ready for it this time, Danny found his attention split between the satnav and the houses they were going past. He tapped the screen, hit the 'state location' button.

'Regent Street,' the satnav responded on cue. That was it.

'No …' he said, frustrated. 'It didn't even sound like its own voice before …'

'Didn't you download some Basil Fawlty voice model for it or something?' Maggie suggested, unable to hide her impatience.

Danny didn't reply. He was staring out at the street as they idled through it. He felt as if he were looking at one of those pictures that seems to be a young woman's body and then, if you looked long enough, suddenly wasn't a young woman's body at all and became an old woman's face: the shoulders became the eyes and the legs the nose and what you thought you were seeing was really something else entirely.

Yes. An old woman's face somehow seemed entirely appropriate. He couldn't shake that feeling, try as he might.

But nothing was forthcoming. No eureka moment. And as the car reached the last few houses on the street for the second time, Maggie pulled onto the kerb and killed the engine, looking over at him. 'Are you okay?' she asked simply, and her impatience had faded to be replaced with concern.

He cast his eyes down, feeling foolish. 'Yes,' he said. 'I'm … I'm sorry. I just, it was the weirdest thing.'

'Look, Danny … you've been working hard. Long hours. And I know you're doing really well in work and I'm proud of you, but maybe, after this go-live, we should go somewhere. Have a break. Just you and me. For a few days or a week. And just … relax. I mean, first that nightmare and then' – and she paused for a moment – 'and then this morning …'

He flushed instantly at the reminder, as he'd known he would the moment it was brought up. 'I'm sorry about that,' he mumbled. 'Really, I am.'

He wanted her to start the car again and get to Steve's, but to his chagrin they remained sitting there. 'I thought we agreed,' she said quietly. 'Not to, you know, take the risk of complicating things before we're good and ready. Or, you know, maybe not even then. Who knows? I thought that's what we both wanted. We have a good life, don't we?'

Sitting in that car, thinking about the house they'd just left, the job he had, he couldn't really argue with her or deny that what she was saying was right. On paper he had everything he'd always visualised having when he worked through school.

'Yeah. We do.'

She smiled and he could see she was genuinely attempting to lighten the mood. 'After tonight you'll probably want to wear three at a time.'

'Don't,' he said sharply, before he could stop himself.

Her eyes widened in surprise. 'What?'

'Don't talk about him like that.'

'Talk about …? Aaron?' she said, now very confused.

'Yeah,' he replied, though something about it didn't seem to fit. 'Don't talk about him like he's some sort of … I dunno, cautionary example, okay? He's a child.'

'Okay,' she said, still a little taken aback. 'It was just a joke.'

'Okay, well …' he looked out of the window beyond her.

And then the colour drained from his face altogether and his expression twisted into one of pure shock. Maggie, on noticing this, felt a twinge of fear and found herself following his line of sight to see what it was that had caused such a reaction.

There was an old woman by the car. She was hunched over, partially from age it looked like, but mostly because she wanted to look inside. Her eyes were fixed on Danny.

Maggie rolled down her window. 'Can I help you?' she asked the woman, feeling some unease herself.

The woman completely ignored her.

'Believe me now?' the old woman said, staring straight at Danny.

Maggie felt Danny's hand on her arm. 'Drive,' he said, his voice strained and faraway, his eyes still locked on the old woman's, seemingly unable to break free. 'Go. Just go.'

They set off, the old dear receding, though she continued staring after the car until they eventually made the left turn towards Fitzwilliam Avenue.

'Wanker!'

'Fuckface!'

Greetings with Danny thus exchanged, Steve turned his

attention to Maggie and smoothly changed gears. 'Maggie,' he said gravely. 'Good to see ye, love.'

'Good to see you too, Steve,' she replied, sounding slightly bemused.

'Find the place all right?'

Walking into the house, Danny and Maggie exchanged a glance. 'Yeah,' Danny answered, carefully. 'No problem.'

'The wee fella's just getting fed,' he said, pointing upstairs to indicate where it was taking place.

'Oh, good – he'll be settled during dinner then,' Danny said instantly.

Steve blinked. So did Maggie. 'Uh, yeah,' Steve nodded, giving Danny a look. 'So, um, feel free to come on through to the sittin' room. You're lookin' well, Maggie.'

Danny cast a sideways look at his friend. Back in the day when Maggie and Ellie had roomed together, the first night he and Steve had met the two girls he'd paired with Ellie and Steve had paired with Maggie. Nothing serious had happened between the two, so far as he knew, but the way he'd said that … was he still carrying a bit of a torch for her?

She smiled and curtseyed exaggeratedly. 'And you,' she returned. 'Fatherhood agrees with you.'

Steve snorted. 'Agrees with what part of me? The bags under my eyes or the spare tyre?'

It was true, Danny had to admit. His friend looked like shit, but Maggie was hardly going to tell him that, was she? She flushed, her attempt at diplomacy thwarted. Danny decided it was time to wade to her rescue. 'You can't blame that on fatherhood, lad,' he pointed out, as they entered the sitting room (tiny, cluttered) and sat down on the settee (bumpy, cheap). 'You've always been prone to bein' a lazy fucker, let's be honest.'

'Danny!' Maggie said, horrified.

'Ach listen to him,' Steve said easily, 'a swanky job and a big motor and he's King Dick. Tell me, Maggie love, is it true what they say about fellas with big cars needing to make up for things in other departments?'

'Fuck,' Danny whistled, 'if that's true, lad, what's your next mode of transport gonna have to be? The space shuttle?'

'I've taken yer ma to heaven and back a few times on my mode of transport …'

'Balls. The only Close Encounters you've ever had are of the Turd Kind, ya big woofter.'

Maggie's head was moving back and forth like a spectator in the front row at Wimbledon. The two boys seemed to notice they were leaving her behind a little and slowed the pace of the back-and-forth with a noticeable downshift. Steve asked Maggie a few questions about her job, giving Danny time to breathe and to think.

The old woman … how did he know her? How had she known him? Why had he frozen when he saw her wizened old face leaning towards him? *Believe me now?* What did that even mean?

'… a drink?'

He surfaced again, and pieced together what he'd missed. 'Yeah, that'd be great.'

'C'mon give us a hand, lad,' Steve said, indicating the kitchen. Danny nodded and met Maggie's eyes; she winked at him for a half-second and he squeezed her hand.

The kitchen was incredibly narrow. He was able to lay a hand each on the counter to the right and the little breakfast bar to the left. Boxes of cereal in various states of use littered the place. Empty bottles stood on the counter. Something was doing in the microwave; he could see the counter counting down from ten seconds. Steve was stooping down to open the under-counter fridge; he had already fished a few bottles of Stella from its interior.

Ding.

Remove steriliser from microwave using safety grips. Spin. Grab tea towel from oven door. Wrap around hand. Unscrew steriliser top. Yank hand away from escaping steam. Place lid on draining board ...

'Lad?'

Danny stopped and looked into the astonished face of his oldest friend. 'What?'

'What are you doing?'

'I'm ...' he began, and then trailed off. Steam was escaping from the steriliser. He looked at the freshly-sterile bottles and bottle tops within and knew that if he lined them up in a row, which wasn't strictly necessary but did look really good, all he had to do then was pour the boiled water from the kettle ...

Danny found that he had no words.

'Not that I don't appreciate the help,' Steve said, and laughed to break the tension. 'All *this* shit doesn't come natural to me, even after months of practice. Ellie says the other day it's like I only just started. You been, ah' – and he grinned and dropped his voice to conspiratorial levels – 'you been takin' a course or something?'

Got plans?' and he made a baby rocking motion with the bottles of Stella he still held in his arms.

'No,' was all Danny said. He took the bottle and cracked its lid off with the bottle opener Steve handed him, sinking a long and cool draught that was as welcome as it was necessary.

They moved back to the living room, after Steve got Maggie a Diet Coke ('sorry no lemon' he'd said apologetically, God love him). Danny sat beside his girlfriend and gave her a little upturned tug of his mouth to indicate things were going well, though to be honest he was growing more and more agitated by the second.

Footsteps down the stairs. And there they were, standing at the living room door.

'You're all right,' he said, up out of his seat, practically collapsing with relief. 'You're okay,' and he was this close to throwing his arms around them both, around Ellie and the little boy she was holding, when the little fella turned around (he'd been dangling over her shoulder while she rubbed his back) and looked, goggle-eyed and bobble-headed, into Danny's eyes.

He stopped in his tracks.

Everyone had.

'Um,' Ellie said eventually, to break the silence. 'It's good to see you, Danny. Steve, have you been telling people you've murdered me again?'

'Only now and again,' Steve offered weakly, looking back and forth at his friend and his girlfriend. Danny could feel Steve's eyes boring into the back of his head, but that was nothing compared to the twin laser beams of intensity being drilled into the side of his face by Maggie. It was a wonder he didn't spontaneously combust. At this point, he would have welcomed it.

'Ach!!! He! Is! Gorgeous!' Maggie said, finally turning off the Stare of Certain Death and standing up to greet Ellie. She placed her glass carefully on the windowsill before approaching mother and son. 'Look at you, wee man! Look at you! Where's the wee man?'

Aaron's head jiggled crazily in response.

'Hey, Maggie. Long time.'

Maggie adopted her usual approach to situations with the potential to develop into awkwardness, which was to adopt a veil of geniality and push through them head-on.

'Yeah, hasn't it? Hard to believe! Uni seems like another lifetime doesn't it?'

'Yes,' Ellie said with feeling and with absolute conviction. 'Yes it does.'

There was a pause.

'I love your dress, Maggie,' Ellie said. 'I used to have one like that.'

Danny could have sworn he heard a slight sigh from Steve when she said that.

'Thank you,' Maggie beamed. 'I was amazed when it fitted. Thought I'd ballooned to a size 12.'

'I wouldn't hold him … he's just had five ounces,' Ellie went on, neatly ignoring the size comment completely – Danny could see she'd put on a little weight since the last time he'd seen her, but she didn't look the worse for it and *he really wanted to hold her*.

Fuck. Christ. This was a huge mistake. How was he going to

get through an entire night of this? For a moment he considered panicking and simply heading for the door, but try as he might he couldn't handle the thought of moving away from Ellie. More than anything right now he wanted to simply touch her, to make sure she was real, that it was really her standing there safe and sound in front of him.

'I'll just leave him in Mummy's capable hands then,' Maggie said, not exactly dismayed at the prospect. She was standing beside Danny now, and he felt her fingers snake around his forearm and hold tight, not a coupley type squeeze of the sort they'd had only minutes before – this one said *I'm watching you*.

They sat and the conversation started between all four, splitting and splintering sometimes on the natural male/female divide when football or clothes shops would rear their heads as topics, or when parenting/social lives came up.

Danny could sense that maybe an hour ago, two at the most, Steve and Ellie had had some sort of argument; certain words, phrases that cropped up in conversation, mostly to do with socialising and the lack of opportunity to participate in the same, would cause a look to be passed between them.

Mind you, he wasn't exactly out of the doghouse himself after his performance when Ellie and Aaron had entered the room. Maggie was being all smiles and pleasantries and teeth-baring grins, her fingers firmly intertwined with his own, but it was more a gesture of forcible restraint than of easy affection.

Aaron eventually conked out in his mother's arms. Steve, Danny noticed, had yet to hold his son. Some part of him burned slightly at this; some other part wondered why.

'Fuck,' Steve said, checking his watch, 'I better go check the chicken.'

'Not in polite company, please,' Ellie replied instantly. Danny laughed, then winced as the fingers holding his grew tighter. Steve stuck his tongue out and disappeared into the kitchen. Ellie looked down at the slumbering little boy in her arms and sighed.

'I'd better go out and help him. He did dinner a month ago for my parents and I swear, we had to get Quincy in to do the autopsy.'

'I heard about that,' Danny chimed in gravely. 'That was no suicide. That … was murder.'

She nodded. 'Thankfully we were able to call in Columbo and just arrest the first person he wouldn't leave the fuck alone.'

Danny laughed. He couldn't help it. Some part of him felt sorry for Steve going up against Ellie in a battle of wits: there was a mismatch made in heaven. Mostly, though, he just found himself marvelling at how many memories the nonsense banter they'd engaged in brought back.

She stood up, awkwardly because she was holding little Aaron, and started looking around for something. 'Steve?' she called.

'Here, let me,' Danny offered, extricating himself from Maggie's death grip and walking to the far end of the room. Reaching down behind the stereo, he picked up a pile of blankets stored there and started to spread them in the centre of the room. Green at the bottom (it was the thickest of the blankets but also the least comfortable for direct skin contact), then the little red one with the teddy bear in the corner, and finally the blue blanket, the one that zipped around the front, spread out on top.

Isn't this when the wee fella's supposed to start crying and we look at each other and sigh?

I bribed him with the emergency fiver.

Staring down at the layers of blankets he'd just organised, he realised the snatches of conversation and fragments of domestic life flashing across his mind didn't feel like fantasies, or daydreams. They were too mundane for that, too normal.

They felt like memories.

He straightened up. Ellie was staring at him in astonishment. Maggie's gaze was moving between him and Ellie, the baby, and the blankets, as if she were trying to add something up but not particularly liking any of the component parts.

'Did I do it right?' he said, keeping his voice level. 'Steve told me where they were.'

Ellie raised her eyebrows. 'Either you didn't hear him right, or Steve actually remembered the correct order for the first time in, um, ever. But yeah, thanks.'

He made his excuses and headed upstairs to the bathroom, supposedly for a piss, but really just to be somewhere that wasn't that room. Staring into the mirror in that tiny bathroom, looking around at the detritus of Ellie and Steve's domestic bliss – the little baby seat that he knew little Aaron lolled semi-limply in when it was bath time, the plastic duckies – he had to fight the wave of nausea that rolled over him.

The revulsion wasn't caused by the objects themselves; it came from the rapid-fire sensations of déjà vu that were thudding through him like some sort of memorygasm, carrying his brain away from where he stood and sending it spinning off, changing his perception of the world. The bathroom where he stood was just as small as it had been a moment ago but now it was formatted a little differently. The bath seat wasn't white, it was yellow ... yellow with little daisies on the side ... and downstairs ... those were the blankets where little Luke slept. He'd known where to get them and how they were ordered because he'd done it one hundred, two hundred times before ... the bottles, Christ Almighty he could make Luke's bottles in his sleep, and often enough he had.

Luke. *Yes.* Luke.

His name is Luke.

That was why he'd stopped in his tracks when the little head had turned to look at him. He'd been expecting a different baby. Sure, Aaron had a look of Luke about him, but he wasn't the same.

He wasn't his.

And now he did throw up, hunched over the toilet, bile filling his mouth as the sense of déjà vu coalesced from formless impressions and half-baked feelings to concrete things – to faces and dates and names and events. It overwhelmed him. His eyes filled with tears, and for a long moment he thought he would pass out from trying to wade through the overload.

A knock at the bathroom door. Maggie's voice. Asking if he was all right. Maggie. He'd almost had sex with her this morning. He would have done if she'd let him do it without a condom. Jesus Christ. Jesus fucking Christ. But that wasn't the worst.

Ellie and Steve were together.

The thought was so patently absurd that for an instant he didn't know whether to throw up again or burst out laughing, not that either option was going to help him.

He cast his mind back, back to the last memory he had of what could be considered 'reality', if that word even still existed. The last two years of memories from this world were still there; but now rather than presenting themselves as the true history, he could see in his mind that they were overlaid on the previous version of his own reality – a superimposed image, a green screen. His entire life had been treated like a special effect.

Anger. Yes, Jesus, yes, anger felt so good. He needed to stop with the self-pity, stop with the wallowing and the crying and the throwing up in toilets. Enough of it.

Bea. Bea and her warning. That was the last 'real' memory he had. Bea whose face had appeared at his car window just over an hour ago and had asked him – *do you believe me now?*

She knew. She had known everything all along, and he'd been too fucking stupid and closed-minded to believe what had been in front of his own eyes.

All of this flashed through his mind in a second, all of this and more; back to him came the synaesthesia, which somehow they'd stolen away along with Ellie and Luke. Why? Why take a neurological disorder? Who, for that matter? Who was doing all of this to him? Who had taken Ellie and Luke in the first place, and replaced them with this impossibly complex looking-glass world?

'I'm fine,' he called, forcing himself to his feet and to the sink. A bottle of mouthwash sat beside the cold tap. He knocked back a capful, swizzed and spat to rid his mouth of the remnants of puke.

The important thing was that Ellie was here. Ellie was back, she wasn't missing any more. Okay, technically in this wanky place she wasn't his Ellie, but Jesus Christ at least she was alive; that was why he had been so delighted, so tempted to wrap her up in his arms the moment he set his eyes on her.

It was time. He opened the bathroom door. 'Sorry, love,' he told Maggie. 'Stomach upset. You're right. Stress. Holiday needed.'

'Do you want to go?' she said, in a tone of voice that suggested that if he said yes she would not treat it as the worst piece of news in the world.

'Go?' he said, shaking his head. 'You joking? I can't wait to get stuck in.'

The Belly of the Whale

It was a mistake. He'd known it had been all along. Somehow they'd mixed up his report with someone else's, one of the other managers. He'd known it the moment it was suggested that he'd lost the respect of the staff. That wasn't him! The staff loved him. Okay, maybe not love – definitely not in the sense of the disabled toilet's extra curricular use – but they respected him, and besides, it didn't do to get too close to the troops, did it? You never knew when you might be called upon to give one of them the bad news. Best to keep a professional distance.

'I'm here to see Mr Black?'

'Go on in, Thomas,' said Sarah, flashing him a dazzling smile. 'He's expecting you.'

In he went. It was late – getting on for after half seven – and Sarah had been most apologetic about the time when she'd rung him to request he come in and speak to Mr Black to discuss his employment situation. He had jumped at the chance; literally jumped out of his chair in his eagerness. He was still had on the work clothes he'd been wearing that morning, when that little fucker Morrigan had given him the news.

Despite the time, the chief executive's office was still stunning, the vista of Belfast just beginning to show pinpricks of illumination here and there, more winking into existence with each passing moment as the streetlights came on, one after the other. He could see the lights of the ferry as it moved up the harbour away from the Lircom building.

'Thomas. Do come in.'

'Yes, sir,' Thomas gabbled, trying to calm down without any degree of success. He'd only been in this office twice before and both times it had been with a group of other junior managers. Standing here alone, he was overwhelmed by it all.

'Sit down,' the chief executive said, indicating the chair opposite his own. Thomas sat.

'Excuse the hour, Thomas. But I didn't want to risk leaving this until tomorrow morning in case anyone had headhunted you by then.'

'Well' – Thomas sucked in a breath – 'to be honest with you, sir, even by being here I'm probably breaking a verbal contract I had with Microsoft. They wanted me to come over and run one of their support divisions at headquarters.'

The corner of Mr Black's mouth twitched. 'Oh?' he said. 'In Redmond?'

'No, sir, at their headquarters,' Thomas said patiently.

Mr Black covered his mouth for a second, apparently to cough. 'Yes, well,' he said. 'I have a role for you.'

'Management?'

'More testing than management. But definitely high-level testing, Thomas.'

High level. Thomas almost fainted in ecstasy. 'That sounds like quite a challenge,' he said.

Mr Black's smile faded. He was deadly serious now. 'It's vital. Pivotal, you might even go so far as to say. And the results of your analysis will be key. Of course to reflect the additional responsibility, we'll have to bring you in as an executive. Seat on the board … fifty thousand a year … company car. Would that suit you?'

'Buh.'

'I'm sorry?'

Thomas tried again. 'Yuh,' he managed.

Mr Black clapped his hands together. 'Excellent! Let the records show you entered into this of your own volition. I'll even text Mr Gates and let him know.'

'Who?'

'Never mind, Thomas. Moving swiftly on! Let's start right now with your duties, shall we?'

And Mr Black moved. Or at least he must have, because one moment he was sitting on his chair opposite Thomas, and the next he was perched on the desk – right on top of the desk and close enough to touch.

Thomas felt a thrill of fear and uncertainty. What kind of job was this … ?

As if at some private joke, Mr Black laughed. Thomas didn't just seem to hear the laughter, musical and melodious though it was; for a moment, the strangest sensation coursed through him – that the laughter tasted of tin and smelled like darkness. He felt it like a pulse, a single throb, and to anyone watching it would have looked as though someone had reached inside Thomas' soul and switched him off and on again.

With an almost audible *whee*, all of his doubts evaporated, along with all thoughts he could have called his own. He stared into nothing, mute and attentive, his mouth hanging slightly open, as Mr Black sat on his massive three-pronged desk, and began to tell him a story. It was a story about a king, and a witch, and her sons ... and as the words washed through him, each one more captivating than the one before, Thomas was warmer and more comfortable and content than he had ever been, or ever would be.

'When it comes right down to it, Thomas,' Mr Black was now saying, a note of regret in his voice, 'nothing much has changed. Oh sure now we have networks and cables where once we had chalk and incense, but the secret is, this is still a single currency market. And that currency, Thomas, is blood. When it gets moving, there'll be no stopping it, but like every engine, the Network needs a little kick to get it going. That's where you come in. Now, take my pen, there's a good man.'

Thomas took it. It was a fountain pen, ornate and heavy, and black ink dripped from its nib. Mr Black leaned forward until his features were thrown into relief by the light cast from the desk lamp. He was not wearing the mini-smile now.

'Good, Thomas. Very good. Now, stab it into your neck.'

Thomas felt the pain like he would have felt a gust of air from someone closing a door half an office away. Warmth spread across the fingers of his right hand, and it became harder and harder to breathe properly, so his breaths started to come in raggedy gasps.

The sticky warmth was seeping down the front of his body now.

'Sarah,' Mr Black said, pressing a button on his desk intercom. 'Can you come in here, please?'

Through fading vision Thomas saw a second figure enter the room and move to stand beside the chief executive, and at some distant level he had the thought that it was the first time he'd seen Sarah move out from behind that desk.

But, considering she had the lower half of a spider, perhaps that wasn't particularly surprising.

'Finish that off and clean it up, will you?' Mr Black said.

'Right away, Mr Black,' Sarah said.

Thomas' eyes were locked straight ahead as Sarah scuttled from beside Mr Black. All eight of her long legs were covered in black chitinous interwoven plates of what looked like armour – with stiff black hairs that jutted out and rippled as she moved.

Thomas wondered, with an odd sense of detachment – no doubt due to the substantial blood loss – if she had just been cramming the immense bulk of her legs and her swollen carapace beneath that expansive desk she sat behind for all this time, wedging herself in with an incredible level of discomfort, yet still managing to smile sweetly at people and wave them in.

He couldn't remember her having rows of needle-sharp teeth before. But as those teeth sank into the loose, tattered folds of skin ruptured by the pen's thrust at his neck, Thomas' brain, now becoming lethally starved of oxygen, managed to focus and for one final moment he came back to consciousness.

He tried to scream, to call out, but it was already over. Sarah's carapace wrenched powerfully, her teeth still locked in his neck, and ripped his head clean off his shoulders.

The receptionist began to feast.

'Microsoft's loss is our gain,' murmured Mr Black, walking to the window and looking out over the city once more. His eyes focused on one street in particular, even as the crunching and snapping of bones behind him told him that Sarah was busy offering Thomas her own unique brand of severance package.

It was all anatomically incorrect of course; real spiders couldn't eat anything solid. They had to liquefy their prey and consume it through a feeding tube, like a milkshake through a straw.

Where was the fun in that?

'Well done, Danny,' he said softly. 'Not long to go now, my boy. Not long at all.'

Slam.

'What was that?' Ellie called from the kitchen, where the smell of chicken and vegetables was getting stronger by the minute. 'Did something fall? Aaron okay?'

Danny lifted his boot from the carcass. Something had been scuttling across the floor; a harmless little money spider, but in his book anything that scuttled in the presence of a child deserved an instant and merciless death. 'It's fine,' he called out. 'Just a bug.'

Maggie was making a face, which he considered a little unfair; their own place in Kensington was occasionally full of the fuckers as well, so it wasn't like creepy-crawlies were class conscious. He remembered one time last September opening their hot press and finding–

Except … it was bullshit, wasn't it?

He turned the memory over in his mind, trying to poke at it from all angles to see if it would deflate like a popped balloon. It didn't. He could clearly remember last September going to their upstairs hot press, looking for a towel because there hadn't been one on the towel rail when he'd emerged from the shower, and when he'd pulled one of the towels down from the shelf, it had fallen, legs kicking crazily, and as soon as it had hit the ground, that horrible tangle of legs had sorted themselves out in an instant and it had raced across the carpet, only to come to an end under his searching heel.

Danny had been terrified of spiders and creepy-crawlies his entire life. Hadn't ever been able to look at one without going somewhere to convulse quietly for a good ten minutes afterwards.

He'd first befriended Steven Anderson in school because in primary four, a big fat spider had been crawling up Danny's desk, getting inexorably closer to him. Little Danny Morrigan had sat there, his eyes filling with tears, unable to move, forced to watch it approach and knowing that either its lazily unfolding legs would cross the boundary from wooden desk to soft flesh, or he would have to give in to his urge to stand up and scream in front of an entire class of ruthlessly judgemental little boys.

Steve, sitting to his left and, until that moment just someone vaguely on his radar, had *splatted* it with a nonchalant hand and – this had been the crucial factor in the immediate gestation of a lifelong friendship – he had seen the naked fear in Danny's eyes and he hadn't mentioned it ever, ever again, to anyone.

Now though – whatever they'd done, whoever 'they' were – his memories remained, but the fear was gone, and Danny had the strangest feeling that for a reason he couldn't begin to fathom, in doing so they'd made a monumental fuck-up.

But how? How had they done all this in the first place? How had they created such perfect lies?

Lies, memories. There was something that could create memories …

His synaesthesia reared up, right on cue. Jesus, how he'd missed that feeling, disorientating though it was. He was in Mr Black's office, listening to cashier guy's Irish mythology stories … yes. Yes.

The Sword of Nuada …? But that was just a myth.

What, like faeries are a myth?

Okay, fine. Fuck it. A magic silver sword was real, faeries were real, and both had decided to fuck around with his life. Brilliant. Where did that leave him? And why was he immune? Why was 'remembering' his power? What made him so different?

'You're miles away again,' Maggie observed.

'Sorry,' he said, and found that he meant it. Maggie … Ellie … Steve … as far as they all knew, this was the way things had always been. They were innocents in this. His eyes fell to Aaron's sleeping form. They weren't the only ones. Aaron wasn't Luke, but that didn't mean he wasn't anyone's either. He was Steve and Ellie's.

What if he was able to find some way to put things back the way they were? What would happen to them all? What would happen to little Aaron?

He already knew the answer. The same thing that had

happened to Luke. He would vanish without trace, with no one there to mourn him because no one would remember his existence. Looking down at that little sleeping bundle snoring quietly through his tiny nose, the truth of this shocked him, but not half as much as the realisation which followed hard on its heels, which was: *Luke was there first. And Luke is mine.* There was nothing civilised about that thought, nothing but primal protectiveness and love for his son.

He had only two real leads: Bea, and Michael Quinn. He knew for a fact that Quinn knew something about what was going on. He went back over his meeting with the older man the day before, and there was no mistaking the fucker's body language. Then there was the comment from Steve about Quinn forgetting his own grandson's name …

As the dinner started, as they sat around the dining table in the front room, Danny took his opportunity to pursue this line of enquiry. 'I met your da yesterday, Ellie,' he said, casually.

'Did you?' Ellie said. 'I haven't spoken to him since yesterday morning – I wonder if he'd have mentioned it to me.'

'He seemed a bit distracted,' Danny observed.

Ellie's face clouded and she shot a quick interrogatory *have you been slabberin' about my ones to your mates* look at Steve, who despite being innocent of all charges, wisely kept his face composed and buried himself in the business of dishing out the mashed potatoes. 'Well, he's been a little … preoccupied with the Lircom buyout of his company.'

'Yeah, we were all a bit rocked by that.'

'He hates Lircom. He always has. It came as a surprise to me too,' Ellie shrugged. 'But he has told me before that the Lircom chief exec can be extremely persuasive.'

Danny felt something form in his mind, a sense of some overall picture, for the first time since all of this madness began. There was some pattern he was missing, some key he wasn't quite seeing. He tried to visualise it like he could numbers; he gave the various strands of information their own colour, their own smell. He wasn't sure whether he did so out of a genuine expectation that it would help, or just because he had missed his synaesthesia so much he wanted another excuse to revel in it like a cat in catnip.

Steve yawned ostentatiously. 'Maggie,' he said, 'what did you think of the Prussian army's decision to mobilise against France in 1870?'

Maggie almost choked on her broccoli. 'I don't know much about history,' she said apologetically.

'Oh it doesn't matter,' Steve said, 'this is the *boring the arse off everyone* section of the dinner. Did you miss the memo?'

'Fuck you up,' Danny said, jabbing a chicken leg at Steve. 'Just showing some concern is all, all right?'

'And I appreciate it, Danny,' Ellie said, skewering Steve with another menacing glower. 'I'm a wee bit worried about Daddy myself.'

'Aye, his memory's fucked,' Steve said casually.

'His memory is not "fucked"!' Ellie said, eyes flashing dangerously. 'Jesus, Steve! Can you ever go a single sentence without using the word "fuck" in some form or other?'

'Ah c'mon!' Steve retorted. 'He called his own grandson … what was it …?'

'Luke,' Ellie said quietly.

'Jesus,' Steve said over the sudden explosion of coughing from Danny, 'you all right, lad? Choke on a chicken bone?'

'Mmm ... fine,' Danny nodded, covering his mouth. When he'd recovered, he sank his teeth into the chicken leg he still held in his other hand, both to hide his expression and, quite simply, to satisfy his sudden urge to sink his teeth into something. Michael fucking Quinn's fucking head wasn't fucking here, so this would have to fucking do until he got his hands on the bastard.

It was true. Quinn knew. At the very least, *he knew*. At worst – what? This whole fuckin' mess was his fault somehow? One way or another he'd find the fucker and beat some answers out of him, find that sword he must be carrying about and create some memories right up his hole if he didn't fix the mess he'd made of everyone's lives ...

What mess, Danny?

He closed his eyes for a second, trying to push the thought away, but it too had sunk its teeth in and wouldn't be shaken loose so easily.

What mess would that be, Danny? The mess where you've a beautiful girlfriend, a big house, a crackin' job, a top-drawer motor, the ear of the head of the company, and where you can fall asleep at night and know that there won't be screams wakening you, or shitty nappies, or bottle making, or the Playhouse-fucking-Disney channel? Where your mates are still your mates, and you haven't scared them off by catching responsibility and them being convinced it's contagious?

All of that righteous anger he'd been building up since his epiphany in the bathroom, strengthened only seconds ago by

Ellie's revelation about her father, was threatening to seep away.

As it turned out, all it took was the tiniest of whimpers from little Aaron sleeping in the next room.

Hearing it, Danny was immediately up and out of his seat, the dinner forgotten.

He caught himself, already on his way to go check on Aaron, as he stared, for the umpteenth time that night, into faces full of incomprehension. Maggie and Steve hadn't so much as moved from their seats.

Ellie had, however. Ellie was out of her seat too, though she'd paused when Danny had done the same thing. She looked at him and he thought … maybe it was his imagination, but he thought, for a second, he saw some flicker there, some buried knowledge in her eyes that at some level she knew something was wrong with all of this too.

'I'm sorry,' Danny said, to Maggie first, and then to Steve.

He took two steps forward, kissed Ellie full on the lips, and walked out of the house, the taste of purple and the sensation of rightness still fresh on his lips.

Back in the dining room, all was quiet.

'Are you not supposed to drop car keys into the middle of the table first or somethin'?' Steve asked into the silence.

He rapped her door, once, twice, three times. On the third knock she answered and, seeing him standing on her doorstep, nodded curtly at him. 'About time.'

'I'm sorry,' he said.

She cocked her head to look at him, giving him possibly the most inquisitive look he'd ever received in his entire life. Body cavity searches had been less thorough. Jesus, Mr Black was less thorough.

'Yes, I think you are,' she said, and he thought he detected approval in her tone. She reached behind the front door and came up holding something he recognised.

He took the spade from her, weighed it, turned it over in his hands. It felt heavy, solid, and real. His fingers curled around it as if drawing strength directly from its very existence.

'What do I do?' he asked her.

'What you were born to do,' she said, and with this, she closed the door.

Or at least, she tried to. She would have, but his foot was jammed in the doorway like only the best *Watchtower* salesmen.

'Oh no you fuckin' don't,' he said firmly, pushing the door back open again. 'Sick of this cryptic ballix, thank you very fuckin' much. None of this wee clues shite and then you close the door all mysteriously and then I stand here and it takes me another fuckin' Christ-knows-how-long to figure it all out. I've seen all them films. Fuck them films. You seem to know all the answers, love. So you're gonna just tell me.'

She looked affronted. 'That's not how it works,' she protested.

He lifted the spade. 'Do I look like I give a flyin' fuck?' he said. 'I'm pretty sure wee old ladies don't get twatted on the head by the hero for wastin' his time either, but let's see what we can do about improvising as we go along, eh?'

It hadn't escaped Danny's notice that since his final dinner-table epiphany back at Ellie and Steve's, his transformative cocoon was almost gone. Even his speech was reverting back to normal. His arse had received a pole-uppendectomy. He'd metaphorically shaved off his evil, mirror-world goatee. Finally, for the first time he could remember in far too long, he felt comfortable in his own skin, something that he could never hope to achieve by sitting in high-powered meetings.

'The hero is it?' she snorted. 'Someone's a high opinion of himself.'

He was about to reply, but she shrugged, reached for a shawl and threw it around herself before joining him outside. She linked his arm, to his surprise, and they began to walk down her path. 'Tell me what you know first,' she said, as casually as if she were discussing the weather.

'I think I have to find some sort of Sword,' he said, being careful to drop the uppercase S in there to give it its proper respect, 'that can reshape memories. I've a feelin' it's not exactly gonna be in the Ulster Museum, is it?'

'The Sword of Nuada,' she said. 'It's held in the Otherworld. Their kingdom. To go there you'll have to pass through a gateway.'

'Right. Gateway. Otherworld. Well that's not so bad is it?' he said, though, truth be told, he had been nursing a hope that, if he stopped to examine what was going on, this world would melt away around him. No, too much had happened, too much raw power had been demonstrated by beings capable of reshaping lives, memories, for it to be that easy.

'It'll be incredibly dangerous. No mortal has been there and returned to tell of it for fifteen hundred years,' she said matter-of-factly, and then shivered. 'Fuck me. It's freezin' tonight.'

'Oh,' he said, absorbing Bea's brand of pep talk.

They were in Regent Street now. Standing in front of his old front gate. Hard to believe he'd driven past this house twice only a few hours previously and not had the memories flood; those countless times returning with the shopping; lugging Luke's pram up the front step; coming in from work exhausted; seeing Ellie getting up to greet him through the living room window.

'Don't worry,' she told him, squeezing his arm. 'I said *mortals*, after all.'

'What's that meant to–' he began, but she had slipped out of his grasp with a spryness that belied her years, and was knocking on the door of his house. No, not his house, *their* house – the couple answering the door to her now.

In the doorway stood a woman with two little girls hiding behind her legs and, coming up the hallway to stand in front of her, a man who looked, with no small measure of confusion and suspicion, at Bea on his doorstep and Danny, spade in hand, standing on his lawn.

'Ach, Casey love, what about ye?' Bea asked easily. 'This is our Danny, my wee nephew. He's doing a degree in landscape gardening at Queen's and his practical examination is coming up in three weeks, God love him!'

'Uh ... okay ...' Casey – who was the sort of burly man that Danny did *not* want to have a disagreement with in the near future – said, with more than a little doubt entering his voice.

'Well, love, would you mind if he flattened out your wee

garden? It's part of his landscape practical only. Free of charge. Isn't that right, love?'

'Absolutely,' Danny agreed. Jesus. Were all old people this devious?

Casey hesitated, clearly smelling something was slightly off about the prospect of a university student offering to landscape his garden at 8.45 p.m. on a Friday night.

'God love ye,' Bea added.

He melted in the face of the God love ye. 'Aye sure, go on,' he said.

'I've been asking him to flatten that thing for months!' his wife chimed in from behind him. She leaned past her husband to address Danny. 'Want a wee cup of tea, love?'

Danny shrugged. What the hell. 'Yeah, thanks,' he said, sending the spade's head into the soil, wondering if he was destined to spend the rest of his life digging up this fuckin' hole. Ah well. It beat rolling a rock up a hill, he supposed.

Bea winked at him. 'I'll see you later,' she said, and disappeared into his – *Casey's* – house.

He got to work.

'He is breaching the rath,' Sarah reported, skittering across from the desk to where her boss stood at the window. Not a trace remained of the late, unlamented Thomas Doonan; not a finger, not a single hair. He had been wiped clean from the face of the Earth.

'I know,' Mr Black said. He could feel the vibrations, as if

275

someone was reaching out and plucking one of the strings of reality itself.

'Again,' she added pointedly.

'I know.'

'He rejected the world we created for him.'

'I know. Wonderful, isn't it? Mother will be thrilled.'

'Should I stop him?'

Mr Black laughed softly. 'In the middle of the city, before night has even fallen?' he said. 'We'd be exposed, my dear.'

'Soon, such concerns won't matter,' Sarah said, betraying her emotions with a trace of hunger in her voice and an involuntary semi-skitter of her legs – a little spider-dance of excitement.

He glanced across at his greatest creation and pursed his lips in amusement. 'Yes, I can see how you'd say that,' he said. 'But we're not there just yet. Much is in the balance.' and he was silent for a moment, deep in thought. 'Leave him be. He's not ready. Let him enter' – and seeing her reaction, he stared at her in direct challenge – 'I said *let him enter*. Do you have a problem with that?'

One of her backmost legs thumped, once, on the ground, her only outward demonstration of the emotions raging beneath. 'No,' she said.

'Good,' he said and he walked back to his desk, pressing a button on its side which Danny, had he been here to see it, would have been slightly disappointed to see did *not* open up a giant trap door in the floor. It did, however, slide back a wall panel to reveal a glass case set into the wall.

The room was bathed in a silver glow.

'Let him enter,' Mr Black said softly. 'And get me Michael

Quinn. I want to see him. Tonight.'

'Yes, sir.'

He watched her move across the room on that flowing mass of legs, as stable as a rock, as deadly as anything that had ever walked the earth. With Sarah outside his door, he feared nothing.

He smiled, luxuriating in the silver glow, before touching the button again. The hidden panel slid back, hiding the sword from view. Mr Black walked to the windows, hands clasped behind his back. The lights of Belfast stretched out in every direction.

When the Network was activated, there would be plenty of fear to go around.

He wasn't prepared for the *clunk*. The *clunk* threw him. Three times he'd flattened this little mound of shit previously, with nary a *clunk* to report on any of those occasions. But this time, as he'd driven the spade into the earth, the rath all but destroyed once more, it had cut through the soft soil and–

Clunk.

In a flash Bea was out the door and at his side. How she'd heard the relatively modest noise from inside the nice, warm, tea-filled house she'd been in for the last forty-five minutes, he had no idea.

'Where's my fuckin' cuppa?' he asked indignantly. 'I was promised.'

'I'm tryin' to keep them busy in there,' she said. 'Anyway, yer woman seemed to have an eye for ye; if she'd have come out here she probably wouldn'ta went back in.'

He prodded the soil experimentally. Sure enough, it met

resistance that it hadn't before – something was buried underneath.

'How come this never happened before?' he asked.

'Because now you believe something's down there,' Bea said.

'Ach, fuck off.'

'You're awful foul-mouthed for such a wee boy,' Bea said mildly.

'Come on, but,' Danny said, exasperated. 'It's there cos I believe it's there? Seriously, like? What a load of ballix. So if I believe hard enough that some supermodel's gonna materialise between my legs …'

'It's magic, son,' Bea said, 'it's not miracles,' and she gestured to him impatiently. 'Well? What are you waitin' for, an invitation? Dig!'

He grumbled but set about it, removing more of the soil around the object until only a thin layer was left. Whatever it was, it was about five feet long and two feet wide and deep enough that he couldn't get the spade under it, even at the sides.

'Wipe off the soil.'

Grumbling forgotten, he dropped to his hands and knees and brushed off the remainder of the covering earth. He heard an intake of breath from the direction of the old woman.

'It's a tablet?' he guessed.

'It's a doorway,' she corrected him.

'So how does it open?'

She looked at him, as if daring him to laugh. 'You have to piss on it,' she said, deadpan.

'What?'

'Ancient magic, son. It was all blood and piss and sweat and tears in them days.'

'The blood and sweat and tears I could do!' Danny exclaimed. 'How the fuck am I meant to pull out the oul lanyard and have a slash in the middle of someone's front garden? Have you seen the size of that fucker Casey? He'll pull my balls off!'

She shrugged. 'It's what ye hafta do. Simple as that.'

'Ach fer fuck's sake,' he sighed. Checking the front room window, he saw that the family were watching TV and had their backs to him. He had a quick peek up and down the street – no one was coming. His hand went to his fly…

'All right,' Bea said, holding up a hand. 'I was only jokin', son. Ya looked a bit tense there, thought it might help.'

He glared at her. 'Thank you so much,' he said.

'Honestly, I don't have a clue how you open these things,' she said, shrugging. 'But then what would I know? – I'm only the silly oul bat reads the tea leaves, eh? You try.'

Try? Try what? He looked in bafflement down at the stone tablet embedded into the soil beneath what had once been – and maybe would be again – his garden. It was big, it was solid, it was depressingly unmagical looking. He'd seen all this sort of shite a million times before in fuckin' movies with wee elves and hairy fuckers with big feet, but all of that seemed to count for exactly zip right at this moment.

Usually in the books or the movies that dealt with this sort of stuff the one trying to open the magic door or get the special sword or complete the Big Important Quest had some sort of advantage, *something* going for them, whether it was a ring or a scar or a group of heavily-armed killers backing them up. What did he have? A neurological disorder and a partially-incontinent octogenarian with three of her own teeth left.

Songs will be sung about this one ...

A switch flipped in his head. He paused in his digging to fish his phone out of his pocket. He'd put it on silent when they'd got to Ellie and Steve's house, for fear that Lircom would try to contact him with some random work thing. He whistled softly. Twenty-eight missed calls, all from Maggie. Twenty-nine ...

He switched the volume back on. As soon as he did so, the mobile burst forth with an insanely up-tempo version of 'La Cucaracha'.

'It's for you,' Bea said.

'Yes thanks,' he snapped, taking a deep breath. *Aw, fuck.* 'Maggie ...'

'Yes, hello,' Maggie replied, with the very, very, precise tones of a woman who wishes to make it crystal clear that she is keeping her voice under control simply out of politeness, and in doing so holds the moral high ground. 'Thanks so much for a wonderful evening. I particularly enjoyed seeing you kiss that fucking slut; although you might have had the courage to at least stick around afterward. Still, an interesting way of telling your girlfriend and your best friend that you've been having an affair.'

He closed his eyes. There really was absolutely nothing he could say. Lying wouldn't help, and the truth was a hundred times less believable than the most outlandish lies he could ever have come up with. 'I'm sorry, Maggie,' he said, 'for what it's worth.'

'Is he yours?'

'Mine?'

'The kid,' she snapped.

He should be.

'No.'

'I don't know why I'm asking,' she said, still in that uber-calm tone, the sort office workers use as they reach inside their holdall on the one Monday morning too many and take out the submachine gun.

'I have to go,' he said, and a second later was good to his word, because he went – not just off the call, but off his feet altogether, the phone thudding into the upturned dirt littering the garden.

'You fucker,' Steve hissed, standing over him.

'Mr Quinn. Mr Black apologises for the time,' Sarah said sweetly.

Michael Quinn regarded her with scepticism. 'I'm sure he does. Can I go in?'

'Yes, please, go ahead,' she said, inclining her head in the direction of her boss' office. Strange: though he could hear the *clackclackclack* of her fingers flying across the keyboard as he walked to the office door, he could practically feel eyes on his back as he moved; almost as if there was more than one person there. Or as if she had more than two eyes.

Mr Black was there, sitting behind his desk, just as Michael had known he would be. The Lircom chief exec looked up with a winning smile. 'Michael,' he said warmly. 'Good to see–'

'Save the shite, all right? This isn't one of your corporate away-days. I know you didn't summon me across town at almost ten o' clock at night for nothing, so let's hear it.'

Mr Black's eyes flashed dangerously. 'Be careful, Michael,' he said, his volume soft but his tone hard. 'Our … arrangement … has entitled you to certain privileges, but that's all they are – privileges. They can be revoked.'

'Like fuck they can,' Michael shot back. 'Who d'you think you're dealing with here? Some bird with clipped wings, like Danny?'

Mr Black shuddered. 'Please. You know my stance on birds. Am I to take it that you admired my work with young Danny, then? I suppose it's a step beyond that old cliché of friends close and enemies closer – why not simply make friends of your enemies?'

'The reverse works too.'

'Meaning?'

Michael leant across the desk to stare into that maddeningly calm face and those big unblinking eyes. 'Why wasn't it instant?' he said.

'I'm sorry? I don't quite follow.'

'Yes, you do. You make a wish and *poof*, wish granted. I made one, and first my daughter and my grandson vanish and everyone notices … and then everyone forgets my grandson existed, and then, days later, they come back?'

'What are you comparing this to, exactly?' Mr Black said. 'How many other wishes have you had granted through supernatural means? Am I suffering in comparison to an animated blue genie with the voice of Robin Williams? Or perhaps I should be a scantily-clad girl hanging around Larry Hagman for want of something better to do?'

When no reply was forthcoming, Mr Black leaned back in his chair and regarded Michael with contempt that he didn't try particularly hard to hide. 'You have no idea what's involved in shifting reality,' he said. 'The complications. The difficulties. So please, do not lecture me, ever, on matters of which you know nothing. You asked for something. It has been given to you. Whether or not it took a few days is immaterial.'

'It has been given to me?' Michael choked. 'Nothing has *changed*!'

'Nothing has changed?' Mr Black laughed. 'How can you say that, Michael? Things couldn't be more different for your daughter.'

'They are exactly the same! I wanted a second chance for my daughter. A good career. A shot at the life she deserved. And she's right back where she was!'

'You wanted Danny gone from her life. I removed him. What your daughter chose to do with the alternative path was entirely up to her. I wonder, Michael, if having a child wasn't simply something your darling daughter wanted to do. Perhaps it wasn't the terrible oversight you believed it to be. Perhaps she – what's the human term for it? – trapped, that's it, first Danny, and now Steve? Like a … like a spider in a web, I suppose.'

Michael, a card-carrying lifelong arachnophobe, was unable to disguise the shiver of revulsion that went through him at that particular image. 'That's ridiculous,' he said hotly. 'My daughter would never–'

'How do you know? How well do you really know her, Michael? How much of her childhood did you miss for this business trip or that three-day conference? What was her favourite toy as a child?'

'What?'

'Favourite television show? Favourite musician? Which posters did she have on her bedroom wall?' Mr Black fired out the questions staccato, one after the other, his mouth and lips contorting incredibly quickly even as the rest of his face remained static.

Michael sat down in the chair and began to laugh. 'I'm getting parenting lectures from you?' he said incredulously. 'Compared to you and your kind, I'm a fuckin' saint.'

'Careful,' Mr Black said very quietly, his face dark. He looked almost regretful as he spoke. 'I'd hate to have to change the nature of our relationship.' Then he smiled, all pleasantries and sunshine again. 'I need you to do something for me. I did a favour for you which means I own you for exactly one year and one day, and it's been' – he made a show of checking his desk calendar – 'two days?'

'You've already taken my company! I'm selling to you. Paving the way for this precious Network of yours. You're getting FormorTech at 20 per cent of market value!'

'Yes,' Mr Black replied easily. 'But that, Michael … that was yesterday.'

Realisation of just how deep the hole he had stumbled into was had begun to dawn in the other man's eyes. 'With the power you have? Why do you need me to do anything?' Michael Quinn asked, with a glimmer of hope.

'Go and visit your brother.'

'Dermot?'

'Yes. Dear old Dermot, the loveable rogue. Wasn't he the one responsible – albeit indirectly – for your recent good fortune in the first place? How is he? Never mind. Go and see how he is for yourself. And while you're at it' – Mr Black leaned forward and licked his lips – 'I'd be grateful if you'd eviscerate him.'

'If I'd what? You can't be serious. He's my brother.'

Mr Black nodded. 'Yes. He is. Curious as to why two brothers have different surnames. How did that come about by the way?'

'Quinn is my mother's maiden name,' Michael replied, suppressing the real reason. It seemed to dawn on him then how ridiculous this impromptu question and answer session was. 'Look, I don't care what agreements we have. You've failed to deliver anything you promised. My daughter is as miserable now as she was before, if not more so. You took my company. Now you want me to kill my brother? You must be out of your mind!'

Mr Black winced. 'I see,' he said, with some regret. He pressed the intercom button on his desk. 'Sarah, could you come through to the office?'

'Absolutely, Mr Black.'

'Why do you want him dead?' Michael asked. 'He's just–'

'He's not just anything.' Mr Black cut him off. 'And I don't just want him dead. I want his intestines spilled and for him to die in unimaginable agonies. Anything else simply won't do, I'm afra– ah! Sarah, glad you could join us.'

Michael Quinn glanced behind him, and it occurred to him that he had never seen Sarah out from behind her desk before.

His jaw dropped – the girl had killer legs.

'You wanted something, Mr Black?' she asked, stopping at the edge of the desk and perching herself on it, so he could almost – not quite, but almost – see a little more than he was supposed to. That was, he reflected, just about the shortest skirt he'd ever seen.

Jesus, how could he be thinking about skirts and legs at a time like this? He'd just been asked to kill his own flesh and blood! And here he was, like some old pervert, unable to keep his eyes off the young woman's perfect thighs …

'I think you're providing it already, my dear,' Mr Black told her.

Sarah turned to Michael and smiled that winning smile and he found his tongue thickening in his mouth, as if he were a lust-struck teenager seeing his first glimpse of a girl's knickers. She had loosened her smart suit jacket and the white shirt she was wearing was stretched over a pair of magnificent breasts that, somehow – Christ knew how – he'd failed to notice as he strode past her desk a short time ago.

And now she was moving toward him, Mr Black watching, reclining his chair in amusement, his hands steepled, as Michael Quinn goggled. Sarah was at the older man's chair now, flicking that waist-length jet-black hair so that it rippled sensuously about her body, almost a living thing by itself.

Mr Black could see what Michael Quinn could not; the stinger emerging from Sarah's carapace, obscured by the effortless pheromone-laden glamour she exuded when the situation called for it, looming over the poor captured man, dwarfing him utterly.

'Shall I?' she asked her boss eagerly.

'Go ahead,' he nodded.

'I don't … I don't understand,' Michael managed.

'No, I don't expect you do,' she shushed him, running a finger (or the barest tip of one of her massive segmented forelegs, depending on how you looked at it) over his lips and causing him almost to pass out from pleasure. The pheromone waves she was pulsing out were effortlessly overpowering him, washing away his reason and logic and making him docile.

The stinger sprang out, and back. His eyes widened for a moment, just a moment, but the needle was so sharp that its prick was practically painless. He would have the barest pinprick on the back of his neck to show for it.

'That will be all, Sarah,' Mr Black said. 'A job well done, my dear.'

His trusty assistant skittered out, leaving Michael Quinn behind, unconscious in the chair facing Mr Black, who took the opportunity to, amongst other things, chuckle at an email Sarah had sent on his behalf to all staff thanking them for their participation in the NI blood donation session that had happened the previous day. There had been no truck, of course, but Sarah had been thirsty, and what had he created her for if not for her very human initiative?

Forty minutes or so passed before Michael's eyes opened.

'Ah, Michael, there you are,' Mr Black said briskly, without looking away from his screen. 'That will be all. You remember what we discussed?'

'Eviscerate Dermot Scully.'

'The very job. Do you have any issues with that?'

'Disobey?' Michael blinked, baffled by the very concept. 'Why would I?'

'Excellent. Have it done by this time tomorrow night. Goodnight, Michael.'

Mr Black watched as his visitor stood up and walked out. He smiled. Humans never failed to amuse him; such simple creatures these days, despite their wondrous technologies. They had made much more formidable opponents back in the old days; but then, that was rather the point of this whole enterprise, wasn't it?

His phone rang. He picked it up, expecting it to be Sarah putting through a call.

It wasn't.

'Brother.'

Mr Black sat bolt upright in his chair, hardly able to believe it. After all these years. 'Dian? Dian, is that really you? Where are you? Who are you? Let me come get you—'

'I can feel it,' the voice went on, ignoring him. 'Someone's crossing over. I thought that was meant to be impossible?'

'All part of some grand scheme Mother's putting together. You know Mother …'

'She's trying to get out.' It wasn't a question.

'Oh, she's already out. Well. Some of her. Not enough of her to do anything grand, and she does love grand gestures. Thinks the world hasn't had enough of them. I think she just misses *Dallas* to be honest. The original, of course, not that remake nonsense … but anyway, enough about her. What about you, my brother? Where are you?'

'Where am I?' There was a laugh from the other side of the line. It lacked any genuine mirth. 'Same place as ever, Dother. Everywhere.'

'You haven't lost your talent for dramatic statements. Excellent!' Mr Black cried. 'I was afraid you'd be out of practice. Oh, it's going to be just like old times, little brother. So who are you being nowadays? You're not that newsreader on BBC1 are you? The one with the lazy eye? I swear I see the same glint of bottomless malice in him sometimes that you used to get when–'

'It's the Morrigan, isn't it?' Dian said, ignoring the question. 'The one who's crossing over?'

'What? Oh yes. The latest one, anyway,' Mr Black said impatiently.

'You've got him, haven't you. The Morrigan's son.'

Mr Black's mouth twisted ruefully. Dian didn't miss a trick. 'Sort of,' he allowed. 'Dian, it doesn't matter–'

'I won't help you. I won't help her.'

'Come, Dian. We're family!'

'Family?' there was only bitter amusement in Dian's voice. 'Family? The things she made us do? She stood by and watched me die. She let it happen. Have you forgotten that?'

Mr Black shrugged. 'So you died,' he said airily. 'You got better.'

'You call going through the Ordeal better? You call what I became better?'

'Disembodied is better than dead, Dian. Come home.'

'I had a home.' The voice was hollow now. 'I had a family. It was taken from me.'

This produced a frown. 'Dian?' he said, an unmistakably older-brother tone creeping into his words. 'Dian, what are you talking about? What have you done?'

'It doesn't matter. You can't help me. I thought I was done with it, all of it, but feeling the Morrigan cross over … I'm making my own plans, brother. I have my own revenge to think of.'

'Get in Mother's way and she'll destroy you.'

'I won't. Why are you calling yourself Mr Black, Dother?'

'Call it a tribute to our trapped brother,' he said impatiently. 'Dian, tell me what–'

'The brother you've always hated.'

'Yes, that miserable bastard. Come and join me, Dian. You and me together. Just like it was; riding out in flaming chariots pulled by fell creatures, crushing the humans underfoot, left and right, by the thousands. Better than it was. You should see my secretary.'

'I've seen her. I was there the day you recruited her, remember?'

'Well then,' he continued without a pause, 'you should see my Audi. This world is a ripe, spoiled, fat, glorious paradise and I've got such plans, brother–'

Click. Dnnnnnnnn.

Dother – aka Mr Black – stared at the receiver for a long time, before sighing and placing it carefully back in its cradle. The baby of the brothers, Dian had always been his mother's favourite. For some unknown reason, she'd consistently refused to acknowledge his shortcomings, whereas he – the faithful middle brother – could never do enough to garner more than a cursory nod in his direction.

He shut down the computer and walked to the office door, turning off the lights as he went. Sarah was on the ceiling of reception above him as he walked through; her glamour gratefully discarded since they were the only two left in the building.

'Early night?' she said, surprised.

'Come on,' he sighed, offering his arm. A leg as thick as a man's thigh snaked around it and she descended to stand beside him. 'I could use a little cheering up. I'm taking you out for someone to eat. My treat …'

Say what you wanted about Steve – and most people took the opportunity to – but the guy could swing a dig.

Danny rubbed the side of his head, which was just beginning to throb from the sucker-punch Steve had landed there. As he tried to get to his feet, Steve came at him again, swinging a foot towards his midriff. Danny threw himself to the side with speed he didn't know he had, avoiding the strike. Steve's foot went in the wet soil and he came crashing to earth. Danny was on him in a flash, pinning his legs to the ground with his knees and clamping his hands over Steve's wrists.

'Stop!' Danny wheezed. 'Stop it, for fuck's sake!'

Steve writhed beneath him like a mad thing, almost throwing him off, but Danny had been through enough in the way of supernatural setbacks to accept such a grubby fate as getting a kicking from his best mate. He held on grimly, pleading with Steve to calm the fuck down and wise up and just stop for a fucking minute …

Sboooosh.

Steve froze in place with shock as the bucketful of cold water hit him right in the face. Danny, who was close enough to experience splash back, did likewise, the frigid water chilling him right down the marrow of his bones as the evening air bit. Both men panted for a moment, waiting for their hearts to start beating properly again.

'Fuckwits,' Bea said, disgusted, an empty bucket swinging limply by her side.

The two men turned to look at her with murder in their eyes. She met their gazes and shrugged. 'And sure what was I meant to do? Wait until you two finished up yer wee pissin' contest?'

'Who the fuck are you?' Steve gasped. He tried to heave himself up and Danny allowed him to wriggle free. Both stood apart, eyeing each other warily as they shook their heads like two dogs, trying to get rid of the excess liquid.

'She's Beatrice O'Malley,' Danny informed him, panting.

'Oh right. Glad I asked,' Steve replied, obviously none the wiser. He turned away from his elderly assailant and back to Danny, making no move to attack him but fixing him with a powerful glare. 'You're my best friend in the world,' he said simply, high emotion overriding his usual need for masculine bullshit. 'I can't believe you'd do this to me. I've been walking these streets for near an hour trying to get my head showered, trying to figure out if next time I see ya I'm gonna have to hit ya or fuckin' call a shrink to put ya in the nearest loony bin, and here's you happy as Larry diggin' up some fuckin' garden?'

Trying to explain would be hopeless, Danny knew. But unlike Maggie, with Steve he felt he had at least to give it a shot. 'It's not what you think,' he began.

'It's not? So yous two haven't been seein' each other?'

Danny gulped for air as he tried to deny it, then had a brain-freeze from the sheer reality-bending mindfuckery of it all.

'I don't even know where to begin,' he said, truthfully enough.

Steve's anger seemed to have cooled now. Somehow that was worse. His friend looked broken, defeated. 'You wanna know something, man?' he said quietly. 'You always got things faster than me. You were always quicker off the fuckin' mark pickin' up stuff. Better at sports and better at touchin' for girls and ya know, if it had been any other fucker I'd have been jealous of it, but it was you. Me and you. Me and you were …' he trailed off and stared at the dirt around his feet.

'I'm away in for another cuppa,' Bea said in despair. She rapped the door. 'Casey! Casey love, I've got yer wee bucket! Stick the kettle on, God love ye!'

'She was mine,' Steve said weakly. 'She was mine and the wee man was mine and even though you had this amazin' job and a big house an all, I thought – well, there we go, finally I've beaten him to the mark on somethin'. I thought, when it's time for him to have a wee one, he'll be the one comin' to me for advice. But then you had to go and take that from me too, didn't ya? What was it we used to say to each other, lad, eh? Bros before hos to a blind donkey,' and he paused to let the impact of those words sink in, standing in a muddy hole in a garden with water dripping from his nose, before repeating this grave proclamation with even more emphasis, 'bros ... before hos ... to a blind donkey.'

Danny felt like tearing his hair out. 'Lad this is crazy,' he said. 'None of this is real! I know it sounds nuts but ya have to believe me. I was the one with Ellie. I was the one had the son with her. Luke – his name was Luke! And this – this fuckin' thing here,' he gestured toward the stone tablet they were both standing beside. 'It's all ... well it's like a parallel universe or something. You're not a da, lad! You must feel it. The bottles and the feedin' aren't comin' natural to you – you said it yourself!'

'Fuck off,' Steve snarled. 'So not only are you fuckin' around with my girlfriend behind my back, but now I'm a shitty da into the bargain, is that it? Some fuckin' best mate you turned out to be. Bastard.'

Face twisted in disgust, Steve turned as if to go. Danny took a step forward, to go after him, his foot landing on the stone tablet.

It happened very quickly.

Danny could feel a strange kind of pressure building up, as if he were suffering the onset of hay fever within a matter of seconds. His sinuses seemed as if they were about to explode. He blinked rapidly, trying to moisten suddenly dry eyes. That wasn't all, though; his synaesthesia was going apeshit – tastes flowed across his tongue at such a rate that his mouth began to water uncontrollably. He tasted fish, and potatoes, chicken, pear, garlic, sesame, *wheatoilbeans Guinnesssoysaucecherriescurrylettucestrawberrysaltcheese*–

And he tasted purple. And red. And Wednesdays. And sarcasm. And Ellie ...

His sinuses, he realised, were trying to shut down, to put up some sort of defence, because he was smelling ten, twenty, fifty, a hundred different smells at once. Like the tastes, there was no order or rhyme or reason to them – some were pleasant and some were awful but they were whirling around too quickly to discern which was which and he was falling, sinking to his knees and throwing out his hands to steady himself, his downturned palms striking the stone ...

... and it got worse. He heard sevens and they sounded like July. He knew the colours of the smells and the sound of the tastes and it overwhelmed him, a lifetime's worth of flashes all screaming for room inside him all at once and the weirdest thing, the absolute weirdest thing about it, was that *it all sort of seemed to come together.*

'Open,' he whispered.

The stone split down the middle with a dry crack. Fragments of it flew this way and that; one sliced his cheek and drew blood. He touched it, felt its wetness, and fought the sudden urge to taste it.

Two shadows fell over him from above.

'You did it,' Bea said wonderingly. The excitement in her voice made her sound much younger, much more alive. 'It's true ...'

'Gimme your hand!' was all Steve said, extending his own down to Danny's. Danny took it, and made to step out of the hole in which he stood.

He couldn't.

As if in a dream, even as he heard Steve's voice above him, ordering him to do something, or try harder, something like that, he looked down, and saw with no great surprise that the crack in the centre of the tablet had widened sufficiently for his foot to fall into.

To sink into.

Steve was pulling as hard as he could on his hand, resisting the tug from below. Danny tilted his head upward toward his friend, a smile of acceptance on his face. Both his legs were gone now, to the knees.

'You have to let me go,' Danny told him.

Steve was leaning over, almost bent double, shouting, refusing, pulling strongly. Sweat made his hand slippery and Danny's fingers began to slide through his grasp. Danny could see his friend make one last desperate attempt to regain his hold, but the pull from below was too strong.

He sank into the earth and it closed above his head. The oxygen died almost immediately with the light and he closed his mouth and eyes, feeling the soil pry and poke at his ears, fill his nostrils, force its way into his mouth. He couldn't breathe, could do nothing but be dragged further downward. The hole he was creating was filling itself in as he kept on going, dropping soil and insects by the hundreds on him.

The pull on his legs increased even as the pressure on his lungs went from painful to agonising to unbearably excruciating; the temptation to open his mouth and try to locate any air, anywhere, was becoming too great to resist and he knew if he complied he would be doomed; the soft disgusting freezing muck would fill his mouth in an instant and he would suffocate. He could not raise his arms to clear his nose, could not move, was only aware of the acceleration of the downward motion.

If only the soil were oxygen.

If only it tasted like air.

Those were Danny Morrigan's last thoughts before the blackness swallowed him whole.

Acknowledgements

My sincerest and warmest thanks to Jo at Last Passage for her belief and to everyone at Blackstaff – especially Michelle and Stuart – for their support.

Finally to my ma and da for teaching me how to be me.

READ ON FOR AN EXCERPT FROM

Folk'd Up
Book Two of the *Folk'd* trilogy

by Laurence Donaghy

Published by Blackstaff Press

The Meeting with the Goddess

Someone sniggered.

He was going to have to open his eyes, he decided at the point of hearing the sniggering, because the sound had coincided rather neatly with the memory of being sucked into the earth through a portal in what had once been his front garden. When something like that happened to you and you found yourself alive, tasting grass and being sniggered at, you at least owed it to yourself to open your eyes.

It was a crow. A crow, perched on his shoulder, as if a crow perching on your shoulder was the done thing, was blasé. And every so often it would lean forward and peck him with its hard little fuckin' beak, right in the crook of his neck, not hard enough to draw blood but hard enough to penetrate right through his unconsciousness and make him emerge into the waking world. What the fuck was a bird's beak made of anyway?

Diamond?

'Get the fuck off, ya fucker!' he said, spasming his upper body in one almighty heave – forcing it to take off in a *phutphutphut* of wings – and pushing down with his palms so he was no longer lying face down in the … *where the almighty fuck was he anyway?*

He got to his feet and blinked in the moonlight, shielding his eyes from the glare until his brain reminded him that, generally speaking, moonlight is not something people have to shield their eyes from. So, ignoring the crow, which had landed a mere six feet or so away, he looked up.

Generally speaking, the moon wasn't usually that fuckin' big, either. It was hanging so low and so huge that if there really was a Man in the Moon Danny could have told him if he'd something trapped in his teeth.

He dropped his gaze to the crow, which regarded him with equal interest. For a moment man and bird stood there, watching one another with intent, on a lonely hilltop in the middle of a great plain lit by the glow of an impossible moon. Danny was the first to break the silence between them.

'You laughing at me, ya big feathery cunt?' he asked it evenly.

'Shouldn't I?' the crow replied.

Talking crow. Danny was vaguely aware that he should be going through all the clichés of disbelief and fear, but right then and there, after the parallel universe and the amazing vanishing baby trick the cosmos had pulled on him, he had very little disbelief left to go around.

'You're not gonna talk only in poetry or somethin' are ya?' Danny demanded. 'If I sniff so much as a *whiff* of iambic pentameter comin' outta that beak—'

The crow hopped a few feet sideways. Insofar as birds could have facial expressions, this one looked decidedly patronising. 'I assume you've never talked to a Creature of Omen before?' it demanded.

'I've been very drunk in some very dark clubs,' Danny offered. 'Chances are I've done more than talked to some Creatures of Omen, mate.'

'Ignorant mortal! I am a crow! Harbinger of the battlefield! Kings and chieftains would await my appearance and the portents for good or ill that it would bring!'

Danny sat on the grass, because he needed a moment to take stock, and as he sat, he gave this information all the grave consideration he could muster, using all his years as a Belfast native to come up with an appropriate riposte.

'So?'

Expert linguists have agreed that the Belfast *so?* is unique among all retorts contained in all dialects of all the world's languages for some simple, yet awe-inspiring reason: there exists no counter-move. Said properly, with exactly the right amount of disdain and nonchalance, coupled with a sneering contempt and flavoured with a soupçon of aggression, the most reasoned and logical statement simply falls apart under its withering gaze.

Had it been said to Moses when he descended from Mount

Sinai with the Ten Commandments, Christianity would have crumbled there and then and everyone would have filed off sheepishly to see if manna could indeed be rolled up and smoked.

'So!?' the crow spluttered, which for a creature lacking lips was not an easy thing to do. 'For millennia the crows served as mystical portents of doom! Divining the chaos of the battlefield and choosing from its infinite variations an unerring picture of the future yet to pass! My magics were ineffable! My conclusions unchallenged!'

'So?' repeated Danny.

'So? So??? SO????' the crow thundered and Danny knew he had the wee bastard.

'Yeah, so?' he concluded, and then sealed the deal. 'And what? What'dja want, a fuckin' medal?'

The crow fluttered up and down a few times, looking for all the world as if were hopping with rage. 'Have you any idea who you address in such a way?'

'No,' Danny said, switching tack, ladling the infinitely wide-eyed patience on with a trowel. 'I thought that's where we came in?'

'I am The Morrigan!'

Danny flashed immediately on the name; back to Mr Black's office, to the on-hold narration playing. The Morrigan ... some sort of warrior goddess. Beyond that, and the obvious fact they shared a surname (surely not a coincidence ...), he didn't know much.

'You have the talent,' the crow said, as if sensing the flash. 'It's true, then.'

His thoughts were not his own. Danny felt his mental guards go up, even as he burned to ask more questions. *Remembering*. That was meant to be his gift, wasn't it? Some gift. It wasn't exactly a double-bladed lightsaber or crimson eye-beams. He was unlikely to threaten the pantheon of the great action heroes with a talent like that.

'You're meant to be The Morrigan?'

'I *am* The Morrigan!'

'You're a fuckin crow!' he exclaimed. 'What's your great power – shittin' on your foes from a great height? Stoppin' them gettin' any sleep by sittin' in a fuckin' tree all night cawing like a cunt?'

'Crows are a form of the goddess Morrigan. An aspect of her whole,' the crow explained, in a tone that suggested it was flabbergasted at his stupidity.

'So where's the rest of her?' Danny asked, deciding to forego the temptations presented to him by the phrase 'aspect of her whole' but making a note of it for later.

The crow didn't answer. 'You have the talent,' it said instead. 'Because of that, I'll choose to ignore the staggering lack of respect you're showing.'

'Ach thanks,' he said. 'I appreciate that so much. Mind if I ask you a few questions?'

'I shall allow it,' the bird said graciously, unruffling its feathers and turning its head away in a somewhat haughty pose.

That was when Danny lunged.

The bird never saw it coming. It squawked, a proper bird *aaaaawwwwrrrrkkk* and it tried to launch itself up and away to safety, but Danny's attack had been timed to coincide with the bird turning its head and that crucial fraction of a second had been time enough for him to clamp his hand firmly around the bird's meagre little body and prevent its escape. The crow went crazy, pecking this way and that, until Danny was able to pinch that wicked little beak shut with his free hand.

'My question is,' he said, ever-so-slightly out of breath, and starting to bleed from a few shallow puncture wounds on his right palm, 'why shouldn't I break your scrawny fuckin' neck?'

What do you think you are doing?

He nearly released the bird from sheer shock. The words had come at him in his own inner voice. It was like hearing your own subconscious rebel against you, and for a long moment he actually wondered if he had finally, somewhat understandably, snapped under the strain.

No. No, the voice wasn't his own, despite coming from inside his head; it smelt different. It smelt of dirt, and blood, of this strange place he'd found himself in.

'I'll tell ya what I'm doin,' he replied, vocalising because it was easier to structure his feelings that way, 'I'm getting sick of all this shit that's been happenin' to me this past week, and you were just the talkin' crow that broke the camel's back.'

I am trying to help you. You have no idea what sort of place you're in. No mortal has been here in—

'Aye,' he broke in, 'hundreds of years. Inexcusable magics or some shit. Blahiddy-blah fuckin blah. And I have some sorta talent. So you said. Whoo-pee-fuckin-doo. Look. All I wanna know is how I make this all stop. How I go back to the way things were. That so hard? That so much to ask, aye?'

There's so much you don't know. So much you don't understand.

The voice was almost pitying now. He felt like squeezing his hand around the little black body he held in his fist until it exploded. If one more person pitied him, just one more …

The landscape around him turned blood-red so quickly and so completely that he was stunned by the speed of it. He looked up, and saw that the massive overhanging moon had shaded itself crimson, just like – and he felt his blood run cold at the memory – just like the one in his dream, moments before the …

The same howl came forth, as he had known it would. Terrifying, ear-splitting, like every wolf in the world howling at once.

The Goddess in his palm promptly crapped herself all over his hand.

Let me go. Let me go now!

He complied, not quite knowing if he did so willingly or as a result of some hitherto unknown power of compulsion the crow had just demonstrated. The bird fluttered up and away, but it didn't abandon him; it hovered about twenty feet above his head. Crows were particularly ungainly things, he could see that now. Little wonder they'd earned a reputation as grim eyeball-guzzling harbingers of death. They radiated menace.

'Something's coming,' the crow called down to him. 'One of their soldiers. One of the elites, by the look of it. Behind you. Look.'

He rotated and from his vantage point on top of the small hillock he saw it almost immediately, lurching across the plains toward him. It moved like the crow flew – in a way that looked clumsy, but was filled with power. It came at him across the red-tinted grass in a stop-start way that put him in mind of those scary fuckin' skeletons in the *Jason and the Argonauts* movie he'd loved as a kid.

'Well! Don't just …! Do something then!' he shouted up at his airborne companion.

'Who? Me?'

'Yes you!' he said, his voice hoarse with terror, as the thing began to rumble on the upward incline, now no more than two hundred feet away. 'You're the fuckin' Morrigan aren't ye?'

'Should I shite on it? Or wait until tonight, perhaps, and keep it up all night cawing like a … what was it …?'

He glared death at the crow. The crow, who had evolution on its side, did the same and won. 'What do I do?' he cried out, taking one step backward, then two, testing the surface beneath his feet, trying to judge how quickly his feet would spring off it, estimating the running speed of the thing moving at him. Knowing it was moving faster than he could ever hope to. There was no getting away, no escape.

'You fight,' said the crow, and flew upward and away from sight before he could say another word, leaving Danny alone with the oncoming nightmare.